Praise for the Faith Hun

CROPPED

MW00592634

"Christina's characters shine, her knowledge of scrapbooking is spot on, and she weaves a mystery that simply cries out to be read in one delicious sitting!"

— Pam Hanson,
Multi-Published Women's Fiction Author

"This was a great read that had me reading non-stop from the moment I turned the first page. The author did a good job in keeping me in suspense with plenty of twists and turns and every time I thought I had it figured out, the author changed the direction in which the story was headed...The writing flowed easily and I liked the cast of characters in this charming whodunit!"

— Dru Ann Love,
Dru's Book Musings

"Witty, entertaining and fun with a side of murder...When murder hits Eden, West Virginia, Faith Hunter will stop at nothing to clear the name of her employee who has been accused of murder. Will she find the real killer before it is too late? Read this sensational read to find out!"

–Shelley Giusti,
Shelley's Book Case

"A cozy mystery that exceeds expectations....Freeburn has crafted a mystery that does not feel clichéd or cookie-cutter....it's her sense of humor that shows up in the book, helping the story flow, making the characters real and keeping the reader interested....And she promises more Faith Hunter books—I hope she writes fast!"

— Cynthia McCloud,
Scrapbooking is Heart Work Blog

DESIGNED TO DEATH (#2)

"Battling scrapbook divas, secrets, jealousy, murder, and lots of glitter all make Designed to Death a charming and heartfelt mystery."

–Ellen Byerrum,
Author of the Crime of Fashion Mysteries

"Read this fun book and you will never think of Washi tape in in quite the same way again, I promise. Christina Freeburn's second installment in her scrapbooking mystery series is full of small-town intrigue, twists and turns, and plenty of heart."

– Mollie Cox Bryan,
Agatha Award Finalist, *Scrapbook of Secrets*

"This is a fun series with very likable characters you will want to visit with again and again with every new book. Even if you are not a fan of scrapping (and I'm not – it's about the only craft I never got into) you will enjoy the series as it is not heavy with information about the hobby – as some hobby series can be. And if you are into the hobby, there are hints at the back of the book."

– Kate Shannon,
Rantin' Ravin' and Reading

CROPPED
to death

To Alesia -

It was great
meeting you at the
crop.

Christina Freeburn

The Faith Hunter Scrap This Mystery Series
by Christina Freeburn

CROPPED
to death

A Faith Hunter Scrap This Mystery

CHRISTINA FREEBURN

HENERY PRESS

CROPPED TO DEATH
A Faith Hunter Scrap This Mystery
Part of the Henery Press Mystery Collection

First Edition
Trade paperback edition | November 2012

Henery Press
www.henerypress.com

Copyright © 2012 by Christina Freeburn
Cover design by Fayette Terlouw
Author photograph by Megan Freeburn

ISBN-13: 978-1-938383-06-9

Printed in the United States of America

To my web person, computer technician, software installer,
financial advisor, plot listener,
who also happens to be my husband, Brian.
Thanks for all that you do!

ACKNOWLEDGMENTS

Writing can be a lonely world filled with lots of nos. If it wasn't for the support of family, friends, and those like-minded people in my life...yes, other writers...I know this book would never have made it this far. A big thank you to my family who don't question me (any longer) about talking to myself, acting out scenes either with action figures, or asking weird "what if" questions. For my writing friends who listened to me talk about the book and helped me plot. A special thanks to Bonner for putting up with me getting pouty because you didn't like a character as much as I did. I hope he grows on you. Also, thanks to Pam for that eloquent email saying "email it!" when I was obsessing with the writer's age old question of "should I or shouldn't I send."

Also, this book won't be as wonderful without the help of the talented Kendel Flaum. I didn't think it was possible for to me to love this book more, but you made it happen. I'm so excited that it will be out there in the world. This couldn't have happened without you.

And a thank you to scrapbooking. It is hard to thank a hobby, but I know without it this book wouldn't have come to be. Through online communities and crops, I've meet wonderful women who have enriched my life, and learned a little bit more about myself.

ONE

The industrial sized straight-blade trimmer sliced through the air. Even from across the room, I heard the blade going through paper – *whoosh, whoosh.* I poked a finger into my left ear and pressed the cell against the other. My grandmother Hope's instructions garbled through the device, the words loud and then soft, an effect that had nothing to do with being in a technological dead zone. Not that keeping a cell phone connection was easy to do in Eden, West Virginia.

Since we started the Scrap This employee crop two hours ago, the whacking hadn't stopped. The blade, like my sanity, was near breaking. I covered the mouthpiece and leaned across the front counter, trying to catch Marilyn's gaze as I avoided jamming my side into the cash register. "Could you adhere something for a while?"

Marilyn Kane picked up the useless part of the picture and dropped it. My gaze followed the fluttering photo cast-off to the ecru colored linoleum floor. A discarded pile of Michaels littered the area beside the eight-foot table.

My friend and fellow employee discovered six weeks ago that her husband, Michael, did more than just commute with his co-worker. I didn't know if she was more upset about the affair or the fact the twenty-two-year-old harlot would give birth to Michael's baby in four months.

"Faith, are you there?" Hope asked. "Are you taking notes?"

"Yes." I tried to keep the chipper in my voice and the exasperation out as I reached for a pen and a piece of paper. My grandmothers had as much trouble leaving me in charge of their store as they did remembering at twenty-six, I was a grown-up.

"We still need layouts for the back display wall. It'll be off-white so use vibrant colors so they'll pop. Also, bring the box of fly-ers and business cards."

"I know." I rolled my eyes, thankful there were no security cameras to catch my attitude.

"Cheryl and I wish—"

"That you could handle the booth." I was perfectly capable of handling a booth at the community art benefit show. I've handled the store just fine. Okay, there was that one incident involving the paper racks but that was almost a year ago. "Grandma, you have to help Cheryl host the show. You can't let her do it on her own."

Not that Grandma Cheryl wasn't qualified to host. She had hosted all of my slumber parties growing up. With a sharp look and even edgier words, Cheryl whipped everyone into shape. I learned the fine art of snarkiness at her knee.

"You're right." Hope sounded resigned to her fate. "I'm just worried about tomorrow. Did you remember—"

"Grandma, I read the list you taped to the front counter by the register. I read the one in the break room. And I've taken my own notes. We'll have everything we need."

"Including the prizes for the contest?"

I squeezed my eyes closed. "What contest?"

Hope sighed. "I told Cheryl to leave a written note   rather than a voice mail."

My forgetfulness for checking phone messages was legendary in my tiny family. No amount of scolding from my grandmothers—or from myself—corrected the flaw.

"Since we're closing the store for the Art Benefit Show, we de-cided to hold two contests to make it up to our customers. And hopefully, it'll draw in some new ones."

Business was down across the county, especially for those of us who offered consumers the non-essentials in life. Hobbies were the first items cut from a budget.

"One contest will be opened for seasoned croppers and the other for novice scrappers," Hope said. "To encourage new scrappers to enter, we'll hold two teaching crops next week. I also need sign-up sheets for those."

I jotted down the time and cost for the crops, then snapped the cell phone shut.

Car lights flooded through the slats of the blinds covering the large display windows. Tunnels of beams bounced off the jars holding fabric flowers and ribbons lining a row of shelves. Shadows flickered across the walls, doubling the inventory of the overstocked store in a dark and menacing hue. We had to start moving the product. A store morphing into a warehouse didn't do well for the bottom line.

"I should've brought sunglasses." Sierra Brodart squinted as the harsh light hit her face. She wiggled her fingers over a glass jar then moved to the next. Fifteen small jars filled with various embellishments were scattered around the work surface. She plucked out two forest green brads from a jar and then pressed them through the cream cardstock.

Whoosh. Whoosh. The slicing and dicing resumed. I held in a long-suffering sigh and glanced at tomorrow's work schedule. In the morning, my grandmothers wanted all the employees at the Art Benefit Show.

Knowing our receivables for the last quarter, I worried about that decision. Scrap This had two full-time and two part-time employees. My grandmothers, Hope and Cheryl, believed part of their purpose in life was helping women through financial transitions. Marilyn was facing a divorce. Sierra's three boys were all in elementary school and her husband Hank was once again out of work. Linda Anderson was an empty-nester who lost her beloved husband of thirty years in a car accident eighteen months ago. I was their prodigal granddaughter who joined the military to take on the world only to have the world slap me back home. Hard.

Eden was a great place to live—well, start over—as no one held high expectations. Here it made sense to go from working in JAG to helping in my grandmothers' scrapbooking store. No one thought a scandal caused the switch in my career path. Here, everything boiled down to family.

Marilyn slapped another picture onto the trimmer. With a whack of the guillotine style blade, she was single.

I ventured from behind the counter and headed toward Marilyn. We needed professional layouts on display tomorrow to demonstrate scrapbooking as a legitimate art, not just a mommy-hobby. The best way to increase income was tapping into the professional art market. I doubted a collage of body parts would entice people into the store. Emerging serial killers probably weren't interested in keeping a scrapbook. Even if they were, they weren't quite the clientele I wanted for Scrap This.

"One day, *your children*," I stressed the last two words, "might want an intact picture of their father."

The evilest of gazes landed on me. I never knew Marilyn's wide blue eyes could look so beady and narrow. "And what would you know about that? Maybe the only good husband is a..."

"Forgiveness, Marilyn. It's a good thing," I said and stole a look at Linda who sat beside the chopping diva.

Linda hunched over her page, lips pinched together, complexion pale except for two red splotches on her cheeks. Her hands shook as she placed a picture of her twenty-something son onto a piece of cardstock.

"What would you know about forgiving a husband?" Marilyn shoved disheveled blonde curls away from her face.

A lot, actually. But I kept the thought to myself.

"Faith's just trying to help." Sierra punctuated her sentence with a snap of her wrist. Two yards of brown and blue grosgrain ribbon furled out. A click of the scissors completed the page starring her three elementary school-aged sons Harold, Henry and Howard, affectionately known by the greater community as the Hooligans.

Sierra swore they took after their father. Having heard of Hank's pranks, which usually ended with a ride in the backseat of a squad car, I agreed with her assessment. Hank was a good guy, but one you never really trusted. The bad boy from high school still lurked inside of him.

Marilyn snorted and returned to hacking her philandering husband from the photo history of her life.

Who was I to judge? I didn't trust anyone with anything other than the sanitized version of my past. Yep, I served in the Army. Yep, I worked in JAG. Nope, it's not like on TV.

I wandered back to the counter and picked up my crop tote. I could only procrastinate so long with administrative duties. My insides squirmed as I dropped myself into a vacant seat at an empty table and pulled out a pack of photos. Public scrapbooking always left me a little anxious as I opened snippets of my life to the scrutiny of others.

Sierra draped herself over my shoulders and stared at the photos. She tapped a manicured nail on the picture of my grandmothers and me at a Renaissance Festival. "Who took the photos?"

I flicked the flap of the packet. "Steve."

"Ah, say no more." Sierra launched a knowing wink at me before returning to her layout.

Steve Davis, my neighbor two doors down, and the one man who could make me think about reconsidering my commitment phobia. Nothing would please my grandmothers more than Steve and I becoming a couple. Nothing could be less likely to happen. A woman couldn't maintain a lifestyle of confidentiality with a significant other in her life.

Whack!

I cringed. I would fall asleep hearing that sound in my head. "I think you should give the cutting tools a break."

Marilyn continued her violent scrapbooking techniques. She held up a picture of a holiday gathering, placed it on the trimmer, and pressed the handle. Michael was dismembered from Thanksgiving dinner.

"You can't cut him out of all the pictures," I said. "It's really ruining the composition."

Marilyn's evil glare returned as she eliminated her philandering husband from two more family portraits. "Yes, I can."

"Think of the children," I said.

"This is my private book. I can crop off whoever I want," Marilyn said.

Linda packed up her supplies and flicked a desperate gaze at me. Unlike her, I didn't have a choice. I had to stay and offer guidance and suggestions. We needed layouts, not body parts.

"It won't look good, Marilyn," I said.

"I think it looks great!" Sierra giggled. "Go, Marilyn, go. Crop that hubby!"

The stress in Marilyn's face evaporated as she laughed. She grabbed more pictures. "Crop you. Crop you. Crop you!" Marilyn slammed the blade down the middle of a picture of Michael. The man fluttered to the floor in two pieces.

TWO

Fog swirled around the Allegheny Mountains on Saturday morning. A fine layer of whiteness dipped into the valley as if the city moved up a few notches during the night and Eden was now closer to heaven. Pinpricks of light broke through the haze. In a few hours, the mist would burn off to leave the day bright and engaging.

Surrounded by mountains, the town of Eden was a mixture of franchise stores, office buildings, farms and quaint Victorian style buildings. The town couldn't decide between evolving into a bustling metropolis or staying true to its roots of a farming community. The loss of landscape, faster pace of living, and rise in crime caused distrust to bloom and lines were drawn in the community. The farmers blamed the problem on the artists who wanted more tourists visiting, and the artists blamed it on the tech people who wanted to enter into the 'new' century. Though everyone took credit for the higher paying jobs and better services.

The drive to the convention center took longer than expected. It appeared everyone in town was at the Art Benefit Show or ABS as it morphed into when texted and tweeted.

I turned into the parking lot and finally found a space at the far end of the last row. Every choice had a consequence, and this was mine for hitting the snooze button one too many times. I switched my beige wedge sandals for dusty rose canvas sneakers. Comfort out ranked cute when a walk turned into a cross-country hike.

I opened the trunk and removed my large brown and pink striped artist tote. I hauled the heavy leather strap onto my shoulder and started across the parking lot.

"Faith, wait!"

I peered through the evaporating mist and spotted Marilyn. I really needed a cup of coffee before I heard about Michael. Again. I was starting to want to hack the man into little pieces myself.

Marilyn rushed over to me. "I'm really sorry about my rant during the crop. I worked on some layouts this morning. I promise all the people remained in one piece."

"Divorce will do that to a woman." I offered an unrestrained smile and mentally patted myself on the back for the quick forgiveness I bestowed.

"Michael says that woman's baby isn't his. He wants us to try counseling. I agreed." Marilyn dropped her bomb and hurried away.

I gaped at her back. A blare of a horn got my feet moving again. I ran and caught up with her. "You don't believe him? You can't. There is no way you can consider getting back together with the louse." I shifted the strap of my tote from one shoulder to the other.

"Weren't you the one talking about forgiveness?"

"Sure, but that meant not chopping up all your photos."

"A decision like this isn't cut and dry when you have children."

"Your kids are teenagers. They'll understand." I gave her the look my grandmothers' gave me when I ignored their wisdom. "What are you teaching your children by accepting that kind of treatment from Michael?"

"That I love them more than I can hate someone." She stomped away but I followed after her.

"Marilyn, no one is questioning your love for your children. Heck, everyone knows you're a great mom. You have terrific teenagers. And terrific and teenagers aren't two words usually linked."

"Liz has been crying for days over the divorce. Mark actually considered not going to an Orioles game with his father. I won't make my children feel it's disloyal to me to love their father. Besides, maybe that woman is lying and not Michael."

"But you don't know that."

Marilyn shot me a triumphant smile. "And you don't know that Michael is."

Touché.

We reached the sidewalk and our conversation stopped. The smell of brewing coffee and fresh baked pastries started my stomach rumbling. Hitting the snooze button also required crossing breakfast off the morning to-do list.

Steve Davis headed toward me carrying a cardboard cup. A tool belt hung around his waist, the metal gizmos clanging with each step he took. "Faith, I've been waiting for you."

The man looked lethal in faded dark blue jeans and a t-shirt. I usually saw him in suits and khakis. Even on the weekends his normal attire was business causal. Not like today...bad boy biker. His shaved head added to the edgy look.

I swallowed my sigh and took my gaze from the man and placed it on the cup of coffee. Also sigh-worthy.

Marilyn tugged the strap of my tote off my shoulder. "I'll start setting up while you flirt with Steve." She continued into the building.

I accepted the coffee from Steve. "I'm not flirting with you. Just being polite since you waited for me."

His expression remained neutral though a twinkle glittered in his deep brown eyes. "I volunteered to help your grandmothers today. They asked me to walk you to your booth. Here I am."

"I can find my way." I took a sip of the coffee and nearly burned my tongue.

"I have a hard time denying a request from Hope and Cheryl. They worry about you."

Poor, unknowing man. Pairing Steve and me together motivated my grandmothers, not worry. Their matchmaking plan had topped every to-do, resolution and prayer list since I moved home fourteen months ago. They turned on the fragile, old women charm whenever Steve and I entered the same orbit. A wasted effort, but I treasured the care and love motivating their antics.

I scanned the large open area and tried locating the Scrap This booth. The art gallery arena was spectacular. Bright, bold signs directed attendees to different exhibits and fabulous art displays. Fans could easily spot their favorite artists and make their way to the booth.

"This is great," I said. "The setup makes it very easy to move around the space."

"Your grandmothers did a good job organizing the traffic flow." Steve draped his arm around my shoulders.

My heart fluttered and I ordered the treacherous organ to stop. What woman wouldn't be thrilled at the attention? But I wasn't looking for a relationship. I was unavailable. My heart still continued at the more rapid pace. A heart was a fickle thing.

Marilyn ran over, exasperation on her face. She raised her eyebrows as she stared at Steve's arm. "Faith, you're needed at the booth."

I stepped away from Steve. "That's where I was headed."

He suppressed a smile and waved goodbye. "I'll let your grandmothers know you're here safe and sound."

"What's going on?" I asked.

Marilyn looked heavenward and shook her head. "One of Linda's layouts was damaged. She stored them without page protectors and one layout with brads poked a hole in the corner of a picture of her husband and son. She ran off in tears toward the restrooms. Sierra is trying to fix the page. And talking about Sierra, she arrived with the Hooligans. Hank's working security today here at the show. Then some photographer is running around taking photos without permission and upsetting the artists."

I stood on my tiptoes to get a better read of the signs. "I'll go after Linda. Point the photographer out to the Hooligans and tell the boys we'll give them a dollar each for every picture they can jump into or disrupt."

"Soothing Linda can wait." Marilyn grabbed my arm and tugged me down the aisle. "We're behind on setting up and they've started letting attendees in."

We only went two steps before Marilyn squealed and rooted

her feet to the concrete floor. I slammed into her.

"What's—" I shut up.

Marilyn's coloring went from brandy red to colonial white. Her husband, Michael, walked down the aisle with his pregnant mistress at his side. He spotted us, blanched, then hurried in the opposite direction with the homewrecker weebling and wobbling behind him.

"That lousy prince-turned-into-a-poisonous-toad stood his son up. His son! He was taking Mark to the baseball game." Marilyn huffed herself red again and started a verbal-roast of Michael. "Heaven better help that man because I'm going to kill him."

She stormed off in a fit, leaving me to face the growing crowd. Smiling, I shrugged my shoulders and asked, "Does anyone know her?"

I hurried to the Scrap This booth—an empty booth besides Sierra.

"The boys are tracking down the photographer. Should you really be encouraging them?" Sierra adjusted one of the framed layouts on the backboard.

"Do you have a better idea?"

"No. And talking about ideas..." Sierra nodded toward Linda's layout near the cash register, "...have any on how to patch up that mess?"

The gaping hole in the layout mocked me. The tear at the bottom of the photograph would be hard to fix without damaging the journaling box. "That's the question of the day."

"Wonderful. You're as much help as Marilyn. What's she doing?" Sierra grabbed a large box of adhesives and dropped it onto the ground.

"Trying not to kill Michael."

"What?" She paused, the box cutter midway through the length of tape.

As I examined Linda's layout closer, I explained Marilyn's disappearing act.

"Maybe now she'll reconsider the reconciliation," Sierra said.

"My thoughts exactly." I glanced at the products we brought with us. None complemented Linda's layout.

Sierra hummed as she rearranged layouts on the temporary wall.

That had to mean one thing. I smiled. "Yesterday's interview went well for Hank?"

Four months out of work took a toll on her husband's confidence and their bank account. The unemployment checks and Sierra's paycheck stretched to cover the basics but that would only last so long. I knew their hearts broke at the inability to buy a few inexpensive extras for their boys.

Sierra nodded. "He told me the builder was impressed with his résumé and talked to him for an hour. We should hear back Monday."

Two mothers with toddlers stopped and asked about our classes. Sierra placed the cutter into her back pocket and walked them over to the table holding our class lists and sign-up sheets. A man entered the booth and I placed the damaged layout down to give him my attention. He examined one of the framed layouts.

"Is that fishing wire?" He squinted and leaned forward, his nose almost pressing against the plastic protecting the page.

"Yes." I smiled and started explaining about mixed media. The man nodded and stepped back. Since he only wanted a yes or no response and not a discourse, I stopped talking and allowed him privacy to browse.

A voice crackled over the loudspeaker. "Ladies and gentlemen. Everyone stay in the building and remain calm. The police are on their way."

From what I could see, security guards approached the exits and stood in front of them. Hands rested at waists near the butts of their guns.

The voice continued. "There's been a murder!"

Pandemonium erupted.

THREE

They asked vendors to return to their spaces and ushered attendees into the main hall. Linda perched on the edge of a wooden stool nervously sipping a bottle of soda, the small drips of condensation splattering her pants. Sierra wrung her hands together and paced around our tiny space. I stood still and worried, the emotion churning the coffee in my stomach. Where were my grandmothers? Where was Steve? Where were Hank and the boys?

Grandma Cheryl was probably chasing Clyde around the building trying to make him victim number two. Who in the world announced a murder over a loudspeaker?

I tried keeping myself calm and rational. Not something easy to do when a person feared for the lives of those they loved. Except for Steve. I liked Steve. I didn't love him.

"They're probably speaking with the police." Sierra placed a comforting arm around my shoulder. We huddled together. "Hope and Cheryl are in charge."

"You're right. And Hank went with them or is rounding up the boys. He wouldn't want them walking around alone."

Those words brought little comfort to either of us. Were the police going to blame my grandmothers for what happened? Would they be sued? I spotted Cheryl, Hope and Steve walking toward the booth and relief flooded through me. They were safe. The tightness in my chest relaxed.

But where was Hank? The boys? I held onto Sierra.

A man in a suit stopped Steve to talk to him. They both looked in my direction, then walked toward me. That wasn't good. Cheryl shot an angry glare at the suited man's back.

"The boys?" Sierra asked.

Steve reassured her with a smile. "Hank took them outside. They were way too interested in the police."

I grinned at Sierra. "I told you Hank was with the boys."

Relief was visible on her face.

"I hate to break up the cheering section, but I have a few questions for you, Miss Hunter." The attractive red-haired man in the dark blue suit flashed a badge.

I squinted and studied the badge. This guy wasn't a security guard. "Officer—"

"Detective Roget." He stood with his legs apart, a stance worthy of any cowboy bent on saving the town from the evil gunslinger.

I didn't know if placing his hands so the jacket opened and revealed the gun was an involuntarily reflex or an act of intimidation. Crossing my arms, I locked gazes with him. From somewhere behind me, Steve groaned.

"When was the last time you talked with Marilyn Kane?" Roget asked.

Marilyn. Marilyn wasn't with us at the booth. Marilyn was dead. Murdered. Detective Roget wavered in front of me, a whirling sound filled my ears. Strong arms wrapped around me and I leaned against a rock of warmth and comfort.

"Marilyn's okay, Faith," Steve said.

"Stay out of this, Davis."

"I would if..." Steve didn't complete the sentence, only tightened his hold around me.

I took in deep breaths and the room came back into focus. My grandmothers stood behind the detective. Cheryl's hands bunched into fists. Hope gripped Cheryl's shoulders to stop her from assaulting the detective. If he wasn't asking about Marilyn because she was the victim then—

"How was he killed?" I asked.

"Him? How do you know it's a him?" A knowing smile tilted the corners of the detective's lips.

"Because you're asking about Marilyn. If she's not hurt then it has to be about her husband." For some reason, I couldn't say dead. Murdered. "Why else would you be asking about Marilyn?"

Steve gestured for me to be quiet. Not something I was good at.

"With an ongoing investigation, the police ask the questions," Roget said.

I stepped closer to the detective. "But you're here to accuse Marilyn."

The detective bestowed a half-smile, half-sneer on me. "You think that because of a little conversation you had with Marilyn?"

So, his search for Marilyn wasn't just based on her being the spouse. I wouldn't admit anything to Roget. "It's because I'm not stupid."

"Faith!" Hope gasped. She looked at the detective and shook her head. "We did not raise her to speak like that to police officers. I'm sure she's just upset."

Great. My poor grandmother was defending her parenting skills. "Listen, Detective, I know the wife is usually the person blamed but it could've been someone else."

"True." Roget walked around the booth, appearing to take a mental note of our inventory.

"So you admit it was Michael." Shivers raced up spine.

"Informing. Not admitting." The detective studied the booth and then me. "You sure do have an unusual way of phrasing things. Maybe I should be questioning you."

I tried keeping my anger from rising. "Now you're accusing me of killing him?"

Steve stepped forward and rested a hand on my shoulder, drawing me away from the detective. "Faith, the detective has to assume everyone is a suspect. It's not personal."

"Of course it's personal." I pushed away from Steve. Being accused of crimes you didn't commit attacked your character, your pride and your self-worth. How could it be anything else?

"I think we should have this conversation in private." Roget took hold of my arm.

"Where are you taking my granddaughter?" Cheryl stepped in front of the detective.

"Steve, stop him," Hope said.

"It'll be okay," Steve soothed my grandmothers. "Faith's been here at the booth the whole time. She's not really suspected of anything. The detective just needs to ask a few questions about Marilyn's whereabouts."

My blood froze. Steve had no idea what Marilyn said to me.

Roget shrugged. "I can either do it here or at the police station."

I pulled my arm away from the detective. "Fine. Let's go."

I wiped my hands on my pants and hoped the detective didn't notice my nervousness. Or if he did, he didn't take the movement as a confession of my guilt. I knew from experience in the beginning of an investigation every action comes across as an admission of guilt.

I looked behind me. Steve stood with his arms loose at his side and left leg bent, a relaxed position the military termed at ease. But his face told me he was far from that state of mind. Of course, his concern could be more on the lines of what kind of trouble I'd get myself into rather than what kind of trouble I was already in.

Detective Roget led me toward the stairwell. "If you need a lawyer, it will be along the lines of a defense attorney rather than a prosecutor." He opened the door and ushered me inside.

"I don't need an attorney." I leaned against the wall, needing the support to keep standing. My heart thudded in my chest and my knees shook. Why was the detective so hostile? I did nothing wrong. I hadn't hurt anyone. Or killed anyone.

Roget pointed at the steps. "Why don't you have a seat?"

"I'd rather stand."

He looked me up and down. A spark of interest gleamed in his green eyes. "You seem a little unsteady and I'd rather not have to catch you."

I walked over to the stairs and sat on the second step.

"When was the last time you saw Michael Kane?"

"I thought you wanted to ask me about Marilyn."

"Just answer my questions, Miss Hunter."

"I saw him a little after nine when he waltzed past with the..." I paused, rummaging through my brain for the correct and least offensive, or less likely to get me into trouble word. "Girlfriend."

Detective Roget grinned, eyebrows raised. "Girlfriend."

"Michael Kane paraded his pregnant mistress right by his wife."

"Right by?"

"Okay, technically, not right in front of her, but where she would notice. I don't know why Michael brought her. His co-workers were going to be here. Why would he want them to know he was committing adultery?"

Roget's features tightened. "Because it isn't a crime. Unlike murder."

I squirmed on the step.

"After Mrs. Kane saw her husband and his girlfriend, what happened?"

Poor Marilyn. Even though she was on the outs with Michael, she loved him. How would his children get over this? I blinked back tears. "How was he killed?"

The detective's look said "that's for me to know and you not to find out," but aloud he said it in a nicer way. "At this time, that's privileged information the public doesn't need to know."

"The public doesn't have the right to know how a man was killed?"

"Not when it could hamper the case. And to clarify this again, it's my job to ask questions. Your role is to sit, listen and answer what I ask. Understand?"

I gave one sharp nod and narrowed my eyes at him.

"So, after she saw him, she walked away?"

"Yes, sir."

He grinned at my answer. "Do you recall which direction?"

"No, sir."

"How did Mrs. Kane react when she saw Mr. Kane and the other woman?"

I'm going to kill him. The statement swirled in my head. Those hastily spoken words would make Marilyn the most likely suspect in her husband's murder. I took a deep breath then answered carefully. "She got very pale and upset."

"Upset as in screaming, yelling, sobbing." He made a circle motion with his hand, encouraging me to elaborate.

"She squealed. Her face turned red, then paled. I where she was looking and saw Michael and the girlfriend."

"Did they approach you?"

"No."

"You're doing good, only a couple more questions. Do you know if Marilyn went home or somewhere else?"

Marilyn was missing. Did the girlfriend kill Michael then his wife? I shook my head and held back the terrifying thoughts. "I don't know where she went."

He winked at me like we were old friends. Confidantes. "Okay, last one. Did Marilyn say anything after seeing her husband?"

"Yes." I stood. I did my duty. Obligation fulfilled.

"Miss Hunter, I need the exact words she said."

"What happens if I don't remember?"

"Nothing. Unless I find out you're lying to me." He stepped toward me. "If you are, your 'forgetting' might fall under aiding and abetting."

I hunched forward, my gaze now directed at the marred linoleum floor. I hated being forced into betraying my friend.

"Let me try again, Miss Hunter, and take note that I have spoken with other witnesses. Did Mrs. Kane say anything after she saw her husband?"

I had to tell Roget. I knew the law. I also knew Marilyn. She said those words because she was angry. She did not want Michael dead. But I couldn't lie. "She said that heaven better help that man because she was going to kill him."

FOUR

The door creaked open and Officer Conroy Jasper, county chess champion and former high school classmate, walked into the stairwell. He nodded at Detective Roget and held out a piece of paper.

I tried to catch Jasper's attention.

He ignored me.

Roget rolled up the paper and tapped it against his palm. "I have a search warrant for Scrap This."

"What?" Blood rushed from my head. I squeezed the stair rail, keeping myself upright. A warrant for the store? Why would the detective think Scrap This tied into Michael Kane's murder?

"I'd like you to open it up for us," Roget said. "Or I could have one of your grandmothers come with me."

I couldn't—wouldn't—let this man upset my family. Pulling myself together, I straightened my posture and centered a go-to-hell look at the detective. "How do I know that's really a warrant? It could be a take-out menu."

Jasper choked back a snicker. Roget thrust the document at me.

With a heavy sigh, I took the offered paper and read it. A legitimate, official warrant. Great, I ran into an officer who used truth, not threats, to intimidate. "Do you mind if I go in my own car?"

Roget lowered his gaze from my head down to my feet and then worked his way back up. From his expression, it appeared he was conducting a character study. I believe he concluded I was lacking something critical.

"I've known Faith for a while, I believe we can trust her," Jasper said.

I crossed my arms and fought the urge to glare at Jasper. Thanks a lot. He "believed" I could be trusted. Why not use knowing?

Jasper pulled the door open. "If she rides with us, someone will have to run her home. And if we find something…"

"Fine." Roget pointed a finger at me. "I'll be right behind you. Don't try anything."

The three of us went out a side door guarded by a patrol officer. What did the man think I would try and do? And why? Okay, so I was the last one seen talking to Marilyn and I didn't want to repeat her figurative threat, but that didn't make me a person to add to the most-likely-to-run-from-the-law list.

Two vans with letters painted on the side pressed the curb. The local newspaper and the radio station arrived. The DJ and his crew started to unload their mobile equipment for their live broadcast. The nearest TV station was an hour away so at least we wouldn't wind up on the evening news.

At least not yet.

"Ignore any and all reporters on the way to your car." Roget opened the door of a white sedan parked in front of the side entrance. "Wait there and I'll drive over."

Reporter extraordinaire Karen England, aka Karen Pancake, watched me with interest. A glow developed in her eyes and she licked her lips, fingers tightening around a pen.

"Don't worry. I have no desire to talk to anyone." I hoped Karen heard and listened. The listening part of any conversation hadn't been one of Karen's best skills. From kindergarten through graduation, she spent more time arguing, questioning, and contradicting everything the teachers said. It was a miracle any of us learned anything besides Karen's opinion on every subject known to mankind. And even a few no one knew existed. It's a wonder she became a reporter rather than a novelist.

Karen's heels tapped behind me. If she wanted to be an investigative reporter, she needed quieter shoes.

"Hey, you. Stop. I want to ask you some questions."

Hey, you? Like that was the way to make friends and influence people. What did they teach her in college? She probably hadn't kept silent long enough to hear the professors. I hummed a Maroon 5 song and placed my hand over my ear, pretending I was listening to music.

A horn blared behind me and I refrained from reacting. That's the problem with pretending. It's hard keeping up when reality changes and a person forgets the perfect act of deception.

"Didn't I tell you no questions?" Roget barked at Karen.

How long had Roget been in Eden? Karen ignoring orders was as reliable as finding a Bible in a church.

I ignored the argument developing between the reporter and the detective and continued to my car. When I reached my Malibu, I took my time unlocking the door then settling into the seat. Detective Roget pulled up revving the engine of his unmarked sedan.

I checked all the mirrors, thrice, then made my way to Scrap This, maintaining the proper speed the entire way. I could almost hear the anxious detective fuming in the car behind me. Served him right. I drove around the corner and made the first right turn into the lot behind the store. Employee parking spaces were near the garbage bins, not choice spots, but we already had incentive to show up: a paycheck. As my grandmothers said, the best spots go to customers.

A squad car stopped behind my car. Great, Detective Roget assumed I'd flee given the chance. Maybe I shouldn't have taken the long way. Without uttering a word, I unlocked the backdoor and allowed the men to enter.

Boxes from a recent delivery were stacked in the middle of the storage area. A few of them had toppled over and made a haphazard trail to the twelve foot wide curtain that separated the storage room from the rest of the store. I placed my hand on the partition. Multi-tasking ruled in a small business. We could accept deliveries, open boxes, and man the store at the same time. Privacy, or a lack thereof, occurred with the simple finger motion of hook and tug.

"Stay here," Roget said.

I made a wide arc with my arms, showing off the storage room with only boxes and shelves. "What if it takes you hours? There's nowhere to sit. No restroom. No caffeine. Can I at least wait in the employee break room? It isn't like this is a secured area."

Detective Roget yanked opened the maroon curtains lined with gold. The metal rings rubbed against the bar and set off a squeal. "All right. Come with me."

Roget nodded at each officer in turn and pointed to a certain area of the store. Jasper headed to the cutting tools. Officer Kline headed for the crop area. "Don't damage any of the merchandise. Miss Hunter, you can wait in the area where the register is."

"You mean the customer service area."

Roget glared down at me. "I don't care what you call it. Just wait over there."

My dislike for him grew moment by moment. From the corner of my eye, I spotted Kline rummaging in the trash can. My breath hitched. Had I emptied it out last night? Was evidence of Marilyn's pictorial rampage still in the garbage?

"Detective Roget, do you want all of them?" Jasper asked from the end of the aisle near the cutting tools.

All of what? I peered down the row flanked by white racks holding different colors of cardstock.

"Just those ones." Roget pointed at the scissor section. He glanced in my direction, raised his eyes in a heaven-help-me plea, then jabbed his finger toward the register. "Now."

"I'm going." I trudged in that general direction.

Roget picked up a box and passed it to Officer Jasper. "Take this to the squad car."

Walking backwards, I watched Jasper head toward the back-door. He weaved through the paper racks. I cringed as he brushed against several stacks of cardstock. Damaged paper meant having to pull it off the shelf. Customers wouldn't buy a sheet with even a tiny bent corner.

Roget moved toward the back of the store. Holding my breath, I diverted my direction and took a few steps toward the cutting tools. My stomach did a free fall. The sharp-tip scissors were gone. Each and every one. Even the new purple handled ones I coveted. Friday night we had an abundant supply. I tapped my finger on the cold, empty, metal hooks.

Like picking out the photos and embellishment for a layout, my mind gathered all the facts and arranged them into a cohesive unit. The police obtained a search warrant to find evidence. Detective Roget took the scissors. Michael had been stabbed with a tool used to help scrappers preserve family memories—or cut people from them.

"What were you told?"

I jumped up and turned around. Two actions a person shouldn't combine. I wobbled and then lost my balance, sending my body toward the racks of paper. A hand snagged my arm and steadied me.

Detective Roget centered his hard gaze on my face and tightened his grip. "If you insist on interfering, I'll put you in the police car."

I pried his hand from my arm, and placed my hands on my hips while raising my chin without making the gesture a challenge. "I'm not interfering. I'm taking inventory."

"Really." He matched my stance, but his hand placements reminded me he had handcuffs and a firearm. His next official business could be giving me a tour of the jail. "Because I'm leaning toward interfering in a police investigation."

I wanted to dare him to prove it. Instead, I kept quiet. I knew my actions weren't as sweet and innocent as I claimed, but I wasn't interfering. I wanted to protect Marilyn. She wouldn't kill Michael.

Talk about it, dream about it, maybe even plot it, but not actually commit it.

Detective Roget cleared his throat. I snapped myself back to the physical present. He kept his green eyes locked on me. I returned his gaze. He continued staring. I stared back but revealed my discomfort by a rapid succession of blinking. I hoped he didn't think I was flirting with him.

He let out an exasperated sigh and repeated the earlier instruction. "Stay out of the way. Do not touch anything."

"Someone else touched something." I pointed at the empty hooks. "All the scissors are gone."

"Are you always so difficult?"

I knew it was a rhetorical question so I went with expounding upon my previous statement. "Being in the process of inventory, those empty hooks caught my attention. I'm guessing you took them for evidence."

"You'll receive a full list of all property removed when we file it with the court."

"I need to know now, for inventory purposes. Or I have to assume they were stolen." I tilted my head and widened my eyes. "Who should I call at the police department to report this robbery?"

"You don't really think those scissors were stolen."

I opened my eyes wider to give him my best innocent-damsel look. "Of course I do Detective Roget. Whatever else could have happened to them?" I fluttered my lashes.

"Officer Jasper, write out an inventory list for Miss Hunter then escort her to the customer service area." Roget pointed to the L-shaped counter in the middle of the store jutting out from the wall.

"Come on, Faith." Jasper placed a hand under my elbow. He leaned toward me and lowered his voice. "If I were you, I'd stop pushing the detective's buttons. You're gonna wind up in trouble."

"I'm not pushing buttons."

"You're either pushing buttons or being stupid," Jasper whispered through gritted teeth. "Knock it off or your grandmothers will be bailing you out of jail. Not to mention Steve seeing this on the blotter."

I decided to keep my opinions to myself. Not that I cared if Steve found out. Of course, I really didn't want my grandmothers storming the police station. Grandma Cheryl would tell off the detective and Grandma Hope would swear upon the family name she raised me better.

But I should share Marilyn's cropping habits with law enforcement. "Marilyn doesn't use sharp-tip scissors. She uses a personal trimmer—"

Cold bands wrapped around my heart.

Marilyn, with her knees pressed against her chin, was squished into the small corner of the register area where we stored our personal items. Tears spilled down her cheeks.

Jasper groaned and shook his head. "I'm going to ask to be removed from this case." He took in a deep breath, and with regret etched onto his face, made an announcement. "Detective Roget, we just found Mrs. Kane."

I hurried into the enclosure and threw a quick glance over my shoulder. Jasper roved his gaze away from us. The detective talked into a cell phone, his burning gaze resting on me. Great, the man probably thought I took the scenic route so Marilyn had enough time for an escape.

"This isn't going to look good," I whispered.

Marilyn scrambled to her feet and pulled wads of paper from her pocket and then thrust them at me. "I didn't have a choice."

The sharp corners of the heavyweight paper poked into the skin of my palms and fingers, a contrast to the smooth texture of the surface. Bile rose in my throat. These weren't slips of paper but remnants from a photograph. Evidence of Marilyn's cropping carnage.

"Hide them." Marilyn whispered between her clenched teeth.

Wide-eyed, I stared at Marilyn. I opened my hands and confirmed my suspicion. Slivers drifted to the floor. Michael's head—minus his body—lay on top of my shoe. The rest of the cropped images slipped from my hands. Roget stepped into the space and looked down. Scattered across the floor were the photo remains of Michael.

"Jasper, collect it and then tag the evidence." Roget removed his handcuffs from his belt.

Was Marilyn going to jail? Was I? Were we?

Marilyn glared at me. Blame clear in her eyes. If I had only thrown out the trash last night when I closed up, the police wouldn't have this evidence against her.

FIVE

Whispers floated around me as I followed Jasper into the police station. Bobbi-Annie, the receptionist and our local town tattler, picked up the phone receiver and punched in a number.

I hoped she wasn't doing me the favor of calling my grandmothers to inform them of my whereabouts.

Jasper opened up the door to a small room with no windows. "You can wait in here, Faith."

I rubbed my hands up and down my arms. "Why? What's going to happen?"

"I don't know. It all depends on Detective Roget."

The words sounded ominous. I stepped inside and fought back the tears. Hurrying over to a metal chair, I sat down and tried thinking about something pleasant to stop from crying. I hated showing weakness. Unfortunately, the only thought creeping into my mind was I wished Marilyn hadn't handed me the cut-up photos.

And that I had thrown out the garbage last night.

The door opened and Marilyn walked inside. Tear tracks stained her face.

Roget narrowed his gaze at me. "Why is she in here? I want them separated."

"Clay Webber is in the other room. Drunk and disorderly," Jasper said.

While Clay wasn't a violent man, he made inappropriate offers to every woman in town. He held the town status of "whipping post" after getting punched at least once by every husband, son, and brother in Eden. Of course that hadn't stopped his comments.

Except for Hilda Pancake, Karen's grandmother. He steered clear after she broke his arm and nearly his skull with a baseball bat. No charges were brought because Clay swore he was too drunk to remember who hit him. More like too ashamed to admit an old woman gave him a beat down.

Leaving the door open, Roget nodded and motioned for Jasper to step closer for a private talk. Marilyn dropped into the chair beside me and shot me a glare that could've melted a glacier. At Christmas time, I'd probably be moved from the handmade card list to the picked-up-at-the-after-Christmas-sale card list.

I inched away. "Do you know what's going on?"

Marilyn slashed her arms through the air. "Are you that dense, Faith? You really can't figure out what's happening? They brought us here because we're suspects."

"But I didn't do anything." The words shook from my throat.

"Oh, and I did."

Heat blazed across my cheeks. "I'm sorry. I didn't mean—"

Marilyn covered her face, hunched over, and sobbed. I froze in my seat at her reaction. From livid to despair in two seconds. Things were going to get much worse for us.

Now I wanted my grandmas.

Jasper stepped into the room and handed me a box of tissues. "Listen, Roget is using the break room to talk to two prosecutors right now, so you both have to stay in here. He wants no talking between you two. Got it?"

I nodded while Marilyn continued sobbing.

"I'll be standing right outside." Jasper took one step outside the small room. "The door will remain open. I mean no talking. Not one word to pass between you ladies. To make it easier, don't even look at each other."

Did Jasper really expect me to just sit here and ignore the fact my friend wept? I squirmed and crossed my arms. I wanted to reach out and hug Marilyn but was afraid that would make the situation worse for us.

Marilyn raised her head and I handed her some tissues. Anguish and anger sparkled in her eyes. She scrubbed her cheeks. "They're going to arrest me for Michael's murder."

Her matter-of-fact tone slugged me in the gut. "No they won't," I whispered.

"I'm the wife," she said. "I was there. They have those photos."

"There's always the girlfriend."

Marilyn shook her head. "It'll be me."

"Everyone knows you wouldn't kill someone."

A throat cleared and I shifted in my seat. Jasper gave me a narrowed-eyed look and placed his finger on his lips.

"Trust me, Detective Roget believes I did it," Marilyn whispered, the words sounding even more threatening. "He'll have me arrested and shoved into a cell by tonight."

"If he does—" I stopped talking as I didn't really know what we could do if Roget arrested her. Besides find her a good defense attorney.

"Good. Then you'll do it."

The triumphant tone in the words regained my attention and the confident smile gracing her face worried me. The last time someone had that I-have-the-perfect-idea smile on their face, I accepted a marriage proposal from a knight in shining armor and later discovered he was a con artist in tinfoil.

"What do you need me to do? I'm in this as deep as you." Hesitation shook my voice. I hoped that gave Marilyn enough of a clue I was asking about—not committing—to her plan.

"I told Roget you had no idea I was at the store."

"Thank you. Because I didn't know."

"Jasper said he saw me hand you the photographs. They should let you out of here."

"Uh huh..."

"I'll need you to prove I didn't kill Michael."

I leaned closer and lowered my voice. "I can't do that. I don't know how."

She shrugged. "You're an expert. Figure it out."

"An expert? Wouldn't that qualification go to the police who are investigating the case?"

"Faith, Detective Roget has already solved this case. He didn't bring the prosecutors in here because he thinks I'm innocent. He's going to arrest me for the murder of my husband." Her voice grew lower and grief etched itself onto her face.

"It's not right."

"And that's why you're going to help me. I thought about it all the way here in the police car." She crossed her arms and glared again. "Besides, you owe me."

"I can't get involved in this. I'm not a private investigator." I tried to erase the responsibility guilt weaved around me.

"You were in JAG."

"I typed reports and Article 15s."

"You told us you transcribed cases."

"Transcribe means taking notes during court. As in the case is being tried in front of judge and jury. CID investigates the crime, the military police arrest the suspect, and then JAG takes the case to court. I didn't interrogate suspects and go to crime scenes."

"Legal experience is legal experience."

I wanted to bang my head against the wall. "Give the police time."

Marilyn opened her mouth, but closed it as Detective Roget entered into the room followed by Steve.

"Marilyn Kane, I need you to stand up," Roget said.

Nausea rose and I covered my mouth with my hand.

"There's a bathroom down the hall, Davis." Roget unclipped his handcuffs from his belt. "Why don't you help Miss Hunter locate it?"

"Come on, Faith." Steve reached for my hand.

I swiveled and his hand touched the empty air. "I'm   fine." Marilyn needed me. I wouldn't abandon her.

"Marilyn Kane, you're under arrest for the murder of Michael Kane." Roget pulled Marilyn's hands behind her back and slapped the cuffs around her wrists. The clink of metal striking metal reverberated through my body.

As he recited the Miranda warning, I numbed my emotions to stop the kindred feelings from dredging up my past.

The tears that threatened to emerge during the drive home tumbled down my cheeks. Using my foot, I shut the front door of my house and dropped my keys and purse. They plopped onto the carpet. I shuffled into the living room and collapsed onto the couch.

I flopped over and pressed a pillow against my face to muffle the sound of my sobs. If my grandmothers heard my cries through the walls, they'd rush over even though I sent Steve over with instructions and reassurance I was fine, but needed to be alone.

Murder. I shuddered. The word was ugly. The deed unimaginable. And the police believed Marilyn committed the action. *Because of the evidence found.* I slapped the traitorous thought away. Marilyn was my friend. Just because someone could've done something—had the motive to do something—didn't actually mean they did it.

My ex-husband Adam, technically my never-was-husband, flashed into my mind. We can only think we know someone. Secrets and hidden agendas lurked inside everyone.

I stood and paced around the living room, avoiding the dining room I had turned into a scrapbooking area. Seeing my cropping tools and photo cast-offs littering the floor only reminded me of Michael's murder and Marilyn's arrest.

My gaze settled on the worn yellow-tinged chair in the corner of the room. An aged blue and yellow hand crocheted afghan was draped over the arm. The blanket Grandpa Tom would tuck around me as he told me stories about him and Grandma Hope and their son, my dad.

Growing up, I sighed at the romantic story of how two best friends meet and fell in love with two best friends. I loved looking at the pictures of the double wedding ceremony and always wished I could've seen it. The story continued years later when the only children of these two couples fell in love and got married. Two loving families merged into one. My grandparents celebrated by purchasing a three-family townhouse unit. The houses my grandmothers still owned. They lived in one unit together and rented out the other two, one to Steve and the other to me.

I picked up a framed photograph of my parents and me taken a week before they left for a three-week mission trip to China. The plane crashed before they left the United States, killing all on board.

Still holding the picture, I settled myself into the worn chair, tucking my feet under me. Even though Grandpa Tom died seven years ago, three months after his best friend and my other grandfather, Joseph, died, I could still smell his pine-scented aftershave. I joined the military right after my grandfathers' deaths. I wanted to see the world. And run away from the grief and fear that my grandmothers would follow their beloved husbands into the afterlife. I wanted to be nowhere around to witness it.

It's A Small World chimed through the house and I cringed. I picked that doorbell chime because of the whimsy and cheerful nature of the song. Today it felt silly and childlike. No wonder my grandmothers forgot that I was a grown-up.

I walked over and wrapped my hand around the doorknob. I paused. What if Detective Roget decided he had more questions—or accusations—for me?

"Faith?" My name in the form of question floated through the door. Steve.

I pulled the door open. Steve balanced a casserole dish and a plastic bowl in his hands. "Your grandmothers sent over some dinner."

"I'm not hungry." I started to close the door.

"Your grandmothers are watching."

I tugged the door back open and stepped outside. Hope and Cheryl wiggled their fingers at me then scooted back into their house. If I didn't let him in, one of them would be over before Steve made it home.

Sighing, I stepped aside. I did have some anger building up

and I'd rather use it on him than my grandmothers. I loved and adored them, but they always smothered.

Steve offered an apologetic smile. "I tried getting out if it, but they seemed determined. I told them I hadn't ate and promised to join you."

"I don't want company."

"I know. And I actually already ate. I can sneak out the back if you like." He flashed a grin. "They'd never expect me to lie to them."

"Fine. You can stay. For now."

I walked to the kitchen, but with each step I took, a voice in my head said I was making a huge mistake. I felt unbalanced by the events of the day. I might let my guard down and lean on Steve. A dangerous activity since my treacherous heart was looking for one hint it could latch onto a romantic entanglement with the sexy neighbor.

I opened the refrigerator and pulled out a pitcher of ice tea. I needed to focus away from the feelings running loose in my head. Marilyn. Think about Marilyn's situation.

Wait, Steve was a prosecutor. He could help me. Her. Help her.

"Roget took all the sharp-tip scissors from the store. Michael had to have been killed with a pair. So, it couldn't be Marilyn."

Steve paused, half of a plastic lid off the larger bowl, the other half remained attached. His unnerving deep brown gaze settled on me. "Why are you telling me this?"

I wandered over to the table and placed the pitcher down. Why in the world did I think this would be easy? I was cute, but not that cute. Actually, a plan like this called for hotness and my attire did nothing for achieving that effect.

Not that I wanted to look hot for Steve.

"Faith," he said through gritted teeth.

I hated that warning tone, especially from a man. "I just thought all the facts about Marilyn's cropping habits should be out in the open."

"Thanks for telling me." He looked around the kitchen. "Where's the silverware?"

I reached up and took two glasses from the cabinet. "In the drawer near the sink. Marilyn hates using sharp-tip scissors. Loathes them, actually. She never uses them when scrapbooking."

Steve sighed in an I-give-up manner. "Since you need to talk about this, I'll grant your wish. Let's start with the scissors in question weren't used in the pursuit of a hobby."

The frosted white glasses clinked on the top of the gold and red toned granite counter top. I planted my hands on my hips, spun, and faced him. "She didn't do it."

"I'm not saying that."

"Then what are you saying?"

He ran a hand over his smooth head. "You should let the police do their job."

A scratch and howl at the back door diverted my attention. I plucked a can of cat food from a lower cabinet and ripped the top off. "I am. I let them search the store and didn't stop them from taking anything they claimed was evidence."

"I'm glad to hear that." Steve roved his gaze to the door then back to me. "Are you still feeding that cat?"

"He's hungry."

Ol' Yowler, an orange tabby tomcat, had taken to me a few months ago. Of course, feeding an animal gained a person some loyalty. I handed Steve the bowl. "You feed him and I'll serve us."

Us. The word caused a jump in my pulse. I switched the subject. "Do you think Marilyn will get released on bail tonight?"

Steve opened up the back door and placed the bowl on the ground. Yowler hissed. Steve jerked his hand back and slammed the door. I pressed back my smile. Yowler was a very jealous male.

"I changed my mind," Steve said. "Let's talk about something else."

There wasn't anything else to talk about for me. My life revolved around my job and hobby, which linked to Marilyn. A chill worked itself down my spine. "Do you think she'll spend the night in jail?"

"I don't know." Steve nodded at the food growing cold. "How about you eat?"

"Could you call and find out? What about her children?" I bit my lip and tilted my head, pleading with my eyes. "Maybe you can talk to someone and let them know the other details."

"What other details?" Steve pulled out a chair and motioned for me to sit.

"Like the fact Michael told Marilyn, who told me, the woman's baby wasn't his. That should be important." I remained standing.

"That's hearsay. Stay out of the investigation, Faith."

"I don't want to be part of the investigation. I only want to give the police all the information. I don't want Marilyn to be charged with a crime because of what I said. That detective wouldn't listen to anything I said unless it hurt Marilyn. He doesn't like me." I heard the whine in my voice and clamped my lips shut.

Steve looked into my eyes. The compassion and care he felt for me clear in the soulful depths. "Whatever happens is not your fault."

"Then why does it feel that way?"

"Because you're too hard on yourself. Don't place Marilyn's choices on your shoulders."

Steve wouldn't understand what was happening to Marilyn. I did. I knew what it felt like for someone to take your words and twist them into the most damaging meaning available.

SIX

After the snooze alarm went off for the third time Sunday morning, I pushed back the comforter and draped my legs over the side of the bed. When guilt brewed inside my heart, church was the last place I wanted to spend time. The feeling always intensified and I felt worse. All the mistakes I've ever made played themselves in my head like a recording of a sports blunder on the evening news.

How could I stay home and feel sorry for myself when Marilyn was in jail? While my tumbling emotions kept me from sleeping, at least I had lain awake in my own bed rather than in a cot surrounded by bars.

I tuned the radio to the Christian music station and cranked it up. On Sunday, I felt guilty listening to anything other than gospel or contemporary Christian music. Before stepping into the shower, I adjusted the water to lukewarm. Hot steamy water would delay me even longer, but I couldn't torture myself with a stream of ice water.

Ten minutes later, dressed in my church finest, I stood in front of the mirror and groaned. There was no way I'd pull the "I'm fine" look off today to my grandmothers. Four hours of fitful sleep didn't leave a person refreshed. Good thing makeup was an option so I could cover up the dark circles. As I blotted on the light beige foundation beneath my eyes, and tried not to think about Marilyn, my mind went to the next logical musing.

Who killed Michael? And why?

Marilyn did had the best reason, and the most evidence against her, but I knew she wouldn't kill her husband. She loved her children too much to hurt them like that. She wasn't a violent type of person. Then again, when reporters interviewed neighbors and friends, no one ever said, "Yep, I knew that one would go off the deep end and kill somebody one day."

The phone rang and I welcomed the interruption.

"Did you see the paper this morning?" Sierra asked.

I squeezed my eyes shut. "Not yet." But I had a good idea the headline announced Marilyn's arrest to all of Eden.

"Harold, do not dump the syrup on your brother. No, you can't butter him either. Howard, I don't care that you love butter and want him to."

Conversations with Sierra always happened in this haphazard manner. It was a miracle either of us remembered the real topic. I went to my dresser and rummaged around for a pair of knee high socks to wear with my boots.

"No one in this house can be lathered in butter or syrup," Sierra said, the exasperation growing in her voice. "I just can't believe it."

"That one of your boys decorated his sibling with breakfast condiments?"

"Concentrate, Faith. We're talking about the newspaper." She took in a deep breath. "Marilyn was arrested for murder."

"Oh." It was the safest response.

"The bail hearing is set for Tuesday. It looks like the prosecution will be asking for a huge bond."

"What?" How would the Bennett's come up with the money? I collapsed onto the mattress and the bed beckoned for me to stay home.

"That's what the article says. I'll talk to you about it after church. We should both be leaving soon as Marilyn's parents will need all the support they can get."

I dragged through the rest of my primping routine. The last thing I wanted was to talk to Marilyn's parents. How would they feel knowing I helped put their daughter into jail?

I trudged out to my car, unlocked the door, and got inside. After uttering a prayer for strength and good sense, I made my way to

Eden Community Church. From down the road, I saw the white cross that topped the steeple of the one hundred and fifty year old church. The freshly painted white wooden building gleamed under the sunlight. Flowers readying to bloom bordered the walkway leading into the church.

"Give me courage," I muttered, gathering up my purse and Bible then opened up the car door. I stepped outside into the air tinged with cold.

I made my way up the steps and tried sneaking inside, but the renovation on the outside hadn't made its way inside. The swinging doors leading from the foyer into the sanctuary creaked. Heads turned. Heat flashed across my face and down my neck.

Eli and Gloria Bennett, Marilyn's parents, settled their gaze on me. I attempted a supporting smile but my mouth froze in a grimace. Lowering my head, I quickly slid onto the nearest pew. The hair on the back of my neck prickled. I shifted in the seat but still felt the sensation of someone staring at me.

Opening my Bible, I rested it on my lap and acted like I was reading while I peered through my lashes at the people around me. No one seemed interested at all. I wasn't quite sure if I should be offended or not.

The choir started singing *All is Well With My Soul*. How I wished I could sing the song as the truth. But as I sung, the feeling of impending doom increased. I scanned the pews and spotted Elizabeth and Mark Kane, Marilyn's teenaged children, glaring at me from the other side of the church. So that's where the hatred originated.

Gloria frowned and twisted her neck. She met my gaze and then blanched. Facing forward, she elbowed her granddaughter and reached over and smacked her grandson on the leg with her bulletin.

Tears burned my eyes. I jumped up and scurried out of the church, praying I didn't draw any interest. The tears raced down my cheeks, blurring my vision. My heel slipped on the edge of the concrete step and I pitched forward.

My breath hitched in my throat as steady footing vanished. I flailed for the rail, relief rushing through me when my hand gripped it. I regained my balance and sat down on the stairs, knowing my shaking legs wouldn't support my weight for one more step. Drawing up my knees, I rested my head on them.

I didn't blame Marilyn's children one bit for being mad at me. My words and actions helped build the police's case against their mother. Why couldn't I have found a way not to tell the police what she said?

Fabric draped around my shoulders. The smell of cinnamon and lilacs enveloped me. I tugged the ends of Grandma Hope's shawl tighter around my body, twisting my fingers into the fringe of the hand-knitted garment.

"Faith, sweetie, please come back inside. It's so cold out here."

"I shouldn't have come today," I choked out, not looking up at her.

Hope settled beside me and gently squeezed my hand. "I'm glad you came. I'm proud of you."

"For coming to church?" I wiped my cheeks with my palm before I looked at her. "Is it that much of a miracle?"

Hope shook her head and tapped me under the chin. "Is that anyway to talk to your grandmother?"

"I'm sorry." I leaned closer to her.

She guided my head to her shoulder and wrapped her arms around me. "Sweetie, I knew it would be hard for you to come today. For some reason, since you came home from the Army, you see judgment from everyone. And I knew you'd expect it today." She kissed the top of my head. "But there's a difference between concern and criticism."

"My being here is upsetting the Bennett family."

"That's nonsense. I talked with them this morning and they are just as upset with how the police treated you as they are at how that Detective behaved toward Marilyn."

"Marilyn's children—"

"Are children. Their father was murdered. Their mother accused. Their world was flipped upside down and it's hard for them to hang on. You shouldn't take anything they do or say as the truth to your character. You're not responsible for the predicament Marilyn is in."

I wiped my eyes. Only Hope would refer to an arrest as a predicament. "I guess I'll need to be an adult and just accept their glares."

Grandma Hope squeezed me and stood up, holding out her hand to me. "I don't think they were shooting daggers at you. That homicide detective was standing behind the last pew. That's who they are angry with."

SEVEN

I went back inside the church and settled between my grandmothers, and pretended to listen to the sermon. Though I did a lousy job at it as Grandma Cheryl kept giving me the wait-till-we-get outside look like I was an errant child. Of course to them, I'd always be a child no matter my age. A blessing or a curse depending on the situation.

When the pastor dismissed the congregation, I jumped up, maneuvered around my grandmothers, and headed for the great outdoors. I even beat the ushers offering the have-a-good-week sentiments to the door. I didn't want to talk to the Bennetts, or Marilyn's children, in case the evil eye was meant for me. I deserved it as much as the detective.

I came to a sudden stop in the parking lot. I wasn't the first one out of the church. That distinction fell to Detective Roget who leaned against my car with that half-smile, half-sneer gracing his face. Why did he want to talk to me now? Hadn't I helped him enough already? There had to be someone else in Eden with information he needed to further his investigation.

I stomped to my car and went around to the passenger door. I unlocked the door with a push of a button on my key ring. "What do you want?"

Opening the door, I tossed my purse into the front seat then gently placed my Bible beside it. The thought of throwing it left me with a vision of lightning bolts streaking from the sky and striking me and the car.

Hmmm... was Roget still leaning against the car?

He followed me with his gaze, his body not moving one inch

from its current position. "You made a hasty escape."

"So did you. Sermon getting to you?" I shut the door and stepped toward the hood of the car. Better for me to peer at him, as I couldn't see over the car roof very well.

"I asked my question first."

"No, that was a statement. Didn't you learn anything in English class?" I finished my question with a superior smile.

"Are you always such a smart aleck?"

I widened my eyes and gasped. "It's a good thing my grandmothers' aren't out here to hear a public servant partaking in such childish name calling. Tsk-tsk."

He grinned and nodded. "Beg my pardon, young lady. I wasn't aware your sensibilities were so delicate."

I rolled my wrist and bestowed onto him a regal smile. "Since forgiveness is divine, and we're standing in the church's parking lot, I'll forgive you."

Voices drifted from the church as people slowly filled the parking lot. Now everyone would see me talking with the detective and think I was ratting on Marilyn. Or being questioned as an accomplice.

"I have plans for lunch." I walked the long way around the car. "Can you just get on with your interrogation?"

"Interesting choice of words you use, Miss Hunter." He watched my every move.

A fluttering motion filled my stomach and worked its way to my limbs. Something in the way his green eyes sparked with a glint of humor unnerved me.

Sighing, I leaned against the car and flipped the keys dangling from the ring out of my palm and then back into it. "Seriously, I need to get going. Why are you here?"

"As I said, curious on why you tore out of church."

"Is that really any of your business?"

His eyebrows rose and he grinned. "Are you kidding me? You're questioning my need to know basis?"

"Yep."

"Why are you harassing my granddaughter?" Grandma Cheryl shouted across the parking lot.

I recreated my mean-person-hurt-my-feelings expression from yesteryears and faced my grandmother. Her complexion reddened and she picked up her pace, stalking toward the detective.

This would be good. And served him right.

Roget held up his hands. "Listen, Mrs. Greyfield, I'm not harassing Faith. I just had a few questions for her."

"On a Sunday? The Lord's day. I've never heard of such disrespect." With a flip of her wrist, Cheryl snapped open her cell phone. "What's your name, young man?"

Roget pulled out a leather case and opened it. "Detective Roget. I'm with the homicide department. If you're planning on calling the Chief, I believe he's at church right now."

"I'll talk to him later." Cheryl poised a finger above the touch screen. "Right now, I'm calling your mother."

Roget gaped at her. "You have got to be kidding."

"I'm serious, young man. Now what's her last name? I'm not familiar with any Roget's in these parts."

"I don't think he's from around here, Grandma." I linked my arm through hers and steered her toward her car.

Roget crossed his arms, his mouth twitching. "Actually, she's on a cruise. I doubt you can reach her."

Cheryl shook her high-tech cell at him. "Don't you underestimate me, young man."

"I see where she gets it," Roget muttered. Before I could respond, Hope glided into the scene and stood beside her best friend.

"Cheryl, he's only doing his job." Hope linked her arm through Cheryl's. "I promised the pastor and his lovely new wife a home-cooked lunch at our house."

"He doesn't have to do his job in the church's parking lot."

Cheryl refused to budge and Roget had the good sense to back away from her.

"I'll wait around, keep an eye on things," Steve said and joined our little entourage.

I pushed down the moan bubbling in my throat and out my mouth. Fury churned in my gut at Roget. This was his fault.

"Well, if Steve's going to be here." Cheryl touched his arm and her mannerisms went from fierce defender to sweet old woman. "You'll make sure this detective doesn't harass Faith anymore?"

Steve met Cheryl's imploring gaze and nodded. "I promise."

She patted his cheek and allowed Hope to lead her away to their car. Great. Now I was stuck with Steve managing my conversation with the detective. Or was it the detective's conversation with me? Either way, I didn't want Steve involved in my business. Unless he persuaded Roget of Marilyn's innocence.

Steve crossed his arms in a protective, proprietary gesture that ticked me off.

"I really want to go home." I shot a glare at Roget then at Steve. "So ask whatever you want so I can leave."

"Not with Davis listening in."

"Get on with it, Roget." Steve placed his hands at his waist and stared at Roget, the defender stance coming through loud and aggravating.

"Aren't you two on the same side of the law?" Maybe I should leave, let the two of them fight it out. "If this is supposed to be discreet, you both sure are getting the attention of the church members. Mrs. Newsome is going to add this to her blog."

Steve and Roget turned. Mrs. Newsome was scribbling in her palm-sized notepad, a look of glee splashed on her face. Nothing like gossip material to get Mrs. Newsome fired up. By tomorrow, I'd either be dating Steve or Roget—or both—or a suspect in a murder investigation. It was nice knowing that at least on the web, I had an interesting life.

"Fine. I'll go wait over by my car," Steve said. He walked away grumbling under his breath.

Roget looked me square in the eyes. "How do you know I'm not from around here?"

"The fact you don't know the standard operating procedures. The biggest threat in small town-life is the I'm-calling-your-mother card."

"So that's why one of the interview questions was where my mother lived and was her phone number easy to find."

"What did you say?"

"It depended on the season and the routes of the cruise ships."

"Your mother lives on a cruise ship?"

"You could say that." Roget smiled, an uncomfortable looking gesture. "Since my parents' divorce, she is either vacationing or performing."

"Your mom is a performer on cruises?" She sounded like a fun lady. I bet her son took after his father.

"A singer." Roget crossed his arms and morphed back into by-the-book detective. "I'm here to ask you questions not talk about my mother."

"That's a shame. She sounds like an intriguing woman."

That comment brought out an unrestrained smile from him. "She is."

An engine revved. A smirk grew on Roget's face. "Your knight in shining armor?"

I waved in a dismissive manner toward Steve. "Like I need one."

The smirk morphed into a small smile. "I have to agree. You do a pretty good job of standing up for yourself." Roget saluted and then pivoted on his heel, leaving me speechless and confused.

What had the detective wanted?

EIGHT

Monday arrived too early. I slapped the button and shut off the alarm. Why had I told my grandmothers I'd open this morning? That's right, our regular Monday morning opener, Marilyn, was unavailable for the foreseeable future.

Hope and Cheryl had a meeting at the bank. Sierra had to wait until her boys were in school before she came in. And Linda didn't have her own key yet and got flustered when she dealt with veteran scrapbookers. Those customers became irate when they dealt with unknowledgeable staff.

I tried shutting up the questions that plagued me during the night. Why had Detective Roget hovered around my car on Sunday? To arrest me? Ask questions? Intimidation?

I crossed off arresting me as an accomplice since he walked away. It had to do with Marilyn's arrest, but what else could he want to ask me about it? I told him everything I knew. Then again, maybe he doubted that since he had to force me to tell him in the first place. First, I avoided repeating what Marilyn said, then badgered him about the scissors disappearing.

Which reminded me, those spaces were still empty. I needed time to rearrange our inventory before customers arrived and questioned the empty shelf space.

After a quick shower, I yanked on a pair of gray jeans and a rose colored t-shirt. I grabbed a lightweight blazer then rushed down the stairs. I snagged a granola bar from the kitchen cabinet. Making coffee would wait until I arrived at the store.

Stepping onto my front porch, I kicked the newspaper behind a bush. Whatever Karen England had to say about Marilyn, I didn't want to read. For a town named after God's pure garden, the people liked operating on innuendos and rumors. Then again, believing the lies of the serpent was what got Eve into trouble, along with the rest of mankind.

The only problem was nowadays serpents looked a lot like friends, family, and others we loved. Had loved.

Like Michael and whoever killed him. Charming snakes that fooled you into believing they were harmless and struck at the first opportunity. Michael broke his wedding vows and flaunted it in front of his wife, then someone who knew of the affair used it to get away with murder. I wouldn't stand by and let someone railroad Marilyn. Been there and someone done it to me.

I needed a plan of action. One, preferably, that didn't get me in trouble. I hadn't the skills for a part-time sleuthing career, but I could learn. My job needed undivided attention, and that might hamper the investigation, but I did work for my grandmothers.

If they thought I was hanging out with Steve to hang out with Steve, they'd be thrilled and help me find the time. I just couldn't let them know there was an ulterior motive. Guilt wiggled around inside of me. I was treading on dangerous ground. I hated being used, and now I was venturing into that area.

But I was planning on helping Marilyn. Making sure she wasn't charged with murder, not forcing another person into paying consequences for my actions.

When I arrived at the store, Sierra's car was in the parking lot. If she was here, Hank was still out of work. Since we had holes in the schedule because of Marilyn's absence, I'd see if Sierra was interested in picking up those hours.

Scrap This would be stormed today as our customers stopped by to get the gritty details of Marilyn's arrest. Nothing like tantalizing gossip to get a small town out and about.

But there was one easy problem I could solve, the empty scissor slots. Customers gloated about buying the last item but did not like staring at blank spaces. That meant they missed out and turned a happy customer into a voice of dissent.

What excuse could I use to explain the missing scissors? Recall? Contest? Donation? Or maybe I'd just direct all the women to Detective Roget. I'm sure the man didn't want me lying.

I placed the key into the back lock and turned. Nothing. Great. I jiggled the key until both it and the lock cooperated with each other. I turned the willing knob and walked inside. I left the door unlocked so my grandmothers didn't have the same trouble.

I maneuvered through the maze of boxes, parted the curtain, and headed for the cutting tools. Rulers were arranged on the hooks usually holding the scissors. I spotted Sierra behind the cash register flipping through a magazine.

Smiling, I headed toward her. "Thanks."

Sierra slapped the magazine onto the counter. "For what, doing my job? I knew Marilyn usually opened on Mondays and after reading today's article about Marilyn's arrest, I figured you might not be up to coming in."

The heat from the windows warmed my back but I felt chilled. What exactly did the newspaper say that got Sierra fired up? I took a deep breath and hoped it settled the churning sea in my stomach. "I couldn't tell you what happened."

Sierra's lips trembled as tears pooled in her eyes. "Marilyn is my friend, too. Why didn't you say something when I called you yesterday? I feel like such an idiot. You still don't trust me."

Still don't trust me. The words twisted around in my conscience even as I tried ignoring the truth. I did trust my friends, just because I kept my past private didn't mean I didn't fully believe in my friends and family. Or did it?

I dragged a stool closer and sat down. "It's not that I don't trust you."

The look in Sierra's eyes spoke of her doubt.

I sighed. "Sierra, the detective warned me if I interfered in the case, I'd be in huge trouble. And I took that to mean not telling anyone anything. I didn't even tell my grandmothers. Maybe if I thought about it, I'd have realized that saying Marilyn was arrested wouldn't get me in trouble. It's not like no one was going to find out." I tried to keep emotions locked up, but the confession at the end trembled my voice.

Sierra's eyes softened and she rested a hand on my arm. "What's wrong, Faith?"

"It was my fault Marilyn was arrested."

"That's nonsense. You had to tell the detective what Marilyn said."

I heaved out a breath. "Marilyn blames me. She says I owe it to her to find the real murderer."

Sierra's mouth fell open. "She asked you?"

The bell above the door chimed. Sierra handed me a manila envelope. "Jasper dropped that off a little bit ago."

I opened up the envelope. The inventory list of scissors. I dropped it into my purse, or as my Grandma Cheryl called it, my "getaway bag." The newspaper lying on the countertop grabbed my attention. I read the headline: *Spousal Revenge. Cheater Dies.*

I couldn't grasp if the headline meant the suspect was right or wrong for offing the cheating spouse. Not that Marilyn killed her husband. Though it sounded like the public held some sympathy for Marilyn—if she did commit the crime.

I started reading the article, but the photograph accompanying piqued my interest. The home-wrecker sobbed over Michael's blanket-draped body. Interesting. How close to Michael had the girlfriend been when Michael died?

I needed the pregnant mistress' name. Referring to her as home-wrecker wouldn't get me very far in questioning people. I started my investigation by reading the article.

Apparently the reporter, Karen England, didn't have the whole scoop. She identified the crying woman solely as Annette Holland, a co-worker of the victim. Self-proclaimed reporter extraordinaire contributed the hysterical crying to pregnancy hormones, not to the fact that the recently deceased was the father of the child. A twinge of pain gathered in my chest. The baby would never have a chance to know his or her father.

If Michael was the father.

Maybe Marilyn wasn't the only person Michael fed that line to. I'm sure a pregnant woman wouldn't be thrilled for the daddy-to-be to deny paternity.

When lunchtime arrived, I visited the office of Allan, Taylor & Gilder. The modern chrome and glass structure was out of place in our rural town. The building could be seen from every point in Eden, making it a landmark from which driving directions branched from.

The Allegheny Mountains rose in the background, dwarfing the modern building and commanding attention for its beauty. Spring was still a few weeks away, but the barren trees cascading down the rolls and dips in the mountain started showing some green.

I pulled into the parking lot and slid off my sneakers and replaced them with classic tan two-inch pumps. I hated driving in heels but the grown-up shoes added a snazzy touch and gave me a more professional appearance.

I gripped the steel handle and pulled open the glass door. A rush of cold air hit me. I headed toward the security station. The sound of my heels grew louder on the gray tile floor. I gave the guard my most winning smile. The man responded with a bored, annoyed look. This was going well. I composed my expression into a more hardened, no-nonsense professional look.

The man turned his chair and looked at the monitors on the desk.

Maybe pestering him would work. I leaned against the counter and cleared my throat, tapping my nails on the black marble top.

He picked up a clipboard and made a tick mark on the sheet. "The conference room is on the fourth floor. Miss Holland is currently speaking with a reporter from channel Nine News. After that, there are two newspaper reporters and then the dude from the radio. You'll have at least a two-hour wait."

I decided against correcting him. Admitting "I'm here to get Annette Holland to confess to killing a man" would get me kicked out of the building. I thanked him and headed toward the elevator. As I waited, my gaze lingered over the building directory. A cafeteria was on the second floor.

The elevator doors opened and I stepped inside and pushed the button for the second floor. As long as I acted like I belonged, I would be fine. I'd ask my questions and be out of there before anyone figured out my intent was proving Annette Holland guilty of murder.

Including—and especially—my number one suspect.

I took a deep breath and hurried, but not suspiciously, to the cafeteria. I choose two different types of salad, one a traditional garden salad and the other a spinach salad with grapes, walnuts and a raspberry vinaigrette dressing. I grabbed two chocolate brownies, and in case Annette wasn't a chocolate girl, a piece of key lime pie.

From down the line, I heard a voice that sounded like the man I most wanted to avoid. I cast a quick glance over my shoulder. Yep, Detective Roget. I strained to hear his conversation with the man and woman standing with him, but couldn't make out if they were discussing lunch options or locating more evidence against Marilyn.

Which I'm sure they needed. A marriage certificate and a flip threat to kill someone had to fall under circumstantial. Even the cropped photographs and the scissors weren't undisputable proof—unless Marilyn's fingerprints were on the sharp-tip scissors.

I quickly handed over my money and asked for a bag. The last thing I needed was someone noticing I was there. Okay, not someone, but Detective Roget, the man who warned me to mind my own business. Mentioning Marilyn asked for my help probably wouldn't persuade him this was now my business.

"We don't have bags," the cashier said. People grumbled about the hold up.

"No problem." I opened up my quilted handbag, glad I preferred my purses cavernous, and placed the items inside. I stopped at the condiment station and fiddled with the plasticware as I waited for Roget to focus on the menu. When he studied the food choices, I scurried off.

Once I was safely enclosed inside the elevator, I let out the breath captured in my lungs. Never did stale air feel so refreshing. The elevator reached the fourth floor.

I walked down the hallway and saw where a large group of men and women assembled. I stood a little away from them and waited. Fifteen minutes later, the conference room door opened. I charged forward, pushing my way through the swarm of bodies.

Annette stood in the doorway, one hand caressing her swelled belly and the other rubbed her back. She looked tired, triumphant, and ravenous.

I pulled out one of the brownies and held it up. "I brought lunch!"

Her gaze pounced on me and she crooked her finger. "You're next."

Complaints erupted around me. Most from reporters wishing they had thought of my scheme. Of course, all they wanted was a story. I wanted to exonerate my friend.

When I was close enough to see her eye color—baby doll blue—Annette snatched the brownie from my hand and unwrapped the plastic from around it. She waddled back into the room and took a large bite of the chocolate treat.

I shut the door and continued toward the large table in the middle of the room. A wall of windows was in front of me, and behind me were bookshelves loaded down with leather-bound books. Annette plopped into a chair at the end of the table. She finished off the brownie and tossed the crumbled wrapper onto the table.

"I also brought a choice of salads." I put the garden and the spinach salad on the table with forks and napkins.

"No more chocolate?" A hopeful expression filled her face.

I smiled and pulled out the gooey, rich brownie I had planned on saving for myself. I held it out to her and she plucked it from my hand, a loving sigh escaped her lips. She motioned for me to sit down and devoured the dessert in two bites. Impressive.

She dusted the crumbs off her hands and picked the garden salad. "I guess you'd want me to start with how I found Michael's body." A sob accompanied his name.

Nice dramatic effect. I pretended to focus on opening the other salad, but peeked at her. "How about some background on why you decided to attend the Art Benefit Show?"

Her fork paused above the plastic bowl. "Why would readers want to know that?"

I scooped up some spinach and walnuts onto my fork, keeping my expression neutral. "People love back story. It really helps to fill everything out. Gives that added personal touch."

A smile flashed in her eyes and then quickly faded. Maybe I could persuade her to admit she killed Michael by pointing out confessing brought even more attention.

"Mr. Allan wanted the lawyers there as a way of supporting the community," Annette said. "Michael knew she was going to be there and didn't want to arrive alone."

"She?"

"His wife. At some craft booth. He was afraid she'd create a scene. They were in the middle of a nasty divorce. "

I shoved a large wad of salad into my mouth, expanding my cheeks to rival a squirrel storing nuts. It was the safest option unless I choked. I needed the truth, the whole truth and nothing but the truth to get Marilyn out of jail. Calling the woman who most likely committed the murder a liar wasn't a wise choice. The boss made us go was such a lame excuse. I had trouble believing Mr. Allan announced on Friday night he wanted his employees to attend the event.

"So, Michael Kane asked you to attend the Art Benefit Show with him, knowing his wife would be there?"

"Yes, he asked me." Collapsing back into the chair, Annette fanned herself with her hands, fingers outstretched and the peach painted acrylic nails fluttered at the air. "Michael feared for his life."

The man should've had a little fear bringing his girlfriend to his wife's job. I shook my head in hopes of silencing the questions growing in my head. "He said those words?"

She stopped the waving motion, but her hands remained raised. She chewed on her bottom lip as her eyes and nose scrunched. "Sure. He said those exact words." She tapped her peach nails onto the table. "Make sure you write that down."

I pushed down the annoyance and worked on settling down my snark. "The reason you accompanied Michael Kane was because he feared for his life? He thought someone would hurt him."

"Not someone. His wife."

"He said he was scared of his wife?" Understandable in a way since the man made a really stupid choice.

"Of course he meant his wife. Who else would he mean?"

I drummed my fingers on the table and gave her my best thoughtful look. "If he was in such fear of his wife, why didn't he just stay home? Being a lawyer, I'm sure he could've come up with a good excuse why he missed the show."

"It was necessary."

"Why?"

She narrowed her eyes. "I guess you'd have to ask Michael. And we can't do that since his wife killed him."

It was time to switch embellishments. "There was a picture in the paper of you kneeling beside Michael's body."

Tears filled her eyes. The brusque manner and the calculated look slipped for a minute as real grief etched itself onto her face. Annette had loved Michael. And now her baby would never know his or her father. Shame skittered along my conscience and I almost stopped the questioning, but a picture of Marilyn behind bars flashed into my mind.

"Were you nearby when he was killed?" I asked.

"No. I was getting a drink when a woman came and told me something happened to Michael."

"Did she call Michael by name?"

A blush crept across Annette's face. "No, she said my boy-friend."

I suppressed my smile. Annette opened up the topic that I hedged around. "Why would this woman believe Michael, Mr. Kane, was your boyfriend?"

She fanned herself again. "She probably saw us together and assumed it since I'm pregnant."

"Could it have been because the two of you were holding hands or acting like a romantic couple?"

Clenching her hands together, she clambered to her feet. "Wait a minute. Why are you asking these questions?"

"Just looking for the truth about what happened."

"The police know Marilyn Kane killed her husband." She lumbered around the table and headed toward me.

I grabbed my purse figuring the question and answer session was over. "Maybe because they don't know he told his wife your baby wasn't his."

Annette charged like a bull in slow motion. I glided away from her and reached the door with no problem. I took hold of the knob at the same time the door was thrust open. I slammed into the wall.

Detective Roget rushed into the room. Sputtering, Annette pointed at the wall I was squished against. Roget's eyes widened then turned into slits. He marched over and grabbed hold of my arm.

"Hey—" I tried tugging away.

"Not. One. Word," he said, between clenched teeth. He kept a grip on my arm and yanked me out of the room.

I watched my feet to make sure I didn't trip over anything, and to not have to look at the detective. I'd call Cheryl to bail me out. She'd handle the news better than Grandma Hope. Hope would rush into the station apologizing for my behavior. Or leave me in jail so I'd suffer the consequences.

Roget found a vacant room, pulled me inside, then released me. He slammed the door and faced me. "What are you doing here?"

I rubbed my forearm and thought about commenting on police brutality then decided remaining silent might be my saving grace.

"I'll ask again, why are you here?"

I took two steps backwards, my pulse fluttering. Truth seemed the better option than evasiveness when dealing with a furious officer of the law. "Helping Marilyn."

His face reddened and his chest ballooned out as he took in a deep breath.

Then again, maybe not. I cringed backwards.

He muttered under his breath, either counting or asking for restraint. "And just how is talking to Miss Holland doing that?"

"I just wanted to know where she was when Michael died. Ask her some simple questions since—"

"On what authority?" He cut me off before I said "the police won't ask her."

I met his gaze head-on, posture straight and regal. "Being Marilyn's friend. I know she didn't kill Michael. I can't see her harming anyone. No matter how horribly they treated her."

"Miss Hunter, did you ever see yourself trying to solve a murder?"

I shook my head and remained standing tall.

"Or see yourself talking to, or rather arguing with, a homicide detective?"

Again I responded with a denial.

"Or see yourself coming really close to being arrested?"

Once. I kept that truth and remained silent.

He rested his hands at his hips, fingers drifting over the handcuffs. "If you can't even know for certain what you would do, how can you be so certain about your friend?"

NINE

I jabbed the blade of the box cutter into the thick tape and jerked my arm downward. The top flaps separated and I yanked the flaps open, the cardboard tearing at the seam. How did Roget know there was no way I could be absolutely sure? I could so know that Marilyn wouldn't murder a person. Cynical cop.

The bell above the door sounded its polite ding. I put on my happy face, stood and placed the box cutter into my front pocket before I turned around.

Steve filled the doorway. My warm smile faded when I saw the closed expression on his face. Usually he greeted me with a flirtatious smile, but the straightened lips said something bothered him.

And it involved me.

"Can I talk with you?" Steve asked.

I continued unloading the paper. "I need to restock. Our customers have been badgering us for more of this brand. Then I need to get the easel boards set up for the layout contest displays."

Hope rushed over. "I'll finish the paper."

I wanted to glare at her, but could never do that to my grandmother. Instead, I rolled my eyes and continued unpacking. "Grandma, I don't want you to strain your back bending over and standing so many times. I can talk to Steve tonight when I'm done working." I flashed a smile at Steve. "That okay with you?"

His mouth remained straight. "It's important we talk right now."

Hope closed the flaps on the box. "This can wait until later, Faith. Why don't you two talk in the office? He did interrupt his day to come over. You should speak with him."

"Thanks, Hope." Steve started in that direction.

Why did my grandmothers always comply with Steve's wishes—or him with theirs? Especially when it came to me. For once, I'd have liked respect for my choice. "Grandma, I know you're in the middle of checking the statements."

"I can use the break." She shooed me back toward the small area. "Take all the time you need."

Unknowingly, my grandmother was leading me to the firing squad. Steve didn't come here for a date. The only interest he had in me right now was delivering a lecture.

Trudging into the office, I made my way behind the desk and sat down. A large piece of furniture between Steve and me seemed like a good idea. I wasn't sure if it was more for my benefit or his.

Steve shut the door and locked gazes with me. "Guess who stopped by my office?"

Even though playing dumb didn't become me, I entered into the game. "Did Cheryl stop by to see if you had a layout for our contest?"

"Faith, this is serious." He braced his arms on the desktop and leaned forward. "You don't realize how much trouble you're about to get into."

I knew. I just didn't really care. Or not care that much. Marilyn needed someone's help and all she had right now was me.

Steve sat on the edge of the desk. "Detective Roget isn't happy with your amateur sleuthing."

"He's going to arrest me?" I peered at the desk and pushed a paperclip around the surface, fighting the emotions wanting released. I wasn't sure if I'd cry or yell at Steve.

"He didn't say anything about arresting you. He just wanted to know if I'd talk to you. Thought you might listen to me."

"Why would he think that?" I grimaced after the question left my mouth as the implied meaning registered in my brain. I would listen to Steve's warning as well as I did the detective's—not at all.

"Because he wanted to offer me a professional courtesy before he took certain extreme measures," Steve said.

I stared at him, hoping he'd elaborate on the statement without my vocal prodding.

He stood and looked down at me. I hated when people did that, it was easy enough to look down on me when standing, sitting while someone did made me feel like a child receiving a scolding.

"Roget has been asking around about you," Steve said.

Sweat trickled down my back and I swallowed down my gasp. Roget had no right asking about me. I pressed my hands against my legs, stopping myself from jumping up. No reason for Steve knowing someone prying into my background was my worst fear.

"People saw us together, in friendly terms, as Roget put it."

"Why wouldn't you be friendly?" I forced out a smile.

"Then there's the fact we live close to each other. A nice, easy arrangement was what the detective called it. Might be the reason you're getting preferential treatment for interfering in a criminal matter."

My cheeks flamed at the assumption the detective made against Steve's character and mine. Pride mixed in with the embarrassment. It was nice to know others thought I had the ability to hook a guy like Steve.

"What did you say?" I asked nonchalantly. Part of me needed Steve to respond that he said there was nothing between us, without him being insulted at the assumption. Another part of me wanted him to have told the detective if there was something between us, it was none of his business.

"I told the detective a man shouldn't go around ruining a lady's reputation because he was irritated at her."

"Oh."

"He then responded you were doing plenty of damage on your own. Like intimidating a witness."

"That's not true!" I jumped up and the rolling chair collided into the wall. "I asked a simple question and the woman blew up. She's lying about why she went with Michael to the art show."

"Faith, the investigation doesn't concern you."

I stamped my foot and crossed my arms. Not grown-up behavior, but I had no idea what else to do to release the frustration shooting through my body. "It does concern me, Marilyn is my friend. That Annette chick is hiding something about what happened when Michael died. I need to find out what it is. Marilyn asked for my help and I owe her."

Steve narrowed his eyes. "You owe her?"

"I need to help her."

"Stay out of this. You're only going to help yourself become her roommate."

"You don't understand."

"I do." Steve wrapped his arms around me and rested his head on top of mine.

"No, you don't," I muttered before accepting the comfort he supplied. This was a temporary lapse of judgment not to be repeated. Ever.

We remained like that for a few minutes before Steve released his hold and took a step back.

"Please, listen. It's not your fault. You had to tell the detective what Marilyn said."

Heaviness filled my heart. "Then why do I feel so bad?"

The aloofness left his expression and softness replaced it. "Because you're a sweetheart." He tucked a lock of hair behind my ear, brown gaze locked onto brown gaze.

The expression in his eyes quaked my knees. I had fantasized about kissing Steve, wondered about it, but never gave him the impression I was interested in him. I fought against the instinct begging me to close my eyes and raise up on my toes. Self-preservation required I avoid a romantic relationship with the assistant county prosecutor.

I stepped back and turned from him. I needed back on safer ground, my choice of defending Marilyn.

"I know she didn't do it. If the police believed Marilyn said she wanted Michael dead because I said it, why won't they even reconsider when I say she wouldn't actually do it?"

"This isn't about believing in someone or not. It's all about evidence." Steve opened the door.

I rushed after him and then grabbed hold of his arm. "What evidence?"

"I shouldn't have said that. You worked in the legal field. You know the police wouldn't unjustly bring charges against Marilyn."

Wrong. People lied. Police bought every made up word and innocent people suffered. I pushed down the brewing anger and the past. "Tell Roget I won't talk to Annette anymore."

"If Marilyn needs help, she should hire a defense attorney. Or if she really wants a private detective, there are professionals out there."

"Are you saying I'm not capable of being a private detective?" I glared at him. "That I would mess up?"

Steve gaped at me. "Do you seriously want to become an investigator?"

I bit my lip. "Well, no. Not really." Heck, I didn't even think I was qualified to track down a murderer.

"Then why are you mad at me?" He raised his arms in surrender. "I can't believe you want to argue about this. Think about it, Faith. If you're right, then the best people to confront a murderer are the police. Not you."

TEN

After Steve left, I minded my own business as well as I could while still being a friendly representative for the store. I kept an interested look plastered on my face as customers swirled around me, gossiping about who killed Michael Kane.

Half the customers believed a displeased client at Michael's law firm killed him. Made sense. Even people who committed crimes didn't like going to jail or forking out loads of money to the plaintiff. The other half sided with the police and felt Marilyn killed her husband. For those who believed Marilyn did it, seventy percent felt Michael deserved it.

Keeping my opinions inside my mind was a tiring job. I feared my head would fall off my neck from all the bobbing up and down. A group of teenagers walked into the store and glanced around. I gave them my entire attention.

"Can I help you find anything?" I asked.

Four awe-struck gazes focused on me.

"Is this where the killer works?" A girl with shiny blonde hair asked. The other three, two boys and a girl, stood behind her and gawked.

"Man, I wonder if she got her weapon here." The tallest boy pointed to the rack with the remainder of our cutting tools. They headed toward that section of the store.

"You think this would work?" One of the boys reached for a pair of decorative scissors.

"You touch it. You buy it," I said, in the tone I used when talking to the Hooligans, Sierra's delightful children.

After shooting me a look of disgust, the teenagers stomped out of the store complaining about the lady with no sense of fun. I knew fun. I liked fun. I didn't appreciate Scrap This becoming a spot on the Criminals in Eden Tour. Other customers in the store redirected their focus to merchandise and the talk of Marilyn fizzled out.

Linda rushed into the store twenty minutes late, and almost collided into a customer. No surprise. Since Linda started working at Scrap This three months ago, she'd never arrived on time. It was an ingrained fault that had lost her other jobs. Scrap This was her sixth job in the last year.

Linda stashed her purse underneath the counter and offered an apologetic smile. "Sorry."

"If you man the register, I'll finish putting up the display boards." I pointed at the mess in the middle of the floor.

"Sure," she said and sat on a stool.

I skirted around the counter and returned to the mess in the middle of the floor. An easier chaos to deal with than the one I created by helping Marilyn. I lifted up one of the display boards and started to pull the wooden legs apart but my tugs were in vain. I let out a puff of breath and eased the display back to the floor. Maybe if I stepped on one of the legs and used both of my hands, I could open it.

As I leaned over to grab hold of the wooden post, a voice snapped behind me. "What are the rules?"

I peered over my shoulder and spotted Darlene, our most competitive and spendthrift customer. Holding in a groan, I straightened and faced her. Cheryl was better at dealing with tantrums, but she had stepped out for a late lunch.

"Rules?" I asked.

Darlene, life artist extraordinaire, whipped out a small recorder from her gigantic Vera Bradley purse and pressed the record button. "For the layout contest the store, Scrap This, is running for the seasoned scrapbookers. I assume the artists competing for the cutting machine cannot have help on their entry. So, if an artist wasn't able to attend the Art Benefit Show, may they use pictures taken by another person who attended the event?"

"How should I know?" I returned to setting up the displays.

"You are an employee here. You are the granddaughter of the owners." She poked me in the shoulder. "You're not allowed to enter are you?"

Releasing a sigh, I gave her more patience than I naturally possessed. "I'm not entering the contest. I was busy running the store's booth and had no time to take photos."

Suspicion deepened the frown on her mouth and the lines around her brown eyes. "But could you if you wanted to? What if a friend took photos and then gave them to you to scrapbook?"

"Darlene, write your concerns down and I'll ask the owners about them."

"I'd like an answer now." She plopped down on the floor and folded her legs into a pretzel shape. "I refuse to leave until the rules are confirmed and written down."

"Fine. I'll go see if Cheryl's back." Right now, I wished Steve was still here. I doubted Darlene would react in such a manner with a hot guy in the store.

Whispers drifted from behind the curtained partition of the storage room. I parted the fabric.

Hope and Cheryl stood huddled together. Hope gestured at the back door, then toward the front of the store. Cheryl's gaze flicked in that direction and widened when she saw me. She elbowed Hope.

The quiet argument stopped and they looked at me as if I was the center of their world.

They were hiding something.

Cheryl grinned at me. "Faith, how's Steve?"

I narrowed my gaze. Grandma Cheryl never grinned like a staged candid moment of children dressed in matching outfits as they skipped through the surf. "You don't care how Steve is."

"Of course I do," Cheryl said.

I muttered in my head and addressed my grandmothers. "I know you two weren't back here clucking about Steve."

Nothing happened. No lecture, no grandmotherly narrowed

gaze. No reminder of how I wasn't raised to talk to my elders like that. The ignoring of my snark concerned me more than their actions.

Hope pointed a shaking finger toward the door. "There's a police car in our employee parking lot."

What did Roget want now? Were the police tying the store into the murder? It was bad enough the police arrested one of my grandmothers' employees for murder. Pinpointing their beloved store as a supply house for weapons would hurt them even more. If Roget wanted a showdown, I'd give him one. "I'll go find out what he wants."

Cheryl puckered her lips. "Maybe the officer wants to question your choice of lunch break."

Steve. The man ratted me out to my grandmothers, which meant the worry I saw on Hope's face resulted from my behavior, not the police's. "I just asked Annette a few questions."

"Faith, stay out of it," Cheryl ordered.

"Marilyn asked for my help."

Hope walked over and hugged me. "We'll find her a better defense attorney since hers isn't doing a good job. We'll even help with the costs of her legal defense. One thing we shouldn't do is personally involve ourselves in the investigation."

"You instilled in me that family means everything. No one should ever turn their back on family when they were needed the most." I held out my arms. "You've always said the employees in this store are family. I can't abandon Marilyn when she needs me most."

Cheryl and Hope exchanged a quick glance, one that said they weren't pleased their words were being used against them.

"This is different," Cheryl said.

"How is it different? Because someone accused her of a crime, we should just forget about her?" I crossed my arms so my grandmothers' didn't see how much I was starting to shake. I didn't know if it was from building anger or fear of what my grandmothers' answer would be.

"Playing detective is liable to hurt you and Marilyn. What's wrong with hiring a private detective?"

Hope smiled. "That sounds like the perfect answer. We need you here doing work for Scrap This. I'm sure a detective would have plenty of resources to get this solved a lot quicker. Not that you wouldn't do a wonderful job, sweetie."

Cheryl rolled her eyes. "You shouldn't encourage her."

"I don't want my granddaughter thinking I don't believe in her." Hope glared at Cheryl. "We never told Faith she wasn't capable of doing something."

"Well she never tried solving a murder before. Do we really want our granddaughter skulking about after a murderer?"

Hope tapped her chin. "That is a good point."

"I haven't been skulking," I said. Somehow my grandmothers forget I was there.

"Faith can do anything she sets her mind on and that's the problem." Cheryl pointed a finger at me. "Messing with the type of people willing to kill isn't something you just decide to do one day."

Hope nodded. "There are professionals for that."

"Like the police who believe Marilyn is guilty," I said.

"How many times have you walked straight into trouble because of being overly helpful when you shouldn't have been?" Cheryl asked.

Thankfully it was a rhetorical question because the actual number was hard to remember. As a child, I could be convinced to ask the teacher the questions resulting in detention. That trait also led me to take every word Adam spoke as truth, so I ignored glaring inconsistencies. Lies that ended my legal career.

And there was one person I wasn't ever overly helpful for, and she was still sitting in the middle of the store. "Darlene wants a written copy of the rules for the layout contest clarifying if the entry must be the sole work of the artist. And if employees are allowed to enter."

Cheryl and Hope exchanged an eye-roll.

"She's holding a one woman protest by the display boards." I tilted my head toward the curtain.

"I'll handle this." Cheryl motioned for me to follow her out into the store. I was either backup or a potential witness in case Darlene decided to take us to court over rule-breaking. Or to hold my grandmother's earrings while she and Darlene tussled.

We entered into the shopping area. I groaned. The problem had escalated while I went for backup.

Darlene was in a heated argument with Robyn and Stephanie, Darlene's bitter rivals in the professional scrapbooking circle. A clear understanding of Darlene's needs for written rules and regulations became apparent. Stephanie was an awesome scrapbooker, but a horrible photographer, while Robyn had the opposite strengths and weaknesses. Since the sisters cropped together, they could share the prize of the die cut machine. The only way Darlene stood a chance was making sure the sisters couldn't compete as one.

Cheryl shoved her way through the threesome, moving them away from each other. "Ladies, what's the problem?"

"They…" Darlene said the pronoun in the tone usually reserved for those who licked their fingers and then touched the pattern paper. "…want to convince you there should be no rules for the Scrap This page contest. But contests need rules. All the good ones have rules."

The ultimate challenge. If we ran a legitimate contest, then rules existed.

"That's not true. We didn't come here to force the store into writing down rules to sway the outcome." Robyn held up a sealed envelope the size of a large pizza box. "We just completed our entry."

Darlene hissed at the news. Stephanie flashed a confident smile. Robyn tried keeping her expression neutral.

"The layout needs to be designed by the entrant," Cheryl said.

"We did design it ourselves," Stephanie said. "We did it together, both of our names are on the entry."

"It should be a blind contest." Darlene glared at the sisters.

"People will play favorites."

"Our names are on a three by five index card. It can be slipped out from the page protector," Robyn said.

I ventured into the conversation. "Since the Art Benefit Show will be the focus of the photos, rather than family members, favoritism shouldn't be a problem. Not that we have any favorite customers." Though for least favorite, I had a nice list building with Darlene's name at the top.

"I don't think it's fair two scrappers can work on a layout together. They have an advantage," Darlene said.

Cheryl smiled at her. "I think a collaboration is fine as long as both artists are willing to share the prize. I'm sure they put a lot of work into their layout and I don't want to disqualify them because they worked as a team."

Darlene's face blossomed red. She sputtered and stopped before lashing out. "It's cheating! If they can't scrap an award-winning layout alone, then they shouldn't enter contests. A great designer doesn't need a partner."

I shrugged. "Most interior designers I know have employees working with them."

"That's different." She shot me a shut-up glare.

"Even authors co-write books together," I continued. "And what about all those layout design books where multiple artists contribute?"

Cheryl, Stephanie and Robyn monitored our discussion with rapt interest.

Darlene continued giving me the evil eye. "That's different and you know it. They each work on separate projects and then those layouts are combined to make a complete design book. The artists don't work on layouts together."

"Are you sure? I've seen some online scrapbook boards where designers give each other tips and pointers," I said. "They critique each other's work and make suggestions on what to take out or add to the layouts. Isn't that collaborating?"

Smug smiles erupted all around. Except for Darlene. She

paled. Everyone knew Darlene participated in a critique group for layout designers. If she pushed hard enough, then her own work would be disqualified. She did have help, though not literal hands-on contribution.

Darlene huffed, then stomped out the front door. The bell jingled and jangled from the violent movement. Robyn and Stephanie smiled their thanks and browsed around the store. Cheryl headed for the storage room.

Since the entries were coming in, I tried setting up the display boards again. This time I'd use my weight as a leverage to pry open the wooden posts. I grabbed hold of the legs and tugged them toward me while keeping my left foot planted on the other post.

Frustration built in my muscles and I hoped it gave me the strength to pry the wooden stand apart so I could set-up the first board. At this rate, I'd be at the store until tomorrow morning getting the displays upright. Or more likely, my grandmothers would call Steve so I could borrow his brawn. Not something I wanted since I was irritated at the man.

"Need some help?" A deep male voice asked from behind me.

Startled, I lost my balance and almost fell onto the wooden posts. An arm snagged my waist and pulled me backwards. I fell back into a broad chest and the arm kept me snug against a well-toned male body. "Didn't mean to startle you."

The words drifted across my cheeks and brushed my ear and the smell of mint and spice wrapped around me. A small trickle of delight warmed my face and danced across my nerves. I didn't even know this guy and I was swooning like a heroine in a Victorian romance novel. Gathering back my equilibrium and wits, I removed myself from the saving grasp that bordered on an embrace. I turned and bit back a gasp.

Detective Roget smiled.

I pressed my lips together and stopped myself from saying something I'd regret. That feeling of shame at being conned wasn't Roget's fault. He didn't expect my mind—for a brief, unsettling moment—would find a little thrill at being in his arms. Of course, if

I'd suspected it was Roget, I'd have elbowed him in the gut.

Wiping my sweaty hands on my pants, I gave my bland customer service smile. "I didn't realize you scrapped."

"I'm not a hobby kind of guy." He kept his eyes on me, the smile never wavering.

The last thing I wanted was to ask him why he was at Scrap This. Linda's gaze was on us, a curious expression filling her face.

"I'll take you up on your offer." I knelt and motioned for him to grab the top of the display board. "If you can lift this up, I'll pull the legs out."

Without argument, he complied with my instructions. In twenty minutes, we had all the display boards raised. Now all I had left was prettying up the wooden elements that would remain unadorned by layouts with some bling. I scanned the store. Yards of ribbon would work, along with some distressing ink. Maybe some faux crystal jewels in a zebra pattern, either pink and black or white and turquoise.

"After all that hard work, a drink would be nice," Roget said. "Why don't you join me?"

"I don't think so." I walked over to the ribbon display and studied the colors and patterns.

Detective Roget stood behind me. His breath whispered against the back of my neck and a shiver worked its way across my body. "I could talk to you here, but I don't think you'd want people overhearing."

I stepped away from him. "Linda and I are the only ones here to man the store."

"What about your grandmothers?" Roget raised one eyebrow and nodded to the area near the pattern paper where they stood, peeking around the display units. "I'm sure they can manage without you for a little while. I just need to clarify something."

"I thought you wanted me to mind my own business." I crossed my arms and gave him a triumphant smile. "You know, stay out of your investigation."

Roget leaned forward. "This is about you."

ELEVEN

A cool breeze blew across the parking lot, whistling through the air, rustling the decorative flags hanging in front of the stores. The wind pierced through the cotton fabric of my t-shirt and I wrapped my arms around myself. The empty parking lot didn't leave any protection from the small gust. The smell of pine drifted in the air, filling my lungs with a purity that existed in the mountains. I rubbed my hands against my arms and hoped Detective Roget planned to go next door to Home Brewed. It was close and Dianne made the best coffee in town.

Though I wasn't sure if what Roget wanted to say, I wanted heard by people who knew me.

I stopped in front of Home Brewed and held out my hand, stopping Roget from opening the door. "Can we just get this over? No need to go through all this pretending."

"You always make such interesting word choices." Roget stepped away from the door and leaned one hip and shoulder against the brick wall.

The look in his eyes told me all I needed to know. He dug. Not too deep to find out what was hidden, but enough to know I buried something. "I'm not planning on getting involved in the investigation anymore."

Just planned on hiring someone to do the work for me.

Roget crossed his arms. "I have a feeling it's the accidental participation I need to keep my eye on."

The icy tone of his voice gripped my scalp and skittered down my neck. His words hinted at too much.

"I wanted to help my friend."

"For the record, twelve years' experience as a homicide detective trumps five years in JAG when it comes to the ability to solve a murder."

My hands shook as he layered on the details of my past. "It had nothing to do with thinking badly about you..."

"So you think about me." He grinned.

"As a police officer." I narrowed my eyes and crossed my arms. The heat of anger took away the chill in the air and the arctic-cold in my heart. "Is this the way you always question people? Doesn't sound very professional."

"I didn't know I was questioning you." He pulled out a small notebook from his pocket and flipped it open. "Should I be?"

"You said you needed to talk to me."

"I just wanted to clarify something I overheard. With you touting yourself as such a good friend of Marilyn's, I decided to ask you."

"Oh." I had allowed my imagination to run away with me and figured Detective Roget discovered everything. How could he, since he couldn't see that Marilyn didn't kill her husband? For some reason, the man brought out my irk. Maybe it was the badge and the gun. Two items that always made me a little paranoid.

Even when I knew I was on my best law-abiding behavior.

"A woman stormed into this coffee shop." He jerked his thumb over his shoulder toward the sign for Home Brewed. "She started ranting about cheating employees and how they shouldn't get away with crimes."

"Blonde, brown eyes, a little taller than me? Carrying a Vera Bradley purse?"

Again, that eyebrow quirked up, but the expression on his face showed confusion instead of sarcasm.

"A fabric purse in a blue and purple paisley fabric. That's a flower-like pattern."

"Sounds like her. Who is she?"

"Darlene Johnson. She's entering into a layout contest at the store and feels the rules aren't fair."

Disappointment flooded his features. Women drama over scrapbooking contests didn't quite compare to murder and mayhem.

"Who's cheating and why the anger at the employees?"

I explained the issue Darlene had with the competition. The last time we had a contest at the store, Robyn's entry had been vandalized, but the ripped elements and splattered ink splotches improved the layout and Robyn won. That had been a huge hit to Darlene's ego and an amusement for the rest of the customers in the store.

We never did find the culprit. I suspected Stephanie messed with her sister's layout in order to give her a better chance at winning and to thwart Darlene's smugness. Nobody could ink or distress a page better than Stephanie. She was a legend at using those techniques.

"Darlene was worried I'd enter the contest. She doesn't think employees should participate." I ended the overlong explanation that caused a glaze to form in Roget's green eyes.

"That makes sense."

"It's not like I could. One, I'm conducting the crops for the contest geared toward new scrapbookers. Two, I was manning the booth at Scrap This with Sierra and didn't have time to take pictures before the show closed."

"You didn't step away from the booth at all?"

I shook my head. "Hope and Cheryl were part of the organizing committee and visited all the booths. That left Sierra and me to run our makeshift store."

"I thought your other employee was also working at the booth that day."

"Linda Anderson was there, but stepped away. Scrapbook layout drama."

He snapped his notebook shut without having written down a word or even making a squiggle line. "Well, if you have any problem with rioting women, call the station and they can send some officers for crowd control." He offered a patronizing grin and turned to leave.

A swarm of uniformed male officers would restore order. Not because of the authority of the police, but most women swooned at the sight of a man in uniform. There was just something unexplainably flirt-worthy about an authority uniform whether it be police, military, pilot, fire department, or even the UPS guy.

"That's all?" I lifted my arms and held my palms face up. "You pulled me away from work because of a rumor?"

"It wasn't actually a rumor since the woman actually felt that way. I just needed to know if it had anything to do with my case. Maybe Michael wasn't the only Kane committing adultery."

Fuming, I stomped back to Scrap This and yanked the door open. The bell jostled and the jingle sounded like a cry of panic. Wasn't it bad enough he arrested Marilyn for murder? Did he really have to insinuate she was having an affair?

"Is everything all right?" Cheryl said.

"Everything's good." I barely refrained from snapping.

"Are you sure?"

The look on my grandmother's face calmed my temper and I relayed the basics without the drama. "The detective overheard Darlene ranting in Home Brewed. He thought it was something more sinister than a scrapbooking contest."

She heaved out a breath and attempted a reassuring smile. "Now, I don't want you to worry..."

My stomach plummeted to my feet. Nothing revved up the worry gene more than the phrase "I don't want you to worry."

Cheryl squeezed my arm. "Hope and I are going home early. Reviewing all the financial records wore Hope out. And while I could let her take the car..."

Grandma Cheryl didn't want her dearest friend driving home exhausted. I hugged her. "Go on home. Linda's still here. We can manage the store just fine." I almost said business was slow, but kept that locked inside my head.

I pointed toward the counter. "It looks like some contest entries have been dropped off, I'll start arranging those on the display boards."

"You'll stay out of trouble?"

Refraining from rolling my eyes, I nodded. "I promise to stay out of trouble."

"Will we see you tonight for dinner?" Cheryl asked.

"Don't wait for me. Our reshelf basket is near overflow and with all the distractions today, I haven't planned any of the upcoming crops. I want to have instructions and samples printed up."

"I'll put some dinner in your refrigerator. All you'll have to do is reheat it."

"That's not necessary."

Love shone in her eyes. "What a silly thing to say to your grandmother."

I gathered up the layouts and walked over to the display boards. I hummed a made up tune as I arranged the layouts on the board. Stepping back, I tapped my finger against my chin. Not quite right. Two pages using black and white as the predominant colors blended together like a two-page layout rather than two separate ones. I placed an entry that used green and pink between them. Perfect.

Linda rummaged around in a box behind the counter, muttering to herself.

"Is everything all right?" I asked.

She nodded and continued the search.

I walked over to the counter, leaned onto it, and then stood on my toes to look into the box. "Can I help?"

Linda turned and huddled over the box, blocking my view from seeing any contents. "Did the police take anything we brought to the Art Benefit Show?"

"Not that I recall. What seems to be missing?"

"It's probably in my bag at home." Tears gathered in Linda's eyes.

"I don't think we've unpacked all the merchandise. If you let me know what it is, I'll be on the lookout for it."

"My layout." Fluttering her fingers in front of her face, she tried to fan away the tears. "I'm sure it's at home."

Sympathy filled my heart. The missing layout was probably the one of her husband and son we tried repairing. "If you want, you can leave now to look. I can handle closing on my own."

She shook her head. "I can't leave you alone."

I smiled. "Sure you can. I've closed alone before, and it's not like we had a large crowd in here today. It won't take long to straighten up."

She picked up her purse and shoved her hand inside, a muffled jingle escaped. "Are you sure?"

"Absolutely. If you don't find the layout at home, give me a call and I'll check here before I leave. "

"Thanks." Clutching her keys, she scurried out the front door.

After Linda left, I locked the door and started cleaning. My mind wandered to Detective Roget. Chewing on my lip, I picked up randomly placed items and put them into a basket. He dug into my background. He knew how many years I spent in the Army. What else did he know about that time?

I should stay out of the investigation so my skeletons remained firmly in the closet, but what kind of person abandoned friends in order to protect their own self-interest? Not the type I wanted to be.

I gently tapped the edges of the cardstock and pushed them back onto the rack. Hiring a private detective would help Marilyn and distract the police detective away from me. I'd let the PI do all the heavy lifting, the real nosy questions, and I'd keep to the more mundane tasks like wrangling information from Steve.

There weren't any PIs in Eden. I needed to check online, see who in Morgantown was reasonably priced, and handled murders. Though I don't know if they'd advertise that in the phonebook. And who wouldn't mind traveling here. With the cost of gas, the hour trip would get expensive. I could always offer expenses on top of the fee.

Walking through the aisles, I pulled damaged merchandise

from racks, shelves and the floor. The calculator in my mind added up the tab. Our bottom line kept getting worse. I picked up a sheet of wedding stickers someone tore from the roll and then crumbled into a ball. If they'd changed their mind on the purchase, they could've brought it up to the counter for us to sell at a discount.

I dropped my finds into the damaged goods bin. I heaved out a sigh, then grabbed my purse, relieved that the long, horrible day had reached its end. Tomorrow could only get better. Or so I hoped.

Stepping out into the dark, I turned my back to the velvet blackness and locked the back door. The night echoed a spookiness I never felt before and a chill danced along my spine, wobbling my knees and my hands. Holding my breath, I strained my ears for any sounds.

For the first time, I didn't feel safe in my community. With shaking hands, I tugged the key from the door and tested the knob. Locked tight. I scanned the lot, hit the button on my key chain, and ran the three feet to my car. The car blipped. I yanked the door open and threw myself inside.

The leather seat felt like a safe embrace. Determined to quiet the irrational terror, I turned on the car and flicked on the high beams. Only three things were in the back lot: me, my car and the dumpster. My heart rate slowed.

I pulled onto the deserted main road. Eden's nightlife drew people away from our town, not toward it. The highlights included bingo, little league baseball, high school football and the occasional summer night vintage car cruise on Main Street. Fun times. The newspaper even listed all baby showers, birthdays, and weddings in the community section. Everyone knew to check with the newspaper before they planned any shindig, unless they wanted low attendance.

Headlights flooded my car and an engine roared behind me. I glanced in the rearview mirror. The car surged forward, then eased back. I squeezed the steering wheel, feeling the grooves of the leather biting into my hands. My neck muscles tightened and I clenched the wheel.

Breath in. Breath out. Breath in. The exercise failed to calm me. Before full panic erupted, the stalker car turned. The breath I held in rushed from my lungs. Three more minutes and I could lock myself safely inside my home.

Turning down my road, the front windows of the three connecting townhouses illuminated the roadway with a burnished yellow light. Leave it to my grandmothers and Steve to welcome me home with a blaze of florescent protection. I pulled my Malibu onto the paved driveway. The porch lamp clicked on and highlighted the garden that would be filled with pink, purple and white haciendas once spring became a stable season in West Virginia.

Stepping out of the car, I reached back inside and yanked out my purse, and used my hip to shut the door. A light touch grazed my arm. I squealed and whirled. The strap of my purse slipped from my shoulder and I clutched it, preparing to use it as a weapon against my attacker.

A nearby door opened. "Faith?"

Cheryl's voice.

Hank Brodart, Sierra's husband, steadied me with a hand to my elbow. "Did I scare you?"

I slowed my breaths. "I'm okay, Grandma, don't call the police."

"Who said anything about the police? I'll go put Charlie back in his corner."

"Charlie?" Hank asked.

"The shotgun she uses for hunting." I unlocked my front door.

"I didn't know your grandmother hunted."

"She hasn't yet, but she's willing to start any day." I looked over my shoulder at Hank. "And was about to start with you."

"Sorry about that."

"Not as sorry as you almost were."

As my anger faded, I realized Hank was at my house. Sierra popped in from time to time, but not Hank. Unless there was an unnatural occurrence created by one of the Hooligans. I took my car key from my fob and held it out. "What did the boys do to the car this time?"

"Long story I'd rather not get into." Hank took the keys. "I'll bring them back in a few. Just need to pick up a part then head back home."

"No problem. I can always catch a ride into work with my grandmothers."

"I'll get them back to you tonight."

"If I don't answer right away, just drop it my mailbox."

"Will do."

Waving goodbye, I closed the door and locked it. An ingrained habit from the short time I lived with Adam. The base was protected and I thought it was silly to lock every door and window. I grew up with unlocked doors and friends walking right in. Adam trusted nobody, said he wanted me safe at all times. I thought he was being protective, cherishing me, but learned he had good reasons for those fears.

Wandering toward the kitchen, I flipped on the reading lamp in the living room. The light on the phone blinked. Voicemail. My finger lingered over the play button. Whoever it was could wait until tomorrow morning.

I made a sandwich, passing on the meatloaf and mashed potatoes Cheryl left, and devoured it in less time than it took to take out the lunchmeat and condiments.

As I put my plate in the sink, a movement near the kitchen window drew my attention. I squinted out. Darkness obliterated anything in the yard. I couldn't even make out the cherry blossom tree smack dab in the middle of the back garden or the deck that stretched eight feet from my house. I stretched onto my toes, leaned closer to the window. Blackness echoed back at me.

TWELVE

Sunlight streamed through the kitchen window the next morning, hitting the beveled glass cabinet doors and dancing the yellows, blues and reds around the room. Pressing my hands on the counter, I rose and studied the backyard, looking for something out of place. Everything appeared as usual.

My imagination had worked overtime last night. In my dreams, I envisioned Roget lurking around the yard, holding up a sign proclaiming all my faults and secrets.

I yawned and filled my travel mug with my second cup of coffee of the day. The scent of the dark, nutty brew filled my being and some of the exhaustion trickled from my bones.

Stepping onto the front porch, I glanced around the cement for my newspaper. I slipped my artist tote from my shoulder and leaned over the railing and looked into the small bush beside the porch. I paid the bill, so the carrier shouldn't have skipped my house.

Another theory wormed into my mind. My grandmothers snitched the paper to keep me from reading about the developments in Michael's murder, a more likely scenario than the carrier having a grievance against me, or a paper thief running amok.

My purse chirped. I rummaged around for the phone. Pen. Notebook. Granola bar. Class sample layouts I needed to complete. On the fourth ring, I finally grabbed the device. I pulled it out and looked at the number flashing on the screen. Hope.

"Hi, Grandma," I answered in my most chipper voice.

"Sweetie, can you run some errands before you come in?"

"Of course." Great. Now I needed the pen and notebook I

dropped back into the cavernous bag.

"Thanks so much, honey. Stop by the pharmacy and pick up my vitamins. Lionel was closed earlier when I stopped by. I called and he said he'd have them at the register for you. Also, grab a package of those mints Cheryl loves. They're located at the front register, by the bell."

I gave up on finding a pen and concentrated on memorizing the list.

"The library called. The romance book Cheryl put on hold is in and she'd like you to pick it up for her."

"The title?"

"You don't want to know."

I could almost hear Grandma Hope blush.

"Then stop at the bank and get some deposit slips."

My morning slipped away from my control. "Anything else?"

"Yes. Pick up a carafe of coffee from Dianne's. Our coffeemaker broke this morning."

"Sure. Not a problem. I might be a little—"

"And hurry. Between the entries coming in, fielding phone calls on the contest, and customers needing help, we're swamped." Hope's voice held a smile. "It's so wonderful to see this place filled to the max. More customers walked in. Must go. Remember, hurry."

Interesting, none of the places she was sending me sold the Daily Eden Tribune. And now I'd have no time to get a copy before I came into work. Something suspicious lurked in the town of Eden.

Offering my most pleasant smile, I handed a purchase to our fifteenth customer that morning. Why did business always pick up on the days I had something to do which required a slow morning? I tapped my nails on the counter as I watched a customer match her photos to different cardstock colors.

She refused my help, afraid any employee assistance would disqualify her layout. Even my reassurances did not relieve her concerns about the rules. Darlene had every contest cropper running scared. Then again, Darlene's antics spread through our scrapbook community, resulting in lots of customers. Buying customers.

Good gossip helped business. Our regulars stopped by for the inside scoop, but stayed and spent money. A few admitted they also wanted to be here in case there was a repeat of yesterday, figuring Darlene's entry would arrive soon. Heaven forbid anyone thought she needed more time than the sisters to complete her layout. Women venturing into the competitive side of the hobby often turned into scrapzillas.

The bell above the door jingled and I greeted the newcomer. Karen England, otherwise known as Karen Pancake during our growing up years, glided into the store wearing a suit that highlighted her trim figure. She glanced around the store. Her mouth dipped into a frown as she took in the rows of pattern paper and the packages of stickers on the far wall.

I had a feeling she didn't enter into the store because of a desire to scrapbook her articles and clippings. But I could be wrong. And she could be the answer for my information dilemma. No need to browse the internet when I could just speak with the reporter holding all the facts.

Giving my best customer service smile, I greeted her. "Welcome to Scrap This. How can I help you?"

She tapped a long red nail against her lips as she walked over. "This is where Marilyn Kane worked?" Disappointment lined her tone. She lifted the flap of her brown leather tote and stuck her hand inside.

I lost my smile. Karen wanted dirt about Marilyn for career advancement. An ordinary story of a woman killing her husband wouldn't make a big splash on the wire service. She needed a unique angle to make this story bigger, catch the interest of a national organization. Well she was on her own.

I plucked a catalog from under the counter and read it. Some new shapes in chipboard caught my eye. I marked the page with a paperclip, circling the item in bright orange ink.

Karen cleared her throat.

After licking the tip of my finger, I flipped the page with a nice resounding snap. If Grandma, either of them, caught me doing that, they'd lecture me as if I was daydreaming during a sermon. Scrapbook shoppers didn't appreciate paper licking. Near riot conditions occurred when someone touched paper with germ-laced fingers.

"Where have I seen you before?" Karen placed a hand on top of the catalog and tried tugging it away.

"Grades kindergarten through twelfth." I yanked the catalog back.

She snapped her fingers. "You tricked Annette Holland into an interview." She made air quotes on the last word. "Sheer genius. I should've thought of it rather than play the take a number game. But you're not a reporter. Why were you talking to Annette?"

"I'm working. No time for questions." I prayed for a customer to walk into the store and beg for help choosing cardstock, pattern paper and other embellishments for their page. I needed Darlene to flounce in and start another argument about the contest.

"Come on, don't you want to help Marilyn?" She flipped open a notebook, her pen poised above a blank page.

"Right, you're here to help her." I glared at her, hoping she'd take the hint. The bell above the door jingled. Hallelujah, a customer. "As I said, I have a customer to help."

The woman waved off my offer and headed toward the adhesives.

"Looks like she knows exactly what she wants."

I wanted to say like you, but kept the comment inside my head. Getting into a word war with Karen seemed like a bad decision.

"One question. I promise."

"I won't talk about Marilyn."

"This isn't about her. I'm interested in what you and Annette Holland, Michael's mistress, talked about."

That raised my eyebrows. So the mistress story was getting

out. "I wanted to know why she showed up at the event with Michael, and how she came across his body. I saw the picture in the paper of her kneeling beside him."

"You don't think Marilyn committed the crime. Even though she did say—to you—that she wanted to kill him."

"I'm sure she's not the first wife to utter those words."

"True. I heard my mom say it to my dad more than once. But then again, my dad is still alive."

"She had nothing to do with Michael's murder. This conversation is over." I spun away from her and frantically looked behind the counter for work needing done.

"If she had nothing to do with it, why was she denied bail? Did you visit Annette to threaten her on Marilyn's behalf?"

"What?" I gaped at her.

A wicked gleam lit her eyes. "I have it on good authority you and Marilyn had a chat before she was arrested. Then you went and had a little talk," she air quoted again, "with Annette. Surprisingly, right after you left, the young expectant mother refused to speak with anyone."

The accusation reeled around in my brain. I didn't know who was in the most danger right now, Marilyn or me. Why hadn't Roget confronted me? Was he gathering more information before he made a move? My stomach churned. How much trouble was my help getting Marilyn into? It wasn't her fault I questioned Annette.

Okay, maybe a little since she asked for my help, but she probably figured I'd be a more competent detective. "We didn't create some elaborate plot to intimidate that woman."

"That's not the way it looks."

"And I wonder who's helping your point of view? Annette?" Detective Roget's name popped in my mind and I kept it there. "Why did Michael show up at the art show with her? He knew his wife would be there, even told her he wanted to put the divorce on hold."

Karen's brows rose. "He called off the divorce?"

"He sure did. So bringing the girlfriend with him doesn't make sense."

"True. Then again, Michael Kane wasn't a bright man if he thought he could have an affair in this small town." Karen shaped her hand into a duck's bill and opened and closed her fingers. "Gossip is our most renewable energy source. He should've known to stop the nonsense when she got transferred from the Morgantown office to the satellite office here."

True. The only secrets in this town were the ones where only the holder knew the details. To continue an affair— "Wait a minute. Did you say Annette followed Michael from the Morgantown branch to the Eden site?"

Karen grinned. "He asked for her specifically when his office needed a new secretary. Funny how Miss Lucy was fine as his secretary until he met Annette at a work retreat."

That was a new piece of information. I needed Karen's sources, they had all the information I craved. "That had to make it worse for Annette. She moves down her to be with the man of her dreams, and when she needs him most, he decides he likes his wife better. Good reason to kill a man."

"I agree with you. The only problem is Annette has a solid alibi."

"She could've killed the cheater, established an alibi, then returned and cried over Michael."

"Most grown-ups don't believe in fairy tales." Karen whipped out a copy of today's newspaper from her purse and dropped it onto the counter. "My compliments," she said, then waltzed out the door.

The headline screamed at me: "Vengeful Wife Kept Behind Bars." Instead of a picture of Marilyn, there was a photograph of her two children being shielded by their grandparents. My heart ached for Elizabeth and Mark.

Why didn't I stop Marilyn before she started spouting off figurative threats? Or throw out the stupid trash from the crop the night before? Right now, she'd be home with her children and helping them through their grief.

Running my finger under the words, I took my time reading the details the story revealed. Marilyn was working at the Art Benefit Show. Michael attended with a colleague, now also revealed to be his mistress. Okay, check mark by those details.

Marilyn arrested. Check. Marilyn denied bailed. Check. Marilyn argued with Michael at the show. New detail. Marilyn spotted screeching at Annette Holland at the art show. Another new detail. At least now I knew why the court denied bail.

But I still didn't believe Marilyn killed Michael.

"Don't even think about it, Faith." Sierra tossed her purse under the counter and grabbed mine. She thrust it at me. "Go get some lunch. And stop feeling guilty about Marilyn."

"How do you know that's what I'm thinking?"

"I can see what you're reading."

I shoved the newspaper into my purse.

Sierra started toward an overwhelmed customer in the blue paper section. "Take your lunch break and think about something happy."

"Tell me what the boys did to the car." I grinned. "I bet it's a great story."

Sierra eyeballed me.

"Okay, okay, I'm leaving." Apparently not a story with a happy ending. I picked up my purse and went next door to Home Brewed. Dianne made a wonderful chicken salad sandwich, and I knew no one would bother me there. She was as protective of me as my grandmothers, only she didn't think Steve was the answer for every problem.

After placing my order, I dropped into a chair facing away from the windows. It was easier to ignore people by eliminating eye contact. I smoothed out the newspaper and read the article again.

If they believed Marilyn killed her husband, then thinking she'd do the same to the woman who was expecting her husband's baby wasn't a stretch. My speaking with Annette didn't help the situation.

But who told the police I had been at both places? Detective

Roget knew Marilyn and I were together at the police station. He also knew I questioned Annette about her whereabouts. But he'd want a reporter in his investigation even less than he wanted me. Would Jasper blab details of the case?

There was evidence out there proving Marilyn's innocence. But where was it?

Someone had to have seen Marilyn during the time of the murder—away from Michael. Someone saw the real last person Michael talked with. All I had to do was find the person who saw Michael alive after the argument with Marilyn. Hopefully someone besides the actual murderer. I couldn't count on that person being forthcoming.

"Worrying about Marilyn?" Dianne placed my order on the table and then sat in the vacant chair.

I tapped the newspaper. "Every day gets worse for her."

Dianne smiled and patted my hand. "It'll work out."

Yeah, right. The homicide detective had this case wrapped up in his mind and the prosecution went right along with his assessment. Conducting an investigation myself meant Detective Roget prying into my life, but he couldn't do that if he didn't find out. I needed to improve my sleuthing and keep it a secret. Or hire another target for his wrath.

"Whatever you're planning, don't get yourself into trouble." Dianne stood and cast a worried glance at me.

"I'm not planning anything."

"And that might be even worse. I'll just put in a word to God to find a way to put a stop between you and anything rash." She walked over to the counter and picked up the next meal.

Lunch break for my first job ended, so I worked at my second job. Private investigating. I pulled out a notebook I usually jotted down layout ideas in and listed my speculations and questions. Who spotted Marilyn talking to Michael?

She should've known not to talk to him with her temper flaring. Then again, she probably didn't think her husband would be found murdered the same day. Someone could've lied about seeing her yell at Michael. And that led me right back to Annette Holland.

But who gave Annette an alibi? Even if I proved   Annette claimed Marilyn saw Michael last, it wouldn't help unless I broke Annette's alibi. I pulled out my cell and dialed Karen at the newspaper. I was transferred to her direct line.

"Karen England."

I hurried into my spiel as lunchtime ticked away.

"I won't reveal my sources," Karen snapped.

I wanted to question her use of "won't" over "couldn't" but knew that would get me nowhere. All during the school years, from preschool to high, Karen was one of the kids who never succumbed to peer pressure, rather she created it. "But you put the information in the paper."

"Not my source's name."

"Please."

"I read the police report," Karen said. "Try doing that."

That response was a little snarky, but helpful. "So, the police report names Annette's alibi?"

A snort sounded in my ear and I winced.

"I'm not going to let some wannabe reporter use my hard work for their benefit."

"I'm not asking for the details about your story. All I want to know is who supplied the alibi."

"Same thing, Faith. This is my story." A loud click signaled the end of our conversation.

Thank goodness my cell phone had web access. I had cringed when I splurged on the phone with internet capabilities. It wasn't a necessity but with all the traveling we planned to do for trade shows, consumer shows, and weekend getaway crops, I thought the entertainment value would be useful. Plus, it allowed me to check out prices when shopping for new supplies. With our limited budget, there was no sense in paying more for chipboard from one company when the next one supplied a similar product for less.

I tapped the screen and brought up a search engine. If I went with the theory Annette didn't kill Michael, and I knew Marilyn didn't, I needed to eliminate love as the motive.

The other type of person who might want to kill Michael Kane, a defense lawyer, was a displeased client. I typed Michael Kane into the search box and hit enter. A lot of hits showed up on the tiny screen, and from a quick scan, most of them appeared useless. I started a new search, this time adding in his firm's name.

A nice supply of manageable links popped up. The first one was of the firm's website. And, the best form of advertisement for a company, their list of victories. I tapped the screen and hit the link on Michael Kane's name.

A serious looking photo of Michael stared at me. The gaze unnerved me. I averted my attention from his photo to the list of achievements listed below his likeness. Insurance claims, employers being sued for discrimination, and a denial of a wrongful death multimillion-dollar claim against a logging company. Quite a victory.

I hit the link and saw a tiny photo of a triumphant Michael walking down the courthouse steps in Morgantown. I back clicked to my original search and read the other entries. I sucked in a breath. The name Roget appeared in the text along side Michael's law firm. I clicked it and was taken to a screen explaining how I could subscribe.

Cheryl walked into Home Brewed and looked right at me. Her brows drew together.

I closed the browser and dropped the phone back into my purse, then gulped down the rest of my lunch. Cheryl's brows hunched even lower over her eyes as she continued looking at me.

An innocent smile wouldn't work as I grew up living with Grandma Cheryl and Grandpa Joseph. She was better at reading my mannerisms than Hope. When Cheryl turned and placed her order, I shoved the newspaper into my bag.

I gave grandmother a hug before I rushed out the door. I wondered if Detective Roget mentioned at the police station or the prosecutor's office that he was tied to the firm Michael Kane worked for. Seemed like a conflict of interest. Roget could be getting revenge on his nemesis by charging the man's wife with murder.

Of course first I had to find out if Roget and Michael were actually enemies and not just people on opposing legal teams passing by each other without so much as exchanging a nod.

As I entered the store, I saw Linda cornered by Darlene near the contest display. I rushed over. "What's going on?"

"I was hanging up the entries." Linda clutched an envelope against her chest. Darlene attempted to snatch it away.

I stepped between the two and avoided Darlene's pink-tipped claws. "Is that an entry?"

"It's mine." Darlene snapped. "I told her I didn't want it up."

"But it has to be," Linda said. "How can the customers judge it if it's not hung up with the rest?"

The rest comprised of eight other entrants work, one of those belonging to the team of Robyn and Stephanie. I motioned for the envelope.

Linda thrust it at me, then retreated to the register.

"Linda has a point," I said.

"No one is voting until Friday. Why does my entry have to be up there for the next three days? I've created a unique technique and don't want anyone else using it." Darlene clamped her hands around her waist and drummed her vicious nails against the pockets of her khakis. She did come up with innovative techniques, but unfortunately for her, she always discovered the newest trend one month too late. By the time her layout and instructions were submission-ready, another scrapbooker already had it published in a magazine.

"No one is going to copy your page. Everyone would know it's a copy, and how could they recreate your design without your knowledge in perfecting the technique?"

The hardness in her expression softened a little, but the scowl firmed again. "I want people to be wowed by my page. They won't be if they get used to seeing it on the display. They'll pass right by it."

"Then maybe I should just take everyone's down." I tried keeping the frustration out of my tone, but even I could hear the clipped end of the syllables. I moved toward Stephanie and Robyn's entry. "Wouldn't want to give you an unfair advantage."

"Please, Faith." Darlene rested a hand on my arms. Tears glittered in her eyes. "Can't you wait until Friday morning? I just feel this is the one page that will help start my design career."

My irritation at Darlene crumbled. Everyone had a dream and believed there was that one moment where it could come true. Darlene believed the envelope contained that time for her. What would it hurt to hold onto her layout? Besides my pride, since I'd be doing a favor for a woman who annoyed me. But that wasn't a reason to deny her request. My grandmothers raised me better.

"Okay. I'll hold onto it for you."

A child-like smile curved her mouth. "Can you put it somewhere so no one finds it and puts it up?"

"I'll keep it in my humongous purse. This way, every night it goes home with me and every morning it comes to Scrap This. You don't have to worry I'll forget it."

"Thank you so very much." A smile trembled on her lips.

Darlene spun on her heel and headed out the door. The humble tone shocked me. I never heard Darlene utter a sincere word. Then again, when had anyone, or I, given one to her?

I walked behind the counter and put the envelope in my purse. "Anything else happen while I was at lunch?"

Linda kept her gaze averted and shook her head. She reorganized the entry sheets for the contest.

My grandmothers always stood up for us when there was a dispute with a customer. In defusing the situation, my actions might have implied Linda did something wrong. "I don't agree with Darlene's behavior, but agreeing to hold onto her entry seemed the easiest way to get her to leave without a fuss."

"If it's that top secret, why did she bring it in today?" Linda spoke to the register though I knew the question was for me.

"Because timing is part of the competition between her and

Robyn and Stephanie. If she waited too long after them, then it would look like she needed inspiration from their work."

"It's not like anyone else would know," Linda said.

I shrugged. "True. But Darlene would, and in her world, she's the only person who matters."

Linda nodded as she alphabetized.

THIRTEEN

Sierra closed that night so I left work early. Pulling onto the main road, I pondered the next step in uncovering who really killed Michael Kane. At the light, I followed Karen's suggestion and headed for the police station. Better to get information first hand rather than second.

Switching on my blinker, I turned onto the smaller access road. The historic buildings housing the courthouse, police station and other city buildings remained in the heart of Eden, a two-mile square. As the town blossomed into a city, it expanded by stretching out in all directions and became more of a lopsided rectangle.

I hoped Detective Roget was off-duty. None of the questions I had about him should be asked to him. I parked in an unreserved space in front of the station, then hurried inside the small foyer and waited my turn. Bobbi-Annie lifted her hand in greeting before feigning interest as Mr. Griffin insisted she take down his complaint.

Wisps of thin gray hair bounced up and down on Mr. Griffin's balding head as he gestured wildly. "In the front yard, she's doing some karate stuff. The front yard! Everyone and God can see her out there doing those kicks and punches."

"Exercising is not against the law, Mr. Griffin." Bobbi-Annie kept a sweetness to her voice. "Now, if she starts waving around weapons, let us know."

"It's indecent, I tell you. No woman, especially a young unmarried woman, should be prancing outside hardly wearing nothing. I know her Daddy and Momma taught her better than that." He turned long enough to shoot me a glare. "That's what happens when these children leave to get more culture."

"And what is hardly wearing nothing?" Bobbi-Annie asked.

Behind her, Jasper paused, and drew closer. "Something you need me to check out, Bobbi?"

She snorted. "You wish, Jasper. I'm sure this is a misunderstanding between Mr. Griffin and Miss England."

"Her last name's Pancake!" Mr. Griffin raised his fists and shook them in righteous indignation. "Ain't nothing wrong with her family name. That's what I'm talking about. These kids thinking there's something wrong with us. Come back from those cities bringing—"

Officer Jasper walked into the foyer area and draped an arm around the older man. "Mr. Griffin, how about I check out this disturbance. I'll give you a ride home."

Mr. Griffin stepped away from Jasper. "I don't need any ride. I can still drive. I ain't feeble, young man."

"I wasn't saying that, Mr. Griffin."

Bobbi-Annie and I smothered our laughter. Jasper settled a shut-up look at us.

"Anyways, she ain't out there now." Mr. Griffin marched toward the door. "Every morning at seven, like clockwork, she's out there in them tight clothes acting like she's going to kick something to pieces."

The two men headed outside with Jasper scribbling down the times the disturbance to the peace took place.

"Are you going to call and warn Karen?" I asked.

"Nope." She grinned. "I'll let Karen handle Conroy. I have a feeling the only reason Mr. Griffin came in is because his wife found out he's been watching Karen exercising."

I shuddered. No wonder the poor man ran down and filed a police report. A real disturbance would erupt if Karen continued exercising "in barely nothing" in the front yard. Mrs. Griffin, who had a heavy right foot, was protective of her man. She believed all women waited in the wings to snatch her seventy-two-year-old husband away from her.

"So what brings you here, Faith?"

Leaning against the counter, I scooted the half-top of my body closer. I wanted a private conversation with Bobbi-Annie. "I wanted to ask about Detective Roget."

"I could go get him for you." She stood.

I grabbed her arm. "I don't want to talk to him. I wanted to ask you some questions about him. "

She eyed me warily, then a grin flashed on her face. She unlocked the door into the dispatch area and waved me in. "This way you don't have to worry about anyone hearing us. Though I'm surprised."

I shut the door behind me and dropped into the chair she rolled toward me. "Surprised?"

"If I had the interest of Steve Davis, I'd be spending time with that man, not asking about Ted."

I let Bobbi-Annie believe I had a romantic interest in Detective Roget. Easier than admitting I suspected the man was setting Marilyn up to take the fall for Michael's death. "Where did he work before here?"

"Near Washington, DC. Arlington, I think. Or was it Alexandria? Annandale? Can't remember. Just somewhere in that area."

"I thought he worked in Morgantown and then moved here."

She squinted at me. "Nope. He grew up in West Virginia, but then hightailed it of here. Attended school in Virginia, stayed in the Northern Virginia area until about six months ago."

"Why did he move here?" I caught the suspicion developing in Bobbi-Annie's eyes. "You know, I don't want to be interested in a man on the rebound or with a vicious ex-girlfriend lurking around the corner."

"He wanted somewhere a little more quiet and slower paced. Closer to family. From what I know, he's available with no known baggage to contend with."

Family? His mom worked on a cruise ship. There were no ports anywhere near West Virginia. "I read in Karen's article someone spotted Marilyn talking to Michael. Is that true?"

Bobbi-Annie pressed her lips together and crossed her arms. "I don't partake in police business gossip."

At least she had some standard. "I'm only asking because Karen charged into the store today and started asking me about Marilyn...and stuff."

The narrowing of her eyes let me know Bobbi-Annie had a good idea what the "and stuff" constituted. I swallowed hard. "She told me I should come here and read the police report, since I didn't believe what she wrote was true."

Bobbi-Annie gave me soft smile and squeezed my arm in a comforting gesture. "Why don't you go home, Faith? I know you're upset about answering Ted's question but you had to tell him. Ted's a good guy. He won't think you're disloyal or something like that. He'd find it admirable."

Heat skittered across my cheeks and I hurried out of there. I prayed this conversation didn't make its way out of the station. I didn't want him—or anyone—thinking I wanted to pursue a relationship. Any man who could run an official background check on me was one I'd steer clear of.

Not that I was searching for a guy.

My unsuccessful attempt at gathering information not only left me frustrated, but also late in starting dinner and I had invited my grandmothers over. I stopped at the grocery store and bought ready-made fried chicken. Homemade macaroni and cheese wouldn't take long, and I could throw a salad together in a few minutes.

Once home, I gathered up the bags of groceries and balanced dinner, my purse, and the keys while I opened up the door. Where was Steve or Hank now? No one ever lurked when a person needed help with the groceries.

I plopped the bags on the empty countertop, then hurried upstairs to change from the nice blouse I wore to work into a Mountaineers t-shirt. I was a messy cook. The biggest clue to what I made for dinner was my shirt.

As I was twisting my hair into a messy bun, the phone rang. I let the answering machine take the call.

Returning to the kitchen, I removed the chicken from the grocery store's self-service bag and arranged the pieces on a serving platter. At least the main entrée could look pretty. I filled a pot with water and set it on the stove.

The doorbell sung. Turning the knob on the stove, I set it on high then raced for the front door. My grandmothers arrived early to ensure dinner got made.

I tugged open the door and shouted an enthusiastic hello. "Hey Gram—"

The grin froze on my face.

Detective Roget leaned against the doorframe, looking me up and down. "I hear you have questions for me."

Everyone in this town, except for the murderer, had a hard time keeping secrets. I stood in the middle of the threshold. "I don't have anything to say to you. I went to the police station to verify something Karen England said."

"Is that so?" He pulled out a small notebook from the pocket of his jacket. "I bet I'm right to assume this has something to do with a certain case I've asked..." He held up his index finger. "Let me correct that, told you, to stay out of."

"I am staying out of it. The reporter came to me and made some allegations about Marilyn. I decided I should check into what she said."

"And what would those allegations be?"

I rolled my eyes. "I'm sure you know because you helped plant them into her story."

"You think well of me don't you?" His sarcasm came through loud and clear.

Sizzles popped in the background. I groaned and ran into the kitchen. The water started boiling. Hard. Grabbing a potholder, I removed the lid to calm the hot bubbling liquid. I blew on the roiling water. For some reason I always thought it sped up the cooling process.

Praying I didn't burn myself, I dumped in the box of macaroni then took the cheese from the refrigerator.

"I guess I don't need to call the fire department."

I spun around. Detective Roget, cell phone in hand, stood in the kitchen and glanced around the area. The open floor plan allowed him a look at my living and dining room. The dining room I had converted into a craft area was messy and disorganized.

"The water just boiled over," I said.

"You shouldn't leave unattended items cooking."

Viciously, I grated the mild cheddar cheese into a bowl. "I thought my grandmothers were at the door. Not you. You were the one who asked questions and distracted me."

"You were the one who came by the police station and played amateur sleuth."

I almost dropped the cheddar. I placed the remainder of the block down then went to refrigerator. I yanked open the door and gazed inside, stalling until I had a good response. Or at least until Roget forgot what he said.

He let out a long-suffering sigh. "Does it occur to you, Miss Hunter, that I'm quite capable at doing my job? People read way too many books where the damsel in distress solves the case and the day."

I slammed the door and turned around to face him full on. "I'm not in distress. And how would I know how capable you are when you arrested the wrong person? You jumped to the first conclusion you could. If what I said can be used against my friend, then why can't what I've learned help her get out of jail?"

"Because this isn't Monopoly. There isn't some kind of get out of jail card up for bartering."

"I'm not bartering. I want you to see the truth. Sometimes the truth isn't just what you hear. It's about what you don't." I stirred the pasta.

"Now I get you." The low tone rumbled from Detective Roget. He rested a hand on my shoulder, kneading the muscle with gentle fingers. "Listen, Faith, you're not to blame for your friend getting arrested. My case is based on a lot more evidence. Evidence you don't know about."

The relaxing touch lulled the anger I had at him. But I couldn't allow it to continue. Stepping away, I tilted my head and looked at his face. His rugged features softened and compassion lurked in his green eyes.

"I can't mention specifics. But I will let you know Marilyn was seen talking to Michael before—"

"He was murdered. I read that. How do you know that person isn't lying? Maybe Annette Holland made it up so you wouldn't suspect her. Why wouldn't a murderer lie?"

"The person I talked with is very reliable. Even you'd agree. You have to realize I'm not the bad guy here." He walked to the front door and paused with his hand on the knob. "And for the record, I'm available."

For the two hundredth time during dinner, my grandmothers exchanged the who's-going-to-talk-to-her look.

I placed my fork onto my plate. "What do you want to ask me?"

Hope linked her hands together and rested them on the table. "I noticed the detective stopped by. What did he want?"

"To ask a quick question."

The evasiveness increased their concern. I read the we-should-tell-Steve message floating between them. I smiled, hoping it eased their worries. "It was a quick, harmless question. All resolved. No problems."

"Are you sure?" Cheryl stood and cleared the table.

"Yes." I pushed my plate away.

"He probably just wanted to know why you visited him," Hope said.

I gaped at her. "I didn't go visit him."

"I heard you stopped by the police station."

"Not to see him. I needed to ask some questions."

Cheryl shook her head and sighed, the sound a weight on my

heart. "Faith, didn't you promise us that you'd stay out of this?"

"I can't believe Bobbi-Annie told you. That can't be proper procedure."

"Bobbie didn't say anything to us," Hope said soothingly. "Her momma was in the back dropping off dinner for the officers and heard you."

The chair scraped against the tile floor as I scooted backwards. I picked up my dishes. "With everyone knowing everyone else's business in this town, I'm surprised the real murderer is still running around."

I dropped my plate, glass and silverware into the sink. It was a good thing I preferred colorful plastic dinnerware than china. I turned the faucet full blast.

"You know," Cheryl's voice carried over the running water. "That is a good point."

I turned the water off.

"Cheryl, don't encourage her."

"Think about it, Hope. Not much goes on in this town that someone doesn't hear and see. Kids around here know if they're going to cut school or pull some kind of shenanigan, they best head a county over because their mommas are going to hear it from somebody."

"So you think this person isn't a local?" I asked.

Cheryl shook her head. "The locals watch outsiders even more than they do their own."

"Then how come no one saw anything?" I asked.

"Maybe they did." Sadness filled Hope's voice. "And we just can't face it."

I clutched the sponge, dishwater dribbled onto the floor. "You think Marilyn killed Michael."

"Honey, I don't know what to think. But the police don't go around arresting people because they can," Hope said.

Heaviness settled into my heart as my past flickered in my mind. I turned from Hope and went back to doing the dishes. "This time they are."

Hope stood beside me and wrapped an arm around me. "If the article in the paper is correct, why didn't Marilyn tell you she argued with Michael that day?"

"Because it didn't matter. She didn't do it."

"I don't think Marilyn should've asked you for help. Her lawyer should hire a private investigator." Anger, an unusual emotion for Hope, shook her voice.

I fixed my eyes on my grandmother. Grandma Hope looked exhausted. She couldn't approve of me involving myself in an activity leaning toward dangerous. We needed something else to think about, bond over, besides my sleuthing issues.

"How about we have an impromptu crop?" I smiled at my grandmothers.

They glanced over into the craft area. Cheryl seemed to consider it, but Hope shook her head. My grandmother probably thought crafting equaled cleaning as the disarray bordered on chaos.

"I'm sorry, sweetie, but I'm kind of tired tonight," Hope said.

"Are you all right?" I asked.

Times like this reminded me my grandmothers were getting older. One day they wouldn't be here. The fear of utter aloneness skittered along my nerves and my heart raced. Without them, I'd have no one on Earth who loved me.

Hope hugged me. "I'm fine. The last two weeks of working late nights to get ready for the show wore me out. I just need to catch up on sleep."

I looked at Cheryl. She winked and left with Hope. The wink said that's-all-there-is-to-it brought some relief. I watched them cross the yard and then go into their house. Once they were safely inside, I shut my door and went into the kitchen. Work first, then play.

After finishing the dishes, I walked into the craft area and stood in the middle of the room. Glancing around, my shoulders slumped forward with the truth of all the cleaning I had to do. Evidence lingered from my frantic night of putting together layouts for the Art Benefit Show.

Bits of different colored ribbon littered the blond wood laminate floor. On the table, small pieces of cardstock filled the basket I used for scraps. In the middle of the table, full sheets of pattern paper and cardstock were stacked to near skyscraper heights. Open magazines took up the small floral couch against the wall. My bottles of flowers, brads and gems were stacked haphazardly on the large table and the shelves bolted into the wall.

From the distance of the kitchen, I didn't get the full effect of what a disaster zone I created in my cropping area. Well, no time like the present for turning chaos into calm. I plucked the basket of scraps off the table, went over to the small couch, shoved the magazines aside and sat down. Most of the scrap pieces were too small and creased for use on another project. I dumped the contents of the basket into the trash.

Gathering up bottles, I returned them to the proper shelf. Using my hands, I swept the bits of ribbons and unusable trimmings into the wastebasket stationed at the end of the table. I eyed the leaning tower of paper. Divide and conquer. I cleared off the remainder of the table and started sorting the paper by color and pattern.

The edge of a photo caught my eye. Gingerly, I pulled it out from underneath the stack of pages. I looked down at myself at the Renaissance festival. In the background of the picture, Steve was captured as part of our family. Every time I turned around, my grandmothers insisted on including Steve in our family gatherings. I wondered how Steve's dad felt about his son's calendar being booked solid with Hunter/Greyfield family events. I'm sure his dad would like to spend time with his only child. Steve's mother died a few years back. He and his stepmom didn't quite get along from the conversations I overheard between my grandmothers. Without his dad, Steve would be alone.

But without my grandmothers—and Steve—I ran the high risk of being truly alone in this world. My mind caught that thought and reeled it in. Maybe my grandmothers' matchmaking efforts were because they saw that reality in my future. Since I moved back home, I kept a distance between others and myself. I had friends. I engaged in their lives, but kept mine private. No one understood I lived that way to protect them.

Collapsing onto the couch, I clutched the photo as memories flooded over me. Trapping me. My grandmothers' dream for me could never happen. Entering a relationship required an honesty I couldn't give. Even to my grandmothers who had given up everything for me.

Because of Adam. Because of myself.

By the time I realized I was a pawn in Adam's life, our finances and future were tied. I trusted him. I loved him. He saw me as a naïve girl from West Virginia whom he could charm and control—and one who held a security clearance benefiting his sideline business.

From the first moment Adam introduced himself to me, I was smitten by the older, handsome man. I never questioned anything he told me. Until it was nearly too late.

I shuddered and pulled myself away from the morbid thoughts.

On the bright side, I never told my grandmothers about him as I wanted our marriage to be a surprise for them. Well, it turned out as more of a surprise for me.

I stood and wandered to the front window and stared out into the vast darkness. Not even one star glimmered, leaving the world ink black. To West Virginians, faith, family and country meant everything. How would my grandmothers be treated once it became known their granddaughter—even unknowingly—betrayed those principles?

There was nothing that could be done about the past except live with it. I deposited the picture into a drawer and got cleaning, focusing on the here and now.

With the amount of time reorganization was taking, I'd call it a night before I completed one page. Clean today, scrap tomorrow. My stomach rumbled. I needed something comforting. Preferably with chocolate. Homemade chocolate chip cookies sounded perfect.

I walked into the kitchen. Something thumped against my backdoor. I froze. The scratch sounded again and I reached for the light but stopped. Turning them off now would only confirm I was in the house. I crept away from the kitchen and headed toward the phone.

A howling meow erupted from behind the door. Ol' Yowler. Opening the cabinet beside the stove, I took out a can of shrimp flavored cat food. I dumped it into a green plastic bowl and water into a red dish. I opened the door. The inky blackness held the coldness of an approaching cold snap. Shivering, I placed dinner out for the cat then retreated back inside.

I scrounged around in the cabinets for chocolate chips. Finding only a half-filled bag, I conceded and declared it an early night. I'd finish organizing tomorrow. I started for the stairs and the red light from the answering machine caught my eye. Sighing, I clomped down the stairs and checked the messages. I hit the play button and examined my chipping nail polish. Time for a new manicure.

"You just can't stop." A voice wheezed from the voice mail and the message ended with an abrupt click.

FOURTEEN

Wrapping my arms around my waist, I stared at the phone. Maybe the high-pitched meow of Yowler wasn't a feed-me-now scream, but a some-idiot-stepped-on-my-tail scream. My legs shook. I made my way to the sofa and dropped onto it. If Annette was involved in Michael's murder, she could've enlisted someone to get me off the case.

Like Roget. He knew where I lived.

"Stop it." I wanted to end the horror flick developing in my mind. Taking in a deep breath, I stood and marched back to the phone.

I replayed the message and analyzed out the creepiness. The wheezing sounded forced. Like someone masking their voice. I hit the caller ID button and looked at the last number that called. Local cell number. Just because someone said "you just can't stop" in a creepy voice didn't mean danger lurked in the backyard. The message could've been meant for someone else. A wrong number.

I placed my hand on the receiver. I could call the number back and find out who called. Though that sounded like something on a top ten list of stupid things for a woman to do. Call and confirm your number to a potential stalker.

It's a Small World chimed. I screeched.

Pressing my hand against my heart, I tried calming myself. An attacker would break down the door, not ring the bell.

"Faith!" Steve pounded on the front door.

That explained the noise in my backyard. Furious, I yanked the door open and faced my would-be knight in shining armor. Every instinct screamed smack him. I balled my hands and squeezed them against my side. Next time, I'd call the police and let Steve explain his skulking to them.

"Stop spying on me." I pushed the door closed.

Steve gripped the doorframe and kept it open. "Faith, what's going on? What happened?"

"Because of you lurking around in my backyard, I got all worked up over a stupid phone call." I blinked at the wetness blurring Steve's image. "You scared me."

He maneuvered around me and stepped into the house. He shut the door and locked it. "I wasn't in your backyard."

My knees quaked and I placed a hand on the wall. Steve walked me to the couch and sat me down. I reached over, grabbed one of the throw pillows, and clutched it against my stomach. Steve knelt in front of me.

"Did you see someone outside?" He asked.

"I heard a scratching. I thought it was Yowler but..." I glanced at the phone and a shiver worked its way up my spine. I heaved out a sigh of defeat. "Someone left a weird message on my answering machine."

"Weird?" Steve stood, walked over, and pressed the button on the machine. His face reddened and he clenched his hands. "When did you get this?"

"I don't know. I didn't think to check my messages until a little bit ago."

Steve pulled his cell phone from the clip attached to his belt. "We should call Roget."

Calling the detective scared me more than calling the person who left the message. "What if it's a wrong number?"

Steve raised his hands in a preaching-was-comin' gesture. "What if it's not? Faith, it's better to err on the side of caution. The police are trained to handle these kinds of matters."

"I don't want anyone getting in trouble." Especially myself.

"Are you listening to me? Safety first. Hurt feelings can be sorted out later."

The McGruff role started annoying me. "If everyone's right,

then Michael's killer is in jail. Who's going to hurt me?"

"Just let Roget hear the message and see what he says."

I crossed my arms. "He'll say I called myself and left the message. It's my new method of interfering. Besides, the voice sounds a little like a woman faking a tough male voice."

The I-know-best expression softened on Steve's face.

"And how dangerous can this criminal be? They used a phone without blocking the number."

Steve glanced at the display screen. "All right. So they're not a professional. That doesn't make them harmless."

"I can take a pregnant woman. Out run her anyway."

"What are you talking about?"

"The only person I've upset with my investigation is Annette Holland." Okay, also Detective Roget, but I decided it best not to bring up that man's name.

Steve's eyes bugged out. Not a good look for him. "Your investigation? You're actively getting involved with this case? After you've been warned?"

I grimaced. Bad choice of word. "Okay, not really investigating in the sense like the way the police handle a case. I've just asked a few questions. Annette is lying. I don't know why no one—"

"Faith, she didn't kill Michael."

"Of course not, she's too sweet and innocent."

Steve walked over and knelt in front of the couch. He gathered my hands into his and took in a deep breath. "I need you to listen to me."

Anger rumbled inside of me, twisting my stomach and threatening to bubble out of my mouth. I yanked away from his touch. "When are people going to listen to me?"

"We have been. You're the one ignoring what everyone has said." Steve dropped onto the cushion beside me. "I need to tell you something."

I scooted as far away as I could, picked up a throw pillow and clutched it to my chest as a barrier. Or an object to bash Steve on the head with—depending on what he said.

Heaving out a sigh, Steve leaned forward and looked at the floor. "I was with Annette when she discovered Michael's body and screamed."

The pillow tumbled from my hand. "What?"

Steve rubbed his head then hooked his hands together behind his neck. He leaned against the couch cushion, staring up at the ceiling. "Marilyn was headed toward Michael and I thought it would be good if she didn't see Annette."

"Did you see Michael?"

He sighed. "No."

"So how do you know Annette didn't kill him and then you intercepted her after the deed? Did she seem upset Marilyn was going to talk to Michael?"

"No. Or at least she didn't mention it." Steve rubbed his hand over his shaved head. "I know it's easier to blame someone you don't know or care—"

"This isn't about ease, it's about the truth."

"I heard Michael talking to someone. Annette turned to go back and that's when I stopped her. I told her we should get her a drink since it was stuffy and she was expecting."

That was Steve, always the knight in shining armor. Excitement wiggled through me at his other revelation. "Who was he talking to? Did you recognize the voice?"

He shook his head. "I told the police everything. I'm only bringing up the part about Annette so you'll back off of her."

A little green worked its way inside of me. "Awful protective of her, aren't you?"

"I'm more inclined on keeping you from being charged with intimidating witnesses. Let the police do the investigating."

"That's the problem. They're done." I slapped my hands onto the couch. "If there was still a murderer to find, I'd be minding my own business. But Roget believes he's found his murderer. He's wrong."

"And you know this because..."

"Because if Marilyn killed Michael, why did she ask for help?"

I asked. "She couldn't have done it."

Steve rubbed his hand over his shaved head. "She shouldn't have asked you to help her."

"Maybe she asked me because no one else would."

Steve cupped my cheek. "Faith, did you ever think there might be a good reason others can't help her?"

"No," I said, keeping still.

"Regardless, it wasn't right of Marilyn to guilt you into investigating her case."

"Sometimes it's not about what is right," I whispered, withdrawing from his touch. "But what's needed."

"And what's needed is for us to call Roget and let him know." Steve flipped open his phone.

"If the police come, my grandmothers will worry. Hope has been stressed enough lately." I couldn't tell Steve the person he wanted to call was the person I planned on investigating—Googling—tonight.

"We have to do something." Steve paced around the room. "Sitting here and testing if this is a joke isn't a smart choice. I don't want you getting hurt."

"I won't get hurt."

"Like you can promise that." Steve peered out the curtains in the living room and then went into the kitchen and gazed outside. "It's possible if we don't call the police, then the person will think they called the wrong number."

I didn't like that theory because it meant the person deliberately called me. I liked my theory better. I was the wrong person pranked.

Steve rubbed his jaw. After a few minutes, he released a loud sigh and nodded. "You can't stay here."

The resolved expression on his face troubled me. "Steve, if I go spend the night at my grandmothers, they're going to know something's wrong. How do I explain a sleepover?"

"You won't stay with them. You'll stay at my house." He walked toward me.

I held up my hands and blocked his approach. "There's no way I'm spending the night with you. That wouldn't look proper."

I didn't believe in toying with temptation. Plus, I was really, really getting into livid territory with Steve deciding my life. I allowed one man to make my decisions for me and I'd never do it again.

Steve shoved his hands into his back pockets. "I don't know if I should be insulted by the assumption or by your utter horror at the idea."

The hurt look on his face revved up my guilt. I took in a deep breath and smiled at him. Friendly, but not flirty.

"I'm not horrified at the thought. It's not like there isn't some appeal. Not that I'm suggesting it, or discounting it because I'm appalled at the idea of us sleeping together. I mean sleeping in the same house."

Steve smiled, the gesture growing broader as I rambled on. Why couldn't I shut up? I'd rather dig a hole and fall into it rather than keep talking my way into an overnighter.

"It's just that, well, what would people think? What if my grandmothers saw me coming out of your place?" I hoped the expression on my face garnered some pity from him.

"You've come up with a much more interesting plan than I had in mind," Steve said, stepping closer to me.

My face flamed and I took some steps backwards, scared by the spark of attraction in his eyes.

"That wasn't what I was proposing," Steve said.

I kept my voice mute and just nodded. My words were venturing me into a place I shouldn't tread.

"I figured we'd switch houses. I'll spend the night here. You spend the night at my place. This way if anyone does come, you'll be safely tucked into my guest room and I can identify the person."

Pictures of a bruised and battered Steve filled my mind. I fought back tears. "What about you? I don't want someone hurting you. It's my home. If someone comes, I'll deal with it."

With a stubborn expression chiseled onto his handsome face,

he held out his hands. In one, he gripped the cell phone, the other hand held his keys. "Then we call the police. Your choice. Choose one."

There was the third choice I inadvertently brought up. "We'll go with my plan. I'll stay at your place. With you. Not with you with you. But..."

"I get what you're saying."

"Good." Because if I tried explaining anymore, who knows what I landed up proposing we do. Wicked, delightful thoughts bounced around in my head.

I went upstairs and packed my fabric weekender bag. I jammed a t-shirt and sweatpants inside. I slowed down so the R-rated movie playing in my head stopped. I thought about Marilyn and all the prison movies I seen. I shuddered.

Fifteen minutes later, I had everything I needed for the night. Tomorrow morning, I'd return home and get ready for work.

Steve opened the front door and reached for my bag. After a slight hesitation, I handed it over and let Steve hold my hand.

The wind whistled in the trees and the branches swayed in the darkness. I peered into the night and tightened my grasp on Steve's hand as we walked across my grandmothers' front lawn.

"My porch light is on. Everything looks okay," Steve said.

I knew he was right, but my senses remained on high alert. My ears picked up every sound of the night, naming them and filtering them into good or evil categories. Were the small sounds just leaves rustling or a person sneaking their way toward us?

We reached Steve's house and he unlocked the door. Jamming my hands into my front jean pockets, I rocked on my heels waiting for him to hurry. After what felt like minutes, the door sprang open and I rushed inside.

Steve set my bag by the stairs. "If you're nervous about me staying here, I can go back over to your house."

"I'm fine."

He leaned against the banister and pointed upstairs. "Second room on the right. I'm down the hall if you need anything."

"I don't need anything. Won't need anything. I'll be totally fine." I plastered a smile on my face and hoped that kept my mouth from moving. Was my nervousness because of the phone call or knowing Steve was a few feet away? I hadn't been alone with a man—in any sense—since the night before Adam was led away in handcuffs three and a half years ago.

Some look of alarm must have flashed onto my face because Steve frowned, concern filling his dark eyes. He stepped forward and wrapped a comforting arm around my back, tugging me forward for a hug.

The cologne Steve wore, a mix of spice and cedar, blanketed around me. The scent held a hint of the rustic beauty and strength of the mountains. A place filled with love and safety, feelings Steve stirred inside of me. Panic rose up and I twisted away from his touch, grabbed my bag, and raced for the guest room.

I slammed the door and locked it, pressing my body against it as I caught my breath. This was going to be a long night.

FIFTEEN

At the first sign of dawn, I peered out the front door looking for any sign of my neighbors. Everything appeared quiet. Taking in a deep breath, I bolted from the house and raced across the lawns, heading for my own house. If my grandmothers saw or heard a word about this early morning dash, by mid-morning, a wedding ceremony would take place.

I checked the front door, no signs of tampering. Good. Grabbing the paper before my grandmothers' did, I opened the door and peeked into the foyer and living room, everything right where I left it. Including my mess. Papers and magazines still littered the small couch and the table in my scrapbooking area. Well, one couldn't expect a rash of rabid housecleaners breaking and entering.

Before I got overconfident, I checked the rest of the house and the backyard. All clear.

Since I was in the kitchen and near the best Christmas present ever, since I never did get my pony, I started the Keurig. As I waited for the magical awakening brew, I snapped open the paper and gawked at the headline.

This was not good. Not good at all.

The front page article written by Karen England mentioned where Marilyn worked and implied Detective Roget believed a coworker conspired to keep the crime quiet. It stated the detective handling the case had stopped by Scrap This more than once to question an employee, a relative of the owners', about intimidating a witness.

My poor grandmothers. We had enough problems attracting customers in the slow economy. People thinking we employed a murderer and an accomplice might run off the rest.

How did Karen find out about what had been happening at the store? Was the woman hiding out in the parking lot or did she have an inside connection? Like Darlene, who was mad enough to blab. Was Roget giving her information in hopes of tripping up the killer? Or maybe force my hand, if he really believed I was involved?

I stomped up the stairs to my room. I paused on the landing and glanced down the hallway toward my home office. This could ruin my grandmothers' business. Time to get my own ammunition.

If Roget was feeding information to Karen, so could I. A quick check on the internet could get me more information about the trial that tied Roget to Michael Kane. Since I was hosting the contest crop tonight, I wasn't scheduled to work until noon. How long could it take to find the information?

An hour later, I finally found an interesting link. Bob Roget, private investigator, Morgantown. Was this the family Ted moved to Eden to be closer to? Maybe his father?

Well, I had thought about hiring a PI, and this man could fit the bill perfectly. I just needed an alias so Detective Roget didn't find out.

I turned off the computer and hurried through my getting ready for work routine. I skipped making a second cup of coffee and headed to Home Brewed where I could grab some caffeine and let someone know my general plans in case my grandmothers checked up on me.

Their third favorite pastime, as scrapbooking and matching-making tied for first.

I shifted the box of specialty coffees in my arms as I popped open the trunk and waited for the male employee to place the steel cappuccino machine in first. My stop at Home Brewed this morning worked out for Dianne, since her machine broke last night. Now, I had a reason for my trip—besides conducting an investigation.

Slipping into the driver's seat of my sedan, I took the GPS

from the glove compartment and typed in the address for Bob Roget's office. Not quite in the heart of Morgantown, but a straight
shot from Dianne's "local" supplier. A bonus since my sense of direction, even with an electronic helper, usually resulted in more
circles and turns than performed on *Dancing with the Stars*.

An hour and three cell phone calls later, I pulled up to a histor-
ical building. The facade was clean and the outside had flowers lining the sidewalk. A quaint area that made me wish I had time to
browse the neighborhood before heading home.

"Glad you found the place." An attractive red-headed man,
who looked a lot like Ted, ambled down the sidewalk toward me.
"Sorry you had so much trouble. Those GPS units can be useless
sometimes."

"I appreciate you still seeing me, considering I'm really late for
our appointment."

I wanted to ask him if he was Detective Roget's brother, but it
was hard being incognito if I gave away I knew Detective Roget—
and in a legal sense.

"How about we head up? I have soft drinks and snacks upstairs if you'd like something."

"That'll be nice."

His green eyes twinkled and he leaned in closer. "Just don't
tell the dentist who has the downstairs office. He thinks I ought to
serve my clients vegetables and whole grain snack options."

My shoes squished against the plush of the gray carpet. The
walk down the long dim hallway made me feel as if I was in an up-
scale country club. My toes itched to feel the softness of the carpet.

Bob Roget stopped at the end of the hallway and opened the
door. "After you."

An ornately carved chair faced an antique desk. Photographs
in maple frames filled in the shelves of the bookcase. One of them
had a picture of a beautiful woman between Detective Roget and
this Roget. A photograph on the corner of the desk showed Bob and
another handsome gentleman enjoying a beer on a fishing charter
boat. "Please have a seat."

"Thank you, Mr. Roget."

"It's Bob. I'm not called Mr. Roget unless some officer of the court is addressing me."

Feeling out of place amid the expensive setting, I carefully walked over and sat on the edge of the seat's cushion. My fingers glided over the smooth wood of the armrests.

"Okay, Miss Shirley Hardy, how about we get started." His eyebrows rose and he pressed back a smile when he said "my" name.

"Well, I have a friend who's in trouble."

"And this friend's name is..."

"I'd rather not say until I'm sure you'll take their case."

Bob settled back in his chair, placed his feet on the desk, and propped a notepad on his legs. "Go on."

"My friend has been accused of something she didn't do, and no one, but me it seems, believes she is innocent."

"Are you're sure everyone else is wrong?"

"Yes!" The word came out more forceful than I intended.

"Noted." Bob scribbled something on the paper.

"There's no one to help her but me. But I need help."

"Help as in a private investigator, and not help as in telling the police what you know?" Bob moved his gaze from the paper to me. "Assuming the people not believing her are the police?"

I squirmed. "Yes."

"Sometimes people do things in the heat of anger they wouldn't normally do. That's why the prisons are full." Bob's tone was soft, almost apologetic.

"I know she didn't do it."

"Sadly, Miss Hardy, there are only two ways to know for certain if she is innocent. You saw who committed the crime or else you were with your friend when the crime took place. Unless the police think the two of you are in cahoots, then neither of those count."

Why did his mini-lecture sound so much like what Detective Roget said, only nicer?

"They shouldn't think..." I trailed off, not wanting to give myself away. Murders didn't happen often in these parts, especially ones at a community art show.

"But they could if your help is seen as interfering. Makes the police wonder what you're motivation would be."

I fisted my hands. "To help a friend, obviously."

"Most people wouldn't risk jail time for a friend."

I almost revealed an arm from my skeleton but slapped my lips shut in time.

"Well, Miss Hardy, I do think it's best for a professional investigator to look into this matter. But I don't take cases someone brings on behalf of someone else. How do I know your friend wants me nosing around?"

"They would."

His eyebrows rose.

"She asked me to help—"

"And you don't have time. Don't want to help. Aren't very good at it..." Bob paused and leaned forward, "or are annoying some officer of the law and thought it best not to do it yourself anymore?"

Was I that obvious or the man that good? "The truth is a little of number one, some of number three is mixed in there, and a large amount of number four."

Bob smiled but it didn't quite reach his eyes. "I appreciate your almost honesty."

I drew in a breath.

"I also don't take cases that put me up against my younger brother."

"Your brother?" I whispered.

He nodded and pointed at the picture as he sat up. "Ted Roget, Eden's one and only homicide detective. Conflict of interest. It's one of the reasons Ted steered clear of working in Morgantown."

"Close, but not too close."

"He has his cases. I have mine. No family ties to be used against either of us." A hardness took away the kindness residing in Bob's green eyes.

Now he and Ted looked exactly alike.

"I'm sorry. I didn't mean any harm. I just—"

Bob held up his hand and cut me off. "Most people don't. But it doesn't change the harm done."

SIXTEEN

Relief flooded through me as I crested the hill and started across the small bridge, the final separation between me and Eden. Soon, I'd arrive at work and my disastrous mission would be over. I could spend time doing something I was actually good at. My foot wanted to punch the gas pedal when I left Morgantown, but any time I'd gain by speeding would evaporate if I got pulled over. Not to mention the unneeded hit to my bank account.

At least I wasn't like Adam. I wasn't setting out to destroy people. But my helping was more likely to get Marilyn in deeper trouble. And now Detective Roget would view my visit to his brother as tampering.

My head pounded. He'd dig into my past. What would happen once he learned I'd been charged as an accomplice in a murder before? The fear centered itself in my chest and squeezed. What had I walked myself into?

My cell phone trilled from the cup holder. I snagged it and flipped it open. "Hello."

"You just can't stop." A choking voice rasped.

I slammed on the brakes. The phone tumbled from my hand and fell near the pedals. As I reached for it, I heard a squeal and my car bumped forward. My forehead struck the steering wheel. A sharp pain swallowed me. Tears and bright lights blurred my vision. Gritting my teeth and hissing, I shoved the gearshift into park and sat up.

Dizziness engulfed me and the pain in my temple increased. I rested my head back against the seat and waited for the world to stop swirling. A fist pounded on the driver side window. I scooted away from the sound.

"What do you think you're doing?" The large man slapped his hand onto the pane. "This ain't a parking lot."

Fumbling with the seatbelt, I unlocked it and stretched, ignoring the rising nausea as I scrambled on the floor for my phone. I grabbed it.

"You're going to call the cops! We'll see about that."

I focused my attention on the wavering numbers on my phone. When they stopped twirling, I punched in Sierra's cell number. There was no way I'd call my grandmothers and tell them I was in a minor car accident. They'd skip the first word and focus on the last two.

The phone rang. And rang. My insides churned and my hand shook. Please let her have it on.

"Hello," Sierra said, a twinge of annoyance in her voice.

"It's Faith."

"When are you getting back? I just got a message I need to see the vice-principal. Something about Henry and a prank."

"Sierra, I've been—"

"If I put this off, the man will upgrade the prank to a misdemeanor."

The fist slammed against my window again. I winced at the loud beat and choked back a cry. Please God don't let the window shatter.

"Faith, what's going on?"

My voice trembled. "I got in a car accident. The other guy is mad at me. He's hitting the window."

Sierra drew in a sharp breath. "Where are you?"

Between sniffles, I rattled off the location.

"Did you call the police?"

A wail erupted from down the street. A small audience gathered on both sides of the street. "I think he did."

"That's good. Sit tight in your car. Keep the door locked. Don't make eye contact. Are you hurt?"

"Not really."

The closer the sirens got, the slower my heart beat. I'd get a ticket for the quick stop, but in exchange I'd get protection from the enraged man. The high-pitched wail bounced around in my head and red lights swirled into my car.

"The police are here," I said.

"Good. Help will arrive soon."

"Thanks."

I closed the phone and lifted my gaze to the rearview mirror. I groaned.

An unmarked white sedan pulled up behind the other car. Stepping from the vehicle was a tall, reddish-haired man. Not many male redheads in Eden. Of all the police officers, why did it have to be Detective Roget?

"Sir, I need you to step away from the vehicle," Roget said.

I squeezed my eyes shut.

"This lady stopped in the middle of the street."

Something thumped against the driver side tire. I cringed and wiped tears from my cheeks. How did those get there?

A hardness entered Roget's tone. "Sir, I'm advising you not to kick that car again."

"She did stop in the middle of the street." A woman's voice joined into the conversation. "There isn't even a light there."

I clutched the phone against my chest. More tears trickled down my face.

Something tapped on the window. "Ma'am, can you roll down the window?" Roget said in a comforting tone I'd never heard him use.

I swiped at the wetness.

The car jiggled as Roget tried opening the door. "Ma'am, I need you to roll down the window or unlock the door."

Tears continued to seep from behind my closed eyelids.

"Are you hurt?" Concern rumbled in his voice. "Can you move?"

Keeping my head dipped so he couldn't see my face, I nodded and unlocked the door. He pulled it open and offered his hand. I ignored the help and clambered from the vehicle on my own stumbling power. Squaring my shoulders, I raised my head and looked at Roget.

A scowl developed on his face. "Care to explain what's going on?"

Apparently an unknown woman deserved his compassion, but not I. "I stopped. Someone ran into me."

An angry blond man surged forward, fists clenched at his side. "This isn't a parking space."

Words buzzed around me, but all I could focus on was the rage the man directed at me. Nausea rolled my stomach and sweat crept down my back. On shaking legs, I stepped backwards and found my retreat blocked by my sedan. The sun-heated metal seeped through my cotton shirt and did little to ward off the chill taking control of my body.

Roget stepped into the small pocket between the angry man and me. "You need to settle down, sir, or I'll have you hauled off to jail."

Stopping in the middle of the road wasn't the brightest choice, but certainly not arrest-worthy. My body swayed and I reached for the car door. I needed to sit down.

Roget slipped an arm around my back and the other wrapped around my shoulders, cradling me to his body. "I'm calling an ambulance."

"No," I whispered. Taking in a deep breath, I tried again. "No. I'm fine. I just need that guy to stop yelling. It's just a little headache. "

"I'm not so sure about that." Roget adjusted his hold so that he took on most of my weight and his back separated me from the irate driver.

"I don't believe this!" the blond guy raged. "The cop is trying to pick up that chick."

"I just called the Chief." A woman announced, snapping closed a cell phone.

"At least she didn't call my mom." Roget loosened his grasp.

"You're sure you're okay?"

"Yeah. Except I don't know if I like being called a chick."

Roget shook his head. "You would decide to get worked up over that. Let me get these people settled down before the Chief arrives."

"I'll just stay here." I pointed over at my car.

"You do that."

I sat in my car and waited for Detective Roget. In less than ten minutes, he strode toward my car with a leather-covered notebook and flipped it open.

"The question of the afternoon is why did you stop in the middle of the road?"

"My cell rang and I answered it..."

"Distracted by a chat," Roget interrupted.

I drew in a deep breath to stop the snark from exiting and to draw in some patience. "Someone called me and said the exact same thing as the threatening call I got last night."

"I wished we could've done this somewhere else." I paced around the Scrap This break room. I moved so I didn't explode. Or cry—an even worse reaction. After I mentioned the threat, Roget felt we should move the discussion indoors. If the phone call wasn't a prank, standing outside with a crowd forming made it dangerous for me.

Sierra attempted to settle me into a chair. "This is better than going to the police station."

"I'd rather face rumors and wagging tongues than cause my grandmothers so much anxiety." I rubbed my temples.

"They would've found out about this," Sierra said. "And hearing you were taken to the police station wouldn't have them less worried."

"Sure it would. They'd be mad instead. Ready to tear into me for whatever harebrained scheme I got myself into."

"Something they should do."

"Thanks for your support," I snapped.

"Is that what you want?" Sierra glared at me. "Me telling you it's okay to be asking questions about a murder? Think about it. What if you find something that points to the murderer? What will you do with that information? Go to the police or keep digging until your positive?"

"I'll figure it out when I come to it."

Where was Roget? He dropped me off at Scrap This, refusing to let me drive myself, then disappeared after stashing me in the break room. I stomped toward the door. "He could at least hurry so we can get this over with."

Leaning out the door, I saw my grandmothers hovering near the beginning of the small hallway. Hope worried her hands together and Cheryl whispered into her ear.

I closed my eyes, blocking everything out. When they discovered the entire reason for Roget stopping by the store, not just verifying some information about a fender bender, they'd become frantic. Why did I ever let Marilyn talk me into playing detective for her? I wasn't qualified or even good at it. Every piece of information I found brought more questions rather than answers.

The bell above the door jingled. I prayed it was Roget. I didn't know if my nerves could handle a longer wait.

"What's going on?" Cheryl asked, her voice growing closer. "Why are you handling a car accident?"

I pulled myself together and met the entourage at the door. Roget carried a white paper sack and a cardboard container with two coffees. My stomach rumbled.

Roget held back a grin and placed the bag on the table in. "I was on my lunch break near the scene. No sense trying to track down Officer Jasper when I was already there. I figured if we came here, I could finish up this little report and eat my lunch. If we go to the station, I'd never get a chance to eat." He smiled at Cheryl. "I hope you don't mind."

Hope opened a cabinet above the microwave. "Of course we don't. Let me get you a plate, it's better for the digestive system to use one."

Grandma Cheryl eyed the detective suspiciously.

"Is that so?" Roget turned sideways to look at Hope.

She pulled out a china plate with a gold trim around the edge and put it front of him. "Absolutely. A person usually eats slower from a plate than from a napkin or a wrapper. That alone is a big help."

"I'll keep that in mind." Roget pulled out three wrapped packages from the bag and put them on the table. He caught my gaze. "I brought extra in case you were hungry. Annabelle makes great sandwiches."

Knowing my grandmothers were watching my manners, I forced out a thank you and picked up one of the sandwiches. Plus, I didn't want word getting back to Bobbi-Annie's mom that I turned my nose up at her food. Hope carried over another plate over and put it down.

"I ran next door and got coffee," Roget said.

"Thanks." This time the word was filled with heartfelt gratitude. The smell of the caffeine improved my mood and cleared my head.

Roget smiled at my grandmothers, unwrapped one of the sandwiches, and placed it on the plate. "I'll be done soon and I promise to clean up."

My grandmothers stood near the door. Roget remained silent and continued smiling at them. Cheryl crossed her arms and locked gazes with him.

I wondered who'd budge first.

Sierra headed for the door. "Is it all right if I go over to the school?"

"She might need a ride Grandma."

Sierra looked at me.

"Or did Hank get the car fixed?"

Sierra winked at me. "It's working fine, but it might be better if you follow me, Cheryl. In case it breaks down again."

"I'll be out front if you need me, Faith." Hope shut the door behind her.

Roget and I were left alone in the room. I spun the plate, doing my best to ignore the sandwich and the detective.

"I'm not going to hurt you," Roget said.

I jerked my gaze up. I wanted to laugh his claim away but I couldn't force the sound out of my throat. My hands shook and I clamped them together.

"Faith, I apologize if I've done anything to frighten you." Roget reached across the table then stopped. "I've been told I can come across rather abrasive."

I shrugged. "I'm not scared of you. It's just this whole situation has me a little edgy."

"Why don't you tell me about it?" He took a bite of his sandwich, his full attention on me.

The unwavering green gaze had nervousness racing through me. "Last night, someone left a message on my machine, 'you can't just stop.' The same thing the person said when I answered my cell in the car."

Roget frowned. "Did you report this last night?"

"No. I thought it was some kid pulling a prank. Or a wrong number."

His eyebrows rose. "So, someone left a vaguely threatening message intended for someone else on your phone?"

"It made sense last night." Lifting up the top bread, I examined what was inside. Turkey, lettuce, tomato, mayonnaise. Using a napkin, I wiped off some of the mayo. "I didn't think I did anything to make someone that mad. Plus, the message sounded weird."

"Weird?"

"Like someone disguising their voice. And if someone was leaving a threatening call, you'd think they'd block the number."

Roget's eyes widened and he put the sandwich down. "The number is on your caller ID?"

I nodded. "That's why I wrote it off last night but..." The air in the room grew colder and goose bumps prickled my flesh.

The humor left Roget's expression. "But the call to your cell phone scared you."

Tears pooled and seeped from the corners of my eyes.

Roget offered me a napkin. "Is there anything that happened right before you got either call?"

"Nope."

"Do you have your cell phone? Maybe they didn't block the number again."

"I think it's still in my car." I crossed my arms. "And I'd rather you not look at my personal items."

"I'll tell you what, I'll get your phone and bring it over later. You can then recite the number to me."

"And I can trust you because?" I narrow-eyed him.

"I've trusted your word."

"Okay." It was the only response my befuddled mind conjured up.

Roget gathered up his lunch. "I'll just finish this back at the station. I think it'll be better if you could relax a little bit."

"Thanks."

He stood in the doorway, head cocked to the side, as he studied me for a long moment. He glanced down the hallway then back at me. "Do you always use the back door when you open and close?"

Why did he want to know that? "Yes. That's the employee entrance."

He looked out to the front of the store. "That parking lot is hidden from the main road. Are there lights out there?"

"A few."

"What are the store hours?"

"Ten until seven. Unless we're having a class, then we're open until nine or later."

He frowned. "Do you have any scheduled this week?"

"Tonight and tomorrow until ten."

His frown deepened and he rubbed the badge clipped at his side. "Don't like that one bit."

"Usually we have two employees on duty for the classes." A varied number depending on the number of students signed up.

"It might be best if you park out front for a few days. Just until we figure out what's going on with these calls."

"Probably nothing," I said.

Detective Roget nodded. "True. But I'm concerned since you have been nosing around in a police investigation."

I tried acting nonchalant. "Why would that mean anything? You believe Marilyn did it. That's why you arrested her."

"That's the way it looked." Roget turned and walked down the hallway.

I watched him go, as my emotions became a mixture of elation and fear. The "but" Roget never said lingered in the air. If he was wrong and Marilyn was innocent, then whoever did do it wasn't happy about my meddling and would let me know.

SEVENTEEN

People stopped in front of the windows of Scrap This and looked at the contest entries displayed. Suspicion wiggled in my gut. Were they interested in the layouts or in spying on me? Three women lingered in front of the crop area, watching as I put together step-by-step samples of different scrapbook techniques. I dusted the chalk off my hands and placed aside the lesson on shading to add dimension. I met the eyes of a spectator and stared back, narrowing my gaze as she continued looking at me. The woman smiled timidly and scurried away.

Great. That helped our finances.

I went to the customer service area. I walked behind the counter and pulled out the class attendance sheet for tonight. Two people signed up for the contest crop. Only two. I tapped my nails on the counter. There was a crop scheduled for tomorrow, so I could cancel tonight. But that decision ran the risk of losing two new customers and they did sign up and pay for a two-night class.

These customers were interested in delving into the competitive side of scrapbooking. The side of the hobby that helped increase our store's bottom line. I sighed. With our current financial situation—and only two students registered—having two employees teaching tonight was out of the question.

The phone rang and I snagged the receiver. "Scrap This. How can I help you?"

"How are you feeling?" Sierra's frustrated voice filtered through the line. I heard the rowdiness of the Hooligans in the background.

"Good." As long as I didn't look at the accounts receivables or our class list.

"I wanted to apologize for snapping at you. Things have been stressful lately. The car incident with Hank and now I'm dealing with my three aspiring juvenile delinquents." There was a slight pause. "Yes, I'm talking about the three of you."

"The school issue was big one?"

"It depended on who was speaking. The principal thinks it's harmless fun gone slightly overboard, the teacher and vice-principal find it invasive and problematic. They've enforced community service at the school tonight and Hank just got an interview also for tonight, so..." Sierra's regret came through loud and clear.

"You need to take tonight off."

She made a noise of agreement. "If either set of grandparents takes the boys to the school, they'd end up doing most of the work rather than the boys. The boys really need to learn this lesson. Lord knows I don't want them pulling a 'prank' one day that ticks off an employer and gets them fired. I keep telling them, someone always sees. But I'm just their mother, I don't know anything."

"You go monitor your community service team and I'll handle the store alone."

"Maybe Linda is available."

"It's only three hours until regular closing time and it's not like business is hopping."

"It could get busy, and you had a rough afternoon. You really should have someone with you just in case you feel sick."

"I'll be fine. It was a minor car accident." Why did everyone want to blow it out of proportion? Okay, I had been a little rattled by the phone call. And a little disoriented after having my forehead collide with the steering wheel, but those were normal reactions and ended a while ago.

Sierra let out a defeated sigh. "Okay. You know your grandmothers better than I do. I'm sure they won't mind leaving you there alone after your accident."

She used the biggest threat of all: calling my grandmothers. They would insist on canceling the class, which we couldn't afford, or one of them working with me. Something I couldn't afford. I didn't want my potential stalker hurting them instead of me. I needed them safely at home.

If I called Linda to come in, I could get her to leave after the normal working hours. She wouldn't insist on staying and hanging around for the crop class. "Fine. I'll call Linda."

Sierra signed off with a triumphant snicker. I dialed Linda's home, and receiving no answer, tried her cell. She answered on the first ring. After hearing about our scheduling crisis, she said she'd come right in.

With the store empty, I ran back to the office to let Hope know of the scheduling shift. Pushing open the door to the office, I stopped in my tracks. The ledger and scattered papers took up the entire space of the desktop. Numbers filled the computer monitor.

Hope knelt on the floor beside the desk, hands clasped, eyes closed while her lips moved in a silent prayer. I hovered in the doorway, torn between interrupting her private time with God and letting her know Sierra needed the day off. Her time with God should come first. I eased the door shut.

"Faith, is everything okay?" Hope placed her hand on the back of the chair and stood. She pushed a crumbled sheet of paper under the desk with her foot.

"Yep. I just wanted to tell you Sierra can't make it back today. I called Linda and she's going to fill in."

Hope frowned. "Is everything okay with Sierra?"

"The boys have required clean up at the school and Hank has an interview so can't take them."

"That might be for the best. Hank would more likely find some more rowdiness for the boys to participate in." She offered a strain smile. Stress deepened the lines around her eyes and mouth. "I'm going to finish balancing the accounts, then call it a day."

"Are you okay, Grandma?" I asked, even though I knew she'd say yes.

"I'm fine. Just tired." Again the tense smile. "I stayed up late last night. Working on layouts."

Doubt reared its ugly head at my grandmother's words. I offered my own fake smile. "That's great. I'd love to see your new pages."

Hope hustled me out the office. "Maybe tomorrow. They're not quite the way I want them. I think one layout in particular still needs a little more pop." She closed the door behind me, ending the conversation.

I wanted to push the issue, but my grandmother avoiding me worked to my benefit. Since Hope and Cheryl shared a car, they'd both leave at closing. Not the way I'd planned on getting them home, but it worked.

The doorbell jingled. I jogged into the shopping area of the store.

Linda rushed to the counter, smiling at me. "I'm here, Faith. You can finish getting ready for the crop. I can handle the register and help anyone on the floor."

Sierra's plan of calling Linda offered a benefit I never contemplated. Needing Linda's help blossomed a confidence in the older woman I'd never seen. Her normal disposition had a gloomy air, not surprising since her beloved husband passed away. Loneliness after experiencing years of devoted love had to be a hard emotion to shake. A person knew exactly what they were missing in life.

"Thanks for coming so quickly." I leaned across the counter and picked up the class supply list. "It shouldn't take me long to pull together some items for tonight. I also want to do one more sample board. I figured I'd do one showing how just choosing a different shape for a brad adds a new look to a layout."

"Take your time. And if anyone brings in an entry?"

"You can just leave it on the counter. I'll put it on the display board after I'm done with the crop prep."

A frown started to develop on Linda's face, but she stopped it. "Sure. I'll put them on the shelf underneath the counter."

"By the way, did you ever find your layout?" I asked.

Linda pressed her lips together and tears surged into her eyes. I took that as a no and dropped the topic.

The door bounced open and the bell went crazy. Dianne stomped into the store and jammed her hands against her hips. "Young lady, were you planning on keeping my machine hostage?"

I groaned. In the excitement of the fender-bender, I forgot to give Dianne her replacement cappuccino maker.

"You did get it from the supplier in Morgantown?" She frowned. "Or did you forget? Please, Faith, tell me you didn't leave it there."

I shook my head and the motion made me dizzy. I reached out and took hold of the edge of the counter. The feeling passed quickly but not fast enough Dianne and Linda didn't notice.

"Faith, are you all right?" Dianne started behind the counter.

"Maybe I should stay for the crop," Linda said.

I placed my finger against my lips then pointed at the back of the store. "Don't let my grandmothers hear you. I don't want them fussing."

Dianne frowned and tried hustling me to a chair. "Maybe they should."

I sidestepped away from Dianne. "I'm fine. I got rear-ended coming back from Morgantown. No big deal. Everything—" I started to say everything was fine then stopped. I hadn't checked the machine in the back. Maybe all wasn't sunshine and roses.

Dianne's gaze narrowed and she walked around me, looking me over. "I'm supposed to buy that?"

"The police towed my car and an officer drove me here. My grandmothers already know everything. If I wasn't okay, don't you think they would insist I go to the doctor?" I raised my arms into the air and then quickly slapped them down to my sides. I didn't need to go all drama queen.

"That's true." Dianne released a defeated sigh of agreement.

"I just totally forget about checking on your machine. I'll get—"

"I can get the machine." Linda stood in front of me and held out her hand. "If you give me your keys, I'll take it to Home Brewed."

"Problem is, I don't have the car. I'm sure one of the officers will be returning it." I didn't want to mention which officer because then Dianne would scold me about having a new career aspiration. "Once my car is here, I'll take it over."

"I'll just call Jasper and ask him to bring it over," Dianne said. "Or Bobbi-Annie. I just made some pumpkin muffins and she'd love a fresh one. I'll have my machine and your car will be returned, in about five minutes."

Dianne hustled off, needing her beloved machine back home.

"Why do the police have your car?" Linda asked.

"Probably because it didn't need any work. The officer didn't want me driving and probably thought it would be easier for me to pick it up from them."

"Mmmm...hmmm." Linda fiddled with the class sign-ups lists on the counter, avoiding eye contact with me.

Linda's comment rankled me. Why else would Roget tow the car there? It was closer to the scene and he needed to get it out of the way before more motorists got angry.

And maybe a way for him to find out what I was up to? Darn it! What if I left a clue about the purpose of my trip? I'd be in serious trouble. I was so not a good amateur sleuth.

Everyone knew the man suspected me, thanks to our resident reporter's tell-all published in the newspaper. I'm surprised Linda came in today to work with a possible murderer, or at least the accomplice of a suspected murderer.

Then again, this might be the highlight of her day and give her something to talk about with her son and friends.

"Is it okay if I run to get a coffee at Home Brewed? I didn't have time to grab a drink and having her in here has made the place smell like pumpkin. Regular coffee just won't do."

I drew in a deep breath. Pumpkin and coffee. Now I wanted one. "As long as you get me a mocha." I grinned. "Let me get you—"

Linda smiled at me. "My treat."

"Thanks. I'll treat next time. "

I headed over to the displayed layouts and studied them, looking for a new embellishing trend that warranted its own class. The store needed to keep up with fresh approaches in scrapbooking, or else our customers sought out online stores for inspiration. I bent closer and looked at a few of the photos. If I didn't know any better, I'd swear my grandmothers took one of the photos. The subject was Steve taking a picture of our booth, but the angle of the shot told me no way.

While Steve did make a nice focus for a picture, especially since the photographer got a lovely rear view, it really wasn't what we were looking for store promotion.

Linda returned with the smell of caffeine and a hint of citrus accompanying her arrival. "Dianne sent over samples of her new specialty drink."

I took one of the lidded foam cups and then picked up a handled basket from the end of the counter. "I'll be pulling the supplies for tonight's class."

I headed into the paper racks, weaving through the reds and yellows to reach the browns. The hues ranged from sand to a brown so dark it could pass for black. What shade and texture should I use tonight?

A smoother paper worked better for beginners, as it was easier for tearing and for making other embellishments, but I had no idea the skill level of the women signed up for the contest class and mini crop. A texture cardstock added an extra dimension to the work and gave the beginning layout a little edge. If using it for a border, tearing the texture paper added a nice jagged effect with feathering detail.

Maybe a sheet of both styles using a monochromatic scheme. That worked. A deeper beige mixed with a sand almost white shade. Neutrals worked well with any photos. I'd take a look at the students' pictures when they arrived and pull complementary colors showcased in the photos.

Time to pick embellishments. I gathered up sheets of letter stickers in a variety of fonts and colors for the layout titles. I stopped in front of the clear stamps and picked out an alphabet set. I'd buy the stamps and share them tonight with the class. Hopefully, they'd love them so much, the two attendees would want a set for themselves. To save some money, I'd go with standard neutral paint colors. If the croppers wanted a hue with a little more pop, they could purchase it.

The bell above the door jangled. I took the items out of the basket and arranged them in piles on the tables. Before the crop started, I wanted to check on the amount of choices offered for the class participants. I snapped my fingers. Items for the prize basket.

A shadow fell over me. I jerked upright, and the wind whooshed in my ears even though I was inside. This fear issue was getting annoying. I hated feeling vulnerable. Taking in a deep breath, my heart rate slowed to normal as I realized a new customer, not a stalker, entered into the store.

A dark-haired woman in her late teens hovered behind me. Two splotches of red bloomed on her cheeks and she stammered. "I was wondering if. Well, if you could...would you mind..."

I smiled and waved my hand over the products on the table. "It's not too late to sign up for the crop tonight."

She pushed a piece of paper toward me. "I was wondering if..."

I held my pleasant smile and waited.

"If I could... like... get..."

The smile strained my cheeks.

"Your autograph."

"My what?" I kept my reaction in check, uncertain if amusement or anger was more appropriate.

"Aren't you the owners' granddaughter? The one mentioned in the paper?"

I went with anger. Before the scolding exploded from my mouth, the young woman turned and fled out the door. Why couldn't the store reach celebrity status because of our awesome customer service rather than because of murder?

I had a crop I needed to finish planning. We also needed a way to draw more to the crops. Door prizes usually encouraged scrapbookers to sign-up, and pay, so I'd add a little incentive and display the goodies in the window.

And if that didn't work...well, I could just start signing prod-ucts and auctioning them off.

EIGHTEEN

With the class materials gathered, I went on to the next project, putting together the prize basket for new scrapbookers. The class attendees had a fifty-percent chance of winning. Good odds. With Linda being new to the hobby, she'd know what would catch a beginner's eye.

Linda hovered over a magazine, biting her lip, as she ran her finger over a page. Scrunching up her eyes, she muttered the steps on how to hand stitch on cardstock. The dedication she showed for learning more about the business touched me. I wished there was something I could do to show my appreciation.

If we had boxes to unpack from the show, Linda's layout could be in one of them. I grinned.

"I'll be in the storage room for a little bit. I need to search for something."

Linda nodded absentmindedly.

Pushing aside the gold-lined maroon curtain, I went into the backroom. Three boxes were inside the room. I stepped closer and read the labels. New paper ordered from an up-and-coming company.

I placed my hands on my hips and turned around in the recently organized space. Grandma Cheryl spent some time in the room. She probably double-checked to make sure Detective Roget hadn't carted off anything else as evidence. If Cheryl had found the layout, she'd have put it in a safe place. The office.

I hurried out of the storage area and tapped on the closed office door. After waiting a minute, I opened it inch-by-inch. Habits died hard. Even with my grandmothers at home, I still felt like I was invading their space.

Hope had left on the desk light. I walked over and snapped it off, my eyes grazing over the financial statement for last month. I winced. We had to get more people into the store, and I feared the contest was a bust. A few entries had trickled in, but the early closing of the Art Benefit Show probably stopped a lot of scrapbookers from getting photos.

I lifted up some magazines and catalogs hoping to find the layout. Nothing. I scanned the rest of the room. Where would my grandmothers put a layout?

Shame skipped into my heart. Actually, where would I have put the layout? Sierra hadn't been able to fix the layout and handed it off to me. I had looked at it and set it down when a potential customer walked into our booth. That page meant the world to Linda. It was the last picture she took of her husband and son together. We tried dissuading her from using that photograph on a display page, but she insisted, wanting to share the day with her husband and son.

Where was that layout? How would I tell her I misplaced her most precious page, or worse yet, left it at the convention center? Who knows what they did with items left behind.

One last place. I dropped onto my knees and scrambled under the desk. A crumbled piece of paper had rolled behind the leg. I snagged hold of it and withdrew the wadded paper from its hiding place.

My name written in Hope's handwriting caught my eye. I tossed the paper ball from palm to palm. Should I read it? It did have my name on it. But if Hope wanted me to know, she'd have told me. Right? I flicked at the edges of the paper.

Once again, curiosity won out. And once again, it crashed my world.

Numbers were written on the top of the page. If it was the financials of the business, not too bad as long as the bottom number was the account balance. If not, the store was in serious trouble.

But it was the two words underneath that made me regret reading the paper.

Tell Faith. No punctuation, but underlined multiple times. Was it a question or a statement? What did she need to tell me? Why was the decision a struggle for Grandma Hope?

"A cropper just arrived," Linda called from the front of the store.

I jumped up, crumbling back up the paper and tossing it into the trash. I didn't want Grandma knowing I found it.

"On my way," I squeaked out.

I yanked a hair band from my jeans pocket and twisted my hair into a ponytail, as hair dangling in my face was a major distraction while I taught. When I was a cropper rather than a teacher, I liked the veil my hair created around me. Hiding my face made it hard for someone to talk to me.

I raced into the main part of the store and started my warm greeting, only to stop in mid-speak. Roget stood in the doorway, surveying the place.

"What are you doing here?" I spoke before I engaged my brain.

Linda's eyes widened. She must not remember the man was the detective investigating Marilyn's murder, and we've never had a male cropper.

Roget headed toward the magazines and picked one up and flipped through it. "Checking out the store."

"You already did that, remember?" I pointed toward the spot where our scissors had been and waged war with my eyes. My glare had no effect on him as he continued flipping through the magazine at a leisurely pace.

"I also brought back your phone and car." He held out my keys and my cell phone.

Linda's mouth popped open.

"Thanks," I grumbled. I took the items and quickly stored them under the counter wishing Linda would stop acting like there was a tennis match going on between me and Roget.

Something was different about him. Watching Roget take an

exaggerated interest in the latest issue of a new scrapbooking magazine, Life Artist Diva, the feeling intensified. The longer I kept my eye on the man, the more I felt—knew—something was off. I studied his stance and then I figured it out. Roget wore jeans and a polo shirt. An off-duty outfit.

Linda wandered over and smiled at Roget. "How long have you been scrapbooking?"

"I don't."

Looking at the clock, I cheered in my head. Two minutes until closing. I pasted on my sweetest smile and turned it full force on Roget. "If you'd like help in choosing some items, please come back tomorrow morning. We're closing—"

He pointed at the table. "What kind of class are you teaching tonight?"

"Scrapbooking," I replied ever so helpfully.

"Actually, it's more of a mini-crop," Linda said. "Women bring their photographs to work on pages together. Tonight's is focused on the contest."

"This class is for those interested in entering the layout contest of the Art Benefit Show," I said. "We're offering prizes for the best layout in two categories."

Roget placed the magazine back in its slot. "The contest the woman was ranting about in the coffee shop?"

"The very one," I said.

Linda kept volleying her gaze from me to Roget. Her brows drew together and she gnawed on her lip.

"Detective, the crop is a teaching crop and starts in a few minutes. I need to make sure I have everything ready." So please go away.

He gestured toward the empty chairs. "Who are you teaching?"

I shoved down my anger and tried a somewhat polite answer. "Croppers sometimes run late."

"Then I guess that means the class...crop...whatever you call it, hasn't started. So, I could take it." He jammed his hands into his back jean pockets.

"You're kidding." My eyebrows rose. "You want to attend our crop? You said you weren't a hobby kind of guy."

"Maybe I just haven't found the right one."

"The crop is forty-five dollars, which is actually scheduled for today and tomorrow," Linda said. "That price also includes supplies for a two-page layout and use of the stores' tools and computer."

"Sounds reasonable." Roget pulled out his wallet and headed for the register.

"What pictures are you going to use from the Art Benefit Show? Crime scene photos?" I said.

Linda paled.

Roget stared at me, his face frozen between shock and amusement. I wanted to grab the snarky words and shove them back in my mouth, but it was too late for a retraction.

"I'll take care of this transaction, Linda." I walked through the small opening and kept my gaze on the floor. "You can go ahead and go home."

"Are you sure?" Her voice wavered.

"Absolutely." I rung up the purchase, took Roget's debit card, and ran it through without ever meeting his gaze.

"If you're sure, I'll head out. And if you need me to fill in tomorrow morning, just call me." Linda exited out the front door. The tinkle added a sound of joy into the mix of snark and baiting wit.

True, I didn't trust the detective's motives—or him, for that matter—but that was no excuse to be rude. As my grandmothers kept reminding me, they raised me better. And I also upset Linda. Since I couldn't apologize to her, I'd have to settle for the only person available.

"I'm sorry. Sometimes..." I didn't know what else to say.

Roget shoved the receipt into his back pocket. "You're not the first or the last person to speak without thinking. I bring that out in people. Mind if I ask a question?"

I grimaced. "Depends."

He grinned. "Have to admire an honest woman."

I rolled my eyes.

Roget's grin deepened. "I thought the backdoor was for the employees. That one just went out the front."

"Linda doesn't open or close yet. She's only been working here a few months, so she doesn't have a key."

A slight frown tugged at the corners of Roget's mouth and his brows drew together. "Don't trust her?"

I wandered from behind the counter into the shopping area, doing my best to stay away from Roget. He was up to something. "I trust her. It's just that we only have four keys. I have one, my grandmothers share one, and Sierra has one. Marilyn does. Did."

Maybe we should get that key back and let Linda use it until Marilyn returned.

"That makes sense." He slapped his hands together and rubbed them back and forth. "Should we get started?"

"If you don't mind, I'd like to wait a few minutes."

"Not a problem." Resting one foot on top of the other, Roget leaned against the wall.

Since he wanted to play student, I'd oblige. I pulled the band from my hair and it fell to my shoulders. "I chose some neutrals paper for the background. If you want, you could pick out a different color or we can find a complementary color of cardstock to use as the photo mat for your project."

"And that would be?" His gaze roamed around the store.

"Are you asking what is your project or what is cardstock?"

"Both."

I let out a huff of breath. "The project is up to you. The cardstock I can show you. It's a type of paper we carry. It's down this aisle." I pointed.

"How would I know cardstock from wide ruled paper?" He asked, humor lacing his words.

"For one thing, we don't sell wide-ruled paper. We're not a stop for back to school shopping."

"I'm a guy. Paper is paper."

Gesturing toward the multitude of color paper, I stepped aside. "This, Detective Roget—"

"Can you call me Ted?" He gazed into my eyes, the green of his a vivid forest. "The detective title sounds out of place."

Flustered by the intensity in his eyes, I looked away. "Sure. Why not, that's your name isn't it?" What is it about Roget—Ted—that caused words to start flowing before the mind engaged?

His lips twitched into a smile and then slipped back into a straight line.

"This is cardstock. It's heavier. Paper. Acid-free..." I clamped my lips shut and stopped the stumbling speech. Hard to inspire confidence when a person sounded like they didn't know what they were talking about.

"I'm supposed to choose one from all of those?" He looked terrified at the prospect.

"It's just paper." Why did men get so bent out of shape by hues? I stood in the middle of the aisle and pointed at the reds and then the blues. "What color is predominant in the photo you're using for your layout?"

He grimaced. "This was a spur of the moment decision. I had nothing else to do tonight."

"I figured that." I refrained from rubbing my hands in malicious glee. It was time to turn the tables. Let him feel uncomfortable and out of his league.

He reached forward and pulled out a burgundy sheet, the color closest to his reach.

The best way to know a person was to see what their private life was like. And this was my opportunity. "If you're not going to enter into the contest, I'm willing to wave the subject of the photograph for your layout. Do you have an idea of what kind of picture you'd like to use?"

"Not really." He returned the burgundy and removed a sheet of Christmas red.

"Please don't tell me you're not a picture-taking kind of guy."

"Not too much in life to take photos of."

I gaped at him. "Of course there is. Everyone's life is worth documenting. What about holiday celebrations, milestones in your life, your work, or family?"

Sadness appeared in his eyes. He pivoted and continued down the row of paper. "My little girl loves green. The brighter the better."

Questions tumbled through my mind about his daughter, but it was none of my business. Besides finding out what shade of green his little girl preferred. A jade green color caught my eye and I pointed it out to Ted.

With a blinding grin, he shook his head. Squatting down, he grabbed a handful of neon green cardstock from the bottom slot of the paper rack.

"This is Claire." He waved the stack at me. "Can I use this as the major color and then use tan as the mat? Or whatever is the technical term you used. I'll make something for her to hang in her room."

The love in his voice for his daughter touched me. I felt my attitude softening toward Ted. Maybe his ulterior motive for stopping by was a good one. Not that I had any clue what it would be. "Sure. We can even work on a few layouts so she can have a collage. I don't think the other croppers are coming."

"They probably forgot," Ted said.

"Right. Both of them."

Twenty minutes after seven meant it was safe to presume the other students were no shows. On the bright side, the class fee was non-refundable. I locked the front door. My hand lingered on the string of the blinds as I debated if it would be more profitable showing my one-person class or would it give the impression I was a lousy teacher.

Then again, Ted's presence could draw in more women. He was an available male. Perfect choice if a woman preferred the tall, good-looking, bossy type. I also wasn't quite sure I trusted the man. I left the blinds open. Better for others to see and know, just in case there was a reason someone asked who I had last been seen with.

"You know, women usually like going places in pairs. If one had to bail, the other wasn't going to show up on her own."

"They changed their minds when they realized they read about the store recently."

He leveled a sidelong glance at me. "You think it's because of Michael Kane's murder?"

"No. I think it's because Marilyn was arrested for the crime. Who wants to shop at a place that hires a killer? Karen England's informative article this morning didn't help much."

"Yeah. I talked with Miss England about that." A hint of anger developed in Ted's eyes. "Apparently she had a reliable source."

"I'd like to know who."

"So would I."

We turned and faced each other. For the first time, we had actually agreed on something. Though I'm sure this harmony would end if he had an inkling I planned on finding out that source.

His eyes narrowed. Drat. He knew. How could this man know me so well when we just met? And we never had a conversation that didn't result in an argument and the reminder I was interfering in a police investigation.

"Our business is tanking because of those articles."

"It's just a coincidence they didn't show up and the article ran today. It's not like your grandmothers hired Mrs. Kane knowing one day she'd commit a crime."

I couldn't keep the venom out of my voice. "Who cares about reality when it comes to passing judgment? Everyone believes you should've seen what was coming. Should've known who that person really was. Saw through the lies." The anger I held for so long boiled out of me.

"Faith, not everyone judges a person based on what they might have known." He rested a gentle hand on my shoulder and kneaded the tense muscles. "Or on what other people have done."

I stumbled away from him and started busying myself with the products on the table. My hands shook as I picked up a pack of chipboard. Geometric shapes wouldn't hold that much interest for a little girl who loved neon lime green over jade. I held the pieces up for Ted's inspection. "Do you think these would work with the project you're planning?"

He glanced at them. "I guess. You're the expert."

Men.

"What picture are you using? That will help make the decision easier on if we should stick with these embellishments or using something else. Personally, I'd choose a photo that went well with lime."

"That's easy." Ted grinned. "Twinkle."

"Twinkle?"

"Yep." He nodded, the little boy smile still splashed all over his face. "My pet iguana. My ex-wife didn't allow pets in the house so my very first purchase for the apartment was a pet."

"So instead of something cute and cuddly, you picked a scaly creature?"

"Hey!" Mock indignation filled his voice. "My five-year-old thinks Twinkle is cute and cuddly. She did name him."

Poor him. "I prefer pets without scales and ones that do not stick out their tongues."

"With my job, I needed a pet that wouldn't mind being left alone. Plus, it's easier to clean up the pet mess when it's in an aquarium."

"Good point."

He rubbed his hands in anticipation. "So, you have any kind of decorations that would go with a reptile?"

I laughed. "Actually, we do."

I walked toward the back of the store where the stickers were located. Five-year-olds loved stickers. At least the ones whose parents brought them into Scrap This. Though we kept an eye on young school age children when they ventured into sticker row.

A rattle stopped me cold. I halted and Ted rammed into the back of me.

He wrapped an arm around my waist and prevented me from tumbling forward. "What's wrong?"

"Did you hear that?"

The rattling of a doorknob shattered our self-imposed quiet.

NINETEEN

Ted tucked me behind him and placed his fingers on his lips. Like I couldn't figure that out for myself. I glanced toward the front windows. A deep rich black had descended and blanketed the area—a perfect time for committing a crime. The door rattled again.

"Stay here." Ted motioned for me to stay low.

I hunched down, my back against the wall, trying to control the tremors racing through my body. Ted pointed at the wall on the right hand side of the store, then the door. He wanted me closer to the front so I could run out.

"You might need backup," I whispered.

"Have it." Ted reached behind and pulled out a pistol. He gestured toward the door with his chin. This time, I went with his suggestions. He was equipped to take on a bad guy. On my hands and knees, I scuttled toward the front door and prayed whoever was breaking into the store didn't have a gun. I didn't want Ted getting hurt.

The jiggling at the back door stopped. The door creaked open.

Ted stood, back jammed against the wall and the gun locked in his grip. His head turned to the side as he waited for the person to step into the area.

Please let Ted grab them and have them not put up a fight. As much as I didn't appreciate someone breaking into the store—or stalking me for that matter—I didn't want that person getting shot.

"Faith," a familiar voice called out.

"Steve?" My intended shriek left my lungs as a squeak.

Muttering undistinguishable words, Ted holstered his gun. As Steve stepped into the main store area, Ted grabbed his wrist, twisted his arm behind his back, and pressed him against the wall. "What were you thinking, Davis?"

A startled expression filled Steve's face. "What are you doing?"

Did Ted think Steve left the threatening calls? There wasn't much I was certain about lately, but I knew Steve would never hurt me.

I shouldered my way between the two men. "Let him go. My grandmothers must have loaned him a key."

"You should've called the lady." Ted glared at Steve. "You scared her."

Casting an unreadable look from Ted to me, Steve apologized. "Hope and Cheryl told me you were working late tonight and asked if I could check up on you."

Of course they would. "I'm fine."

An image of Ted holding the gun popped into my mind. A shudder wracked my body and I felt the blood drain from my head. "You almost weren't," I whispered.

Steve pulled me into his arms, resting his head on top of mine. "I'm sorry, Faith. I didn't mean to frighten you."

"You might have been sorrier, Davis. I had my gun drawn." Ted tapped his side. "It's a good thing Faith recognized your voice."

"Are you the shoot first kind of cop?" Steve asked.

"No. I'm the protect-and-serve kind of cop, not the look-the-other-way kind." Ted stood like a gunfighter preparing for a duel. "This woman, as you know, has been receiving harassing calls. I took precautions. And since you knew about the calls, it'd been nice if you let her know you were stopping by. Sometimes surprises aren't appreciated."

"I apologized," Steve said.

I pushed away from Steve, hoping if I wasn't secluded in his arms the men would remember I existed in the same room. "Listen—"

"What if she'd been alone, Davis? How scared might she have been then?"

I saw red and marched toward Ted. "I would've managed on

my own. I know self-defense. I don't need you."

"It seemed that—" Ted started.

"Lots of things seem a certain way and aren't that way. That's what the word assumption is all about. I don't need you coming in here and berating Steve. If his apology is good enough for me, then what happened is no concern of yours."

Ted crossed his arms. "Maybe Steve doesn't need you defending him."

I clamped my mouth shut and peered at Steve.

Instead of anger or embarrassment in his expression, he had a grin on his face. "I don't mind at all."

Ted pointed toward the table. "Now that you know she's safe and sound, I'd like to get back to my class. Have a nice evening, Davis." Ted went and unlocked the front door.

"You're taking a scrapbook class?" Steve roved his gaze from Ted to me.

"It's a crop," I corrected. Not a very successful one.

"Hobbies make a man well-rounded," Ted said.

Steve snapped his fingers. "That's right, the crop for the contest is tonight and tomorrow. Maybe I should enter."

"You took pictures at the Art Show?" Ted asked.

"Sure," Steve said. "I told Hope and Cheryl I'd get shots of their setup from different angles. Faith couldn't as she was in charge of the booth."

"So they asked you?" Ted crossed his arms.

Steve smiled. "They know they can trust me to help whenever they need it."

How long would Steve and Ted continue talking around me? Pretty soon the men would start circling each other, beat their chests and prepare for war because—I had no idea. This crop was a bust. I didn't want the room wrecked because the two "students" decided they'd rather brawl than scrapbook.

An advertising brainstorm flashed into my mind. I tilted my head and studied Ted and Steve. It could work. It had possibilities. Both men stopped talking and looked at me. They each took a step back.

"Steve, do you have your camera?" I asked, looking up at him through my lashes.

He gave me a dubious look. "In my car. Why?"

"I just wanted some photos of you and Ted working on your contest entries."

Ted held up his hands. "Now wait a minute. I didn't say I would enter into some contest. I don't even have photographs from the show. The ones I do have access to wouldn't be appropriate."

"Steve will share."

Steve grinned. "Sure. And a contest sounds like fun."

"Like you know how to scrapbook," Ted said.

"I'm a quick study." Steve crossed his arms, a hint of challenge in his gaze.

I tugged Ted and Steve toward the tables. "This will be great. We can start your layouts tonight then finish them tomorrow."

"Hold up." Ted locked his knees, cementing his feet to the ground. "What about the crop fee?"

"That's right." I held my hand out. "Forty-five dollars, please."

With fanfare, Steve pulled out his wallet and handed over the cash. "I'm ready to learn the fine art of scrapbooking."

Ted looked disappointed that Steve had cash readily available.

"You can pick something out later. Right now, I'd like to get started." I picked up two sheets of 12x12 beige cardstock and placed one in front of each man. "This is the foundation for your layout."

Steve raised his hand.

I couldn't help smiling. "Yes."

"Can I have a pen and some paper?"

Ted snorted.

Steve looked at Ted. "Do you think what Faith is teaching us isn't important?"

Ted shot his hand into the air. "Me, too."

Almost skipping, I made my way to the counter and retrieved two pens and narrowed-ruled writing paper.

Not one second later, the front window splintered and glass

flew in all directions. Screaming, I covered my head, and dropped to the floor.

TWENTY

Footsteps pounded on the floor, heading toward the door. The bell rattled, then the door slammed shut. Uncovering my head, I remained on my knees and attempted to look around the store but my hair blocked the view.

Steve pushed my hair from my face, his desperate gaze roaming over me. "Faith, are you okay?"

Besides soreness in my knees, nothing hurt. I ran my fingers through my hair, tiny shards of glass dropped around the floor but I didn't feel any wetness or cuts. "I'm okay," I said. "What happened? Are you okay?"

"I'm fine. Someone threw a rock through the front window, right at the displays."

I scrambled to my feet. "How are we going to afford to fix that window? And the layouts. Please don't let the layouts be damaged." I headed for the entries.

Steve grabbed my arm and herded me toward the storage area. "Stay away from the windows."

"I need to check—"

"No. After Roget returns. For now, we keep you safe."

Keep me safe? The threats. Whoever made the calls wanted me to know they were serious. My legs shook and I tripped. Tears wavered the room.

Steve wrapped an arm around me. "Do you want to go into the lounge?"

"I want to sit. Now."

He loosened his hold and I sat on the floor, staring at the gaping hole in the front window.

"We'll get this fixed. I promise."

"Cheryl and Hope will be devastated."

"Who says they have to know?"

I looked at Steve. He'd keep something from my grandmothers? "You won't tell them? You'll help me get this straightened out tonight?"

"Absolutely."

"They'll find out we kept this from them."

"They'll get over it."

I laughed, almost manic. "Did the rock hit you in the head?"

He encircled me in his arms. "Just tell them it was a secret between you and me. They'll forgive us."

I melted into Steve's protective embrace and swiped away the tears forming in my eyes. Hopefully, Ted caught the person and everything would be fine. I didn't want them to come back and hurt someone because of me.

"Where exactly did Ted go?" I asked.

"After the person who threw the rock. He took off into the parking lot and Roget followed him."

I jumped up. "We have to help him."

Steve gripped my shoulders, blocking me from moving toward the door. "He can handle it. I'm sure he has back up by now."

I worked out an argument, but before I uttered a word, an angry Detective Roget strode toward the store dragging a man behind him. As they got closer, I realized it wasn't a man, but a teen. Mark Kane, Marilyn's teenaged son.

Roget pushed the boy into Scrap This. "Sit down."

Mark dropped into the chair in the crop area, avoiding looking at Steve or me.

Stalking to the door, Roget crooked his index finger and narrowed his eyes. "Get in here."

Elizabeth Kane shuffled into the store, tears streaming down her pale face. She picked a chair far from her younger brother.

"Sorry, Lizzie," Mark muttered.

"We are so in trouble." Lizzie picked at her nail polish.

A picture formed on why Marilyn's children were sitting in the store. Steve stood behind me and rested a comforting hand on my shoulder. How could this get any worse?

On second thought, I really didn't want to know.

Ted crossed his arms and glared at the teens. "Would either of you like to start explaining?"

"Lizzie didn't do anything," Mark said.

"She drove you here," Ted said.

Mark stood. "That's all!"

"Sit down!" Ted stepped toward the boy and pointed at the chair. Mark sat.

"She didn't know that—" The teen clamped his mouth shut.

"Start talking." Ted towered over the teen.

I had enough of the bullying. I walked over and picked up the phone receiver on the desk. "Do you need me to call your grandparents?"

"Faith, let me handle this," Ted said. "You have no idea what's going on."

"I have a pretty good idea. They're kids. I think we should have their grandparents here."

"I called them. Once Mark..." Lizzie rested her head on the table.

"It's okay, Lizzie. You can tell them I did that," Mark said. "Please don't be mad at her. It's all my fault. All of it."

A car stopped in front of the store and the headlights blinded me. Eli Bennett rushed inside, gaped at the broken window, then turned his attention to his grandchildren. "Mark Benjamin and Elizabeth Noelle, what have you two done?"

Lizzie wailed.

Mark's bottom lip quivered, but he stood up and faced his grandfather. "I threw a rock, sir."

Eli pointed at the window. "You did that?"

"Yes, sir."

"Faith, I'm so sorry." Eli pulled a cell phone from his jacket pocket. "My nephew is a contractor. I'll see if he can come board up the window. "

Ted jutted his chin toward the window. "What happened here tonight is a crime. I'm taking these two down to the station."

Lizzie cried louder. Tears trailed down Mark's cheeks.

"That's not necessary, Detective Roget," I said. "As long as the window gets fixed—"

"What about the phone calls?" Roget glared at me.

"The calls?" I squeaked out.

"Calls?" Eli looked from the detective to his grandson.

"I just wanted her to keep helping Mom," Mark said.

"It's my fault," Lizzie turned pleading eyes to me. "I'm the oldest. I'm almost eighteen and should've known better. I drove him to your house, Faith. He couldn't have gotten there by himself. And tonight. I brought him. But I didn't know he'd break the window."

The noise I heard in my backyard wasn't Yowler. Someone had been lurking in my backyard. While I felt better knowing it had been Mark, it unnerved me that someone easily hid in the bushes without me knowing, or seeing, them.

"She really didn't," Mark said. "I just wanted to talk to Faith. Not hurt her. Or cause problems."

"But?" Steve asked.

Mark looked at the floor. "I saw her in here with you and the detective. I figured she turned on Mom. Wanted my mom to go to prison."

Roget sat down and motioned for all of us to do the same. He leaned forward and rested his elbows on his knees. "How about you kids start from the beginning?"

I dropped into the nearest chair. Steve dragged another one over and sat beside me. Mark looked at his grandfather. Eli nodded his encouragement.

Clasping his hands together, Mark started explaining, occasionally meeting my gaze. "When we went to visit Mom, she said you were helping her. You know, find who really murdered our dad."

Ted groaned and slapped his forehead, shaking his head back

and forth.

Way to go, Marilyn. What was she thinking telling her children that? Then again, what other hope did she have to offer her babies?

"The papers kept saying worse things about Mom, so I thought you quit. I wanted you to keep helping Mom. So I called and left you a message."

The cryptic words of 'you just can't stop' no longer held an ominous meaning to them. Mark needed a little work on his communication skills, like remembering to leave a name when he left a message.

"Then this morning, I called you between classes and you yelled at me. So I decided to see you in person."

I didn't correct his interpretation and tell him I screamed because I ran into a car. The boy felt guilty enough about the situation.

"Seeing Mr. Davis and me here made you angry?" Roget asked.

"Yes, sir. Like I said, I thought she was giving up on my mom."

"I'd never give up on your mom," I said.

Roget glared at me and Steve shook his head.

What else was I supposed to say to a distraught teen?

"My mom's not guilty. She didn't do anything. This is all my fault." A sob tore through him and he sank to the floor. His grandfather knelt down to comfort him. "All of it."

With tears now brimming my eyes, I tried catching Steve's gaze. I wanted this over. The teen's pain tore through me and I didn't even want to imagine what it was doing to his grandfather and sister.

Roget frowned and knelt by Mark. "What do you mean by that?" The friendly tone evaporated. Roget was using the police interrogation voice he used on me.

I stepped forward and wiggled between Roget and Mark. "He wasn't at the event."

"Stay out of this." Roget looked up at me.

"I'm not going to let you..." The term railroad stuck in my mouth as Roget's unpleasant expression intensified. The two teenagers and their grandfather watched us. Taking a breath, I took a step back and found myself slamming into Steve. He gripped my shoulders and maneuvered me off to the side.

"Mark, don't worry about the phone calls." I blurted. "I understand you made a mistake. I will accept an apology and want to drop the matter. It really wasn't that big of a deal. Heck, I just thought it was a prank."

Roget stood. "Faith..."

"Well, I did." I wouldn't let Roget bully Mark. The boy's mom got arrested for his father's murder. That was more than enough turmoil for one family. What were a couple of misunderstood phone calls between people in a small community?

Mark stood and wiped his nose on his sleeve. "Miss Hunter, I'm sorry. I was mad when I threw that rock, but I didn't want to hurt you."

I smiled at the boy. "I wasn't hurt, Mark. Don't worry about it."

"He isn't quite off the hook yet, Faith." Eli glared at his grandson. "Though I appreciate your understanding in this."

Lizzie touched my arm. "Mark wanted you to keep helping Mom. Since no one else would." She fired the accusation toward Roget with a small gesture of her head. "Mark and Dad were supposed to go a baseball game that day."

Mark hunched his body forward, almost trying to fold it in half.

Eli wrapped an arm around his grandson's shoulder. The older man's pain filled gaze locked with mine.

"Mark." Steve cautiously approached the teenage boy. "If you were angry at your father for canceling your plans, that's understandable. It has nothing to do with what happened to him."

"Davis..." The warning from Roget bounced off the walls.

Steve continued. "I knew your father. He wouldn't want you to blame yourself."

"You don't understand," Mark grumbled.

I sat down, hoping it would ease the tension radiating from the teen. "I'd like to understand, Mark. Can you explain it to me?"

Mark stared at me and minutes ticked by. I stayed still and maintained eye contact. I figured he'd either leave the room or tell me. Finally, he released a shuddering breath and then his secret. "I cancelled on Dad."

I pushed back the memory of the righteous anger Marilyn felt when she believed her husband stood up her son in favor of his mistress. We had been wrong. I had been wrong. We all labeled Michael a scoundrel, a bad father, a horrible person for an action he never committed. Maybe Michael had also told the truth about the baby not being his. We automatically assumed he was cheating on Marilyn because of the baby. Though Michael never denied the affair.

Did we ever really listen to him?

I know no one listened to my explanations that Adam was lying about my involvement. The authorities figured the reason Adam and I planned a honeymoon to Las Vegas was to go AWOL and never return to Germany. They figured we'd take all the black-market money earned from selling stolen military items and assume new identities.

"I was sick of him defending his right to have 'women friends' and hurting mom. I told Dad I wouldn't be caught dead with him." With tears streaking down his face, Mark's gaze rested longest on his grandfather.

Lizzie took hold of his brother's hand. "Mark thinks if he went to the ball game with Dad, he'd still be alive. I think someone would've hurt Dad anyway."

Roget started scribbling into his notebook. "Why do you say that? Was someone threatening your father?"

The air crackled around us. I could feel the change in the room. Roget's mannerisms were different, not just confident and cop-like, but alert.

Mark shook his head. "No. But someone hated him. Mom didn't. She didn't kill him. Someone else there did. They killed our dad."

TWENTY-ONE

When I pulled into the employee lot of Scrap This early the next morning, the sun filled the sky with a beautiful pinkish hue a paper company could never reproduce. I yawned and took a slug of the coffee in my travel mug. When I finally fell asleep the night before, the dreams playing in my head woke me up again.

How was I going to get through this day without saying something stupid? Tough enough when I got plenty of sleep. The contractor was arriving at seven to replace the window before my grandmothers arrived. It seemed a good idea last night. Of course, I thought I'd fall right to sleep, not have my mind what-if itself into worst-case scenarios.

I turned off the engine and then leaned forward, resting my head on the steering wheel. My heart hurt for Elizabeth, Mark, and their grandparents. They were just as much victims in this case as Michael. All the gossip about Marilyn had to be killing them and the only person they could rely for discovering the truth was me.

Well, I couldn't just sit in the car all day. I flung open the door and fresh mountain air filled my lungs as I clambered from the car. Contorting my body into a weird position, I pulled out my purse and large tote.

Reaching the back door, I shifted the bags farther up on my shoulder and wrestled with the lock. Of course it'd get jammed today. One, I needed to get inside quickly, and two, I had my hands full. After a few minutes, I finally jiggled the key in the right pattern and the lock budged.

The glass guy arrived on time and quickly put up the new window while I cleaned up the mess left from last night. Steve and Ted took care of the large pieces, but the tiny shards were still on the floor. A thorough sweep, then I deposited them in the dumpster in the back.

I tidied up the crop table, leaving out the supplies, hoping it enticed someone to sign up for tonight's crop. I'd throw in some extra goodies and more prize drawings so the price was worth it.

The phone rang. Was it nine already? I ran to the counter and snagged the handset.

"Scrap This."

"When's the next store event?" A woman asked, anxiously.

"We have a crop tonight—"

"Is it full?"

"No."

"Great." Her utter glee came through loud and clear. "I'd like two spots. One for me and a friend."

"The fee is forty-five dollars since it was a two-day learning crop. But we'll be having—"

"Not a problem. We'll pay the full amount."

"We can't guarantee a spot without payment." I doubted anyone else planned on signing up, but I had to stick with the rules or risk a countywide incident once Darlene found out. She always found out.

"Can you take a credit card over the phone?"

"Sure."

The woman rattled off her number and I copied it down. "Don't forget the pictures you and your friend plan to use for the contest."

"Pictures. Right. We'll bring some."

As I placed the phone on the cradle, I heard the woman yell "we're in."

The phone rang again. Busy morning.

"Scrap This."

"You have any openings for the thing tonight?" a woman asked.

"Do you mean the crop?"

"Yeah, that. I'd like to get in on it. How much is it?"

I told her and she eagerly gave me her credit card number and reserved a spot.

The back door slammed opened. I jumped and knocked the phone to the floor. The back sprang off the receiver and the batteries tumbled out.

"Faith Patience Hunter!" Cheryl exploded from behind the curtain.

I spun around and placed my hands behind my back. Not that I had anything to hide, but old instincts and all that. Her tone plus my full name meant Grandma found out something I didn't want her finding out. "Yes, Grandma?"

She waved the newspaper at me. "Why didn't you call?"

The smell of newsprint hit my nose as the pages fluttered close enough to give me a paper cut. Darn it! Of course the glass-breaking incident would be in the newspaper. I should've bribed Karen England to keep it quiet. Though that might have just made her more eager.

I opened and closed my mouth a few times as I worked on a good reason.

Hope stood beside Cheryl and tapped her foot on the ground. "We'd like an answer, young lady."

"For what?" I went with feigning ignorance.

"Not telling us that someone threw a rock through the window."

"Oh that."

Hope shook her head and tsked.

"I didn't want to worry either of you." I gave them a gracious I'm-such-a-helpful-granddaughter smile. From the scowls on their face, it wasn't working. "Mark felt really bad about throwing the rock, and since Mr. Bennett arranged for the replacement this morning, there was nothing to tell you."

An assorted melody of voices outside the store ended our discussion. Cheryl and Hope gaped. A line formed in front of Scrap This entrance. Women shifted large satchels from one shoulder to the other. Others shifted anxiously from foot-to-foot, weaving their head back and forth around the crowd.

"We should unlock the door," Cheryl said.

"Are you sure?" Hope asked. "It looks like someone said George Clooney was here giving out his phone number."

Cheryl rolled up her sleeves. "Hope, you take the register, keep the phone beside you, and Faith and I will handle crowd control. Get ready to open those doors."

I moved into action.

"Did you read the paper?" Sierra shouted, running through the store toward the register.

"No. But I was yelled at about it." I stepped out of the way of the stampeding crowd. Some women thrust layouts at me while others bee-lined for the counter, asking about the crop. When—and why—had the contest crop become such a hot item?

Sierra shoved a newspaper into my hands and started managing the crop schedule. As I read the article about the vandalism, everything became clear. The paper made it sound like the store sponsored a singles night. The reporter, not Karen England, stated that homicide Detective Ted Roget and Assistant Prosecuting Attorney Steve Davis and a young lady were attending the store's evening get-together when the malicious act occurred.

Bobbi-Annie made it to the front of the line. Leaning against the counter, she caught her breath. "Why didn't you tell me about these get-togethers?"

"We've been advertising the crop since Saturday," I said.

"A crop. Nowhere did it say it was a singles mixer."

If that is what the women of Eden wanted, that's what Scrap This would give them. Now I needed more men attending the class. While Sierra rang up purchases, I tugged the class book toward me. "The crop fee is forty-five dollars, Bobbie-Annie."

"Is there room for four?" She drummed her fingers on the counter. Her cell phone sang *I'm Every Woman*. She flipped it open. "Yeah, Jasper, I'm here. Taking care of it."

Jasper wanted to attend also? Awesome! Another available, attractive, employed male—what every single, marriage-minded woman wanted in a man. I'd need another teacher for tonight. "We have room for four more croppers. Tonight, we're focusing on creating layouts for the contest."

Bobbie-Annie shooed away my words. "Sure. Pictures."

"From the Art Benefit Show."

"Fine. I'll see what I can do." She hit a button on the phone. "Aunt Gussie, I got the spaces. Yep, I'll be here and keep an eye on them."

I suppressed a shudder at the implication of those words. "Them" had to be Bobbie-Annie's cousins, Wyatt and Wayne. Please let them not bring pictures of their hunting successes or their mug shots, I thought.

"I'm so excited." A red-haired woman headed to the contest display board, now showcased by a brand new, sparkling windowpane. "I know my entry is the winner. The die-cutter is coming home with momma."

The woman behind her laughed and shouldered past her. "That's what you think. That machine is so mine. You should see the yummy page I made. My photos are fantastic."

The good-natured ribbing between the friends continued. Before I could even wish the other contestants would be so fun-spirited about the competition, an argument broke out in the front of the store. Hope and Cheryl emerged from the paper aisles where they had been helping customers. Cheryl charged toward the melee.

Hope pointed at the boards. "Faith, arrange the entries. I'll handle the cash register."

A line that rivaled the auditions for *American Idol* weaved itself through the paper aisle and ended at the register. Some entrants decided to add more embellishments to their layouts before they entered them into the contest.

"They're all gone!" A shriek came from where we kept the Prima flowers.

I switched directions and headed toward the wail. A woman shook with anger as she glared at the empty shelf. Yesterday, the shelf contained at least thirty bottles of the flowers.

Near the cash register, another woman pressed a basket against her chest, the top hidden so no one could look inside. I had a feeling the inventory of fabric flora was hidden within. Before a riot erupted, I distracted the lady without the flowers away from the woman with all the flowers.

"Now how did that happen?" I gave a wide-eyed look and tapped my chin. I took hold of the shaking woman's elbow. Leaning forward, I whispered, "I have a secret stash of Prima flowers in the break room. I like to have supplies on hand in case I get an inspiration during my lunch break."

"What color and style do you have?"

"I have a mix." I led her from the front of the store to the back. "You're welcome to pick what you'd like to use."

The offer of free scrapbooking embellishments cheered her and she left with half my flowers. What an employee must do to keep the peace. Luckily, I knew where I could get more. Grandma Cheryl had a weakness for the flowers even though she didn't use them on her pages. She owned every type of Prima flower available. Shelves lined with the colorful bottles of flowers encircled her scrapbooking room like decorative molding.

A vise-like grip wrapped around my arm. "Just what did you think you were doing?"

My head reeled from a sudden spinning movement and I found myself looking into the fury-filled face of Ted. I yanked from his grip. His clasp tightened. I kept my voice low but firm. "Let me go."

"Not until you answer some questions." He shook my arm, adding emphasis to his demand.

Last night, Ted acted like a friend, a protector. Today, he wanted to throttle me. What happened in those few hours to turn him into this raving lunatic?

Did he know about Adam and now suspected me of killing Michael?

I swallowed hard and pushed the fear aside. "You're hurting

me. You better let go. Now."

Ted released my arm and stepped back, nearly colliding with a rack of paper. If it weren't for the anger on his face, I'd almost believe he was shocked at his own behavior.

I walked away, keeping my pace slow, showing him he hadn't won. I wasn't scared. I took in deliberate breaths and ran through some self-defense moves in my head. If he tried that again, he'd answer for it.

"Don't you dare drag my brother into this."

I froze. I knew he'd be annoyed if—when—he found out, but not furious. "People aren't allowed to speak to your brother?"

"Don't play Miss Innocent with me. It won't work," Ted said. "I suspected your questions to Bobbi-Annie weren't for innocent reasons, but I decided to give you a chance, think the best of your prying."

I pivoted and faced him. His eyes snapped with anger and betrayal. I bit my lip. Why did he think I betrayed him? He arrested my friend for murder. He charged into my grandmothers' store and ruined our business. I didn't owe him anything.

"Bobbi told me you always lent a helping hand, stuck up for people," Ted said. "One of the most loyal people she ever knew. So I believed your motive in sticking your nose into the investigation was all about helping."

"That is what I'm doing. Nothing more." I stared into Ted's eyes, hoping he'd see the truth in my eyes. "I know she's innocent."

"Then why pry into my background and track down my brother? Decided maybe threatening to parade my brother's lifestyle around would get you your way? If you want to hurt me," Ted slapped a fist against his chest, "go right ahead. Here's something for you, I was an alcoholic. That's why my wife left, also why the only detective job I could get was in Eden. Other police departments were leery of me and my past. But have at it. Use it to your heart's content, but leave Bob alone."

I recalled the vacation picture on Bob's desk. Ted thought I planned on "outing" his brother as vengeance or blackmail. It broke my heart that someone in the past hurt the brothers in that way. I blinked back tears and placed my hand on his arm. "Ted—"

"I came here yesterday to make sure you'd be safe. I knew I could use a friend and figured so could you." He shoved a piece of paper at me.

I jammed my hands into the front pocket of my jeans. "I'm sorry."

Ted crumbled the paper into a ball and tossed it at my feet. "You're sorry because you got found out."

"I admit I tried to hire Bob as a private detective, and maybe learn a bit about you. And because it would be fun if your brother took the case. If someone else was annoying you then—"

"You could continue investigating the case because I'd be busy with the private eye." He let out a bitter laugh. "You expect me to believe that?"

I bit my bottom lip.

He studied me. "You're serious. That was actually your plan? You were going to hire a private detective, preferably my relative, so I'd be distracted by them and not notice your antics?"

I smiled and shrugged. "It was absolutely brilliant when I came up with it."

"Darling," he drawled, for the first time showing a hint of his accent, "you're the only woman I'd ever believe that from."

"So, how did you find out?" I rocked back and forth on the heels of my pink sneakers.

"I shouldn't tell you, but I will." He crossed his arms. "Maybe it'll convince you detective work isn't a talent of yours. You left notes on the front seat of your car. Miss England peered inside and jotted them down. She came to me last night and asked about my brother's connection to the case and if it was a conflict of interest."

"Oh." Rule number one of amateur sleuthing, hide any and all notes. "Well, in my defense, I had been distracted by a car accident and didn't think of hiding the notes. But I'll remember that."

Ted groaned and smacked himself in the forehead. "I'm not giving you pointers, Faith. I'm giving you a warning. For crying out loud, hire Bob. Heck, hire him and my mother, but stop investigating this case yourself."

"What do you care? Maybe it's my new hobby."

His eyebrows rose. "Annoying me?"

"Marilyn is the murderer, so what harm can come of it? If you have the murderer locked up, then I can't really find any trouble."

"So, Mark Kane throwing a rock through your window isn't trouble? Having Karen England peering into your windows—"

"Window. And it was only once," I corrected.

"That you know of."

That shut me up.

"Asking people personal questions can set them off. There are things people want kept private. It will make them nervous, even angry, if they think someone will find out."

The knowing look in his eyes punched me in the gut. Too many times his eyes said he knew something about me, but not the actual what. And if anyone could relate to what Ted spoke about, it was me. The second biggest secret in Eden was one I held. The biggest was the one Michael's murderer clutched.

"Hire an investigator, a professional one, if you truly believe Marilyn is innocent." Ted jotted down two phone numbers on the back of a business card. "Bob said he'd give you recommendations since he couldn't take the case."

"Conflict of interest." I took the offered card.

Ted made a sound that was a cross between a snort and a growl and walked away.

Hope rushed over to me. "What was that about?"

"Pointers."

Hope's eyes grew wide.

"I'm kidding, Grandma. Sorry." I showed her the card. "He thinks me involving myself is an act of stupidity."

"I guess the man does have some sense," Hope said.

"So he gave me a name of a PI. He'd rather I mind my own business and is steering me in a safer direction."

Hope's eyes narrowed. "He seems fond of you."

"He's not a bad guy, Grandma."

"You know, people are thinking there's something going on be-tween the two of you."

That was a good reason to start minding my own business. I didn't want anyone thinking I was dating a police officer, or had a thing for him. "Trust me, there's nothing between us. Except for annoying each other."

"I don't want to see you or Steve getting hurt."

"Steve?"

"He cares about you."

I knew that, and if I was truthful, I cared about him. But caring about each other was enough for me, and my grandmothers needed to realize that. I looked around the store. Cheryl and Sierra had everything under control, not surprising. Anyone who herded the Hooligans would have no problem keeping a group of scrappers under control.

"Can we talk, Grandma? Like now?"

"Of course, sweetie."

We linked arms and headed into the employee lounge. Alone in the small room with the door closed, I couldn't figure out the right words to say. I didn't want to hurt her feelings. I dropped into a chair and then rested my head on the table.

"Honey, what is it?"

"Steve," I said and sat up.

Grandma tsked. "Does he think you and the detective are de-veloping a relationship, so he's giving you space? I'll talk with him."

I put my hand over hers, really noticing for the first time the thinness of her skin. "Grandma, I want you to stop sending Steve over when you think I need help. If I need him, I'll call him. I know his numbers, work and home. I also know where he lives and works."

"You keep to yourself too much."

"I'm here with you and Grandma Cheryl all the time. We crop together. I go out to lunch with Marilyn and Sierra. Okay, not Mari-lyn right now, but I'm not a hermit."

"You don't go out. Cheryl and I would love to see you find a nice man. Go on some dates. Have some fun. Even spend time with girlfriends."

"I do."

"At work. Not on your own. It makes us worry." Hope stood, the chair scraped across the floor. She poured coffee into two mugs. "Ever since you got home from the Army, you act like you don't really want anyone in your life. You just 'tolerate' everyone."

I knew she was right, but I couldn't explain it. "I love you and Grandma Cheryl."

"We know that." Hope placed a mug of coffee in front of me. She turned a chair so that it faced me and then sat down. "But others want to—"

"Like Steve."

The delicious, rich scent of the caffeine filled me with comfort. I remember waking to this smell every morning. My grandfather Joseph downstairs singing as Grandma Cheryl banged pots looking for the egg frying pan.

"It's just not Steve," Hope said. "Though, I can tell he'd like to know you better."

I knew that about Steve, along with everyone else in Eden. "I don't want a relationship right now."

Or maybe ever.

"I have a confession," Hope said.

I paused mid-sip and stared over the rim of the cup.

A sad look flittered onto her face. She thrust her shoulders back and sat up straight. "I wish I told you earlier. Maybe things wouldn't have gotten out of hand and you wouldn't be spending so much time with that detective."

I wanted to correct Hope again, but kept quiet before she changed her mind.

Hope took hold of my hand. "The night before the Art Benefit Show, Steve called the store and asked if someone could bring a pair of skinny scissors. He needed to hang a banner and the string originally used wasn't strong enough. They found a stronger twine, but a remnant of string still hung down. The larger scissors they had couldn't cut close to the grommet. Marilyn offered to bring them to Steve. She wanted to avoid seeing Michael at the show that morning, so she planned on arriving an hour earlier than the rest of us."

Wait a minute. Marilyn and I ran into each other in the parking lot. She was angry because Michael stood Mark up. She knew Michael would be there, so that meant her son told her he cancelled with his dad. Marilyn lied about that. And if she got there later than planned, she had the scissors with her, because I didn't see her hand them to Steve.

"I told Detective Roget about the scissors," Hope said. "That's why he thought they came from our store and took the other ones. I think he wanted to see if they could compare them in some way."

My heart twisted. "Grandma, you had to tell the police what you knew."

"I know. Just like you." Hope heaved out a sigh. "When Cheryl wanted to encourage you to help Marilyn, I told her."

I sat down beside her. "Why didn't you tell me?"

Hope gazed down at the table. "I knew it would break your heart that Marilyn didn't trust you with the whole truth. In a way, it might seem like Marilyn was using you. I couldn't let you get hurt over a misunderstanding."

My leg started twitching and I fisted my hands.

"Are you okay?"

"Yeah. I just need a few minutes alone." I was taken for a fool. Used. Did God stamp puppet across my forehead where only others could read? I'd have thought I learned my lesson the first time and not be so easily duped again.

Grandma Hope squeezed my hand. "If you need us, just holler."

Was it possible Marilyn did kill her husband?

TWENTY-TWO

I kept my mind occupied by hanging up and rearranging the layouts coming into the store. I wanted to stop thinking about Marilyn before I marched to the police station and had it out with her. Maybe I should call Karen and let her know the newest scoop.

I didn't know why Marilyn kept those facts from me. Maybe she was afraid she'd look guilty when she wasn't. I knew all about that. Focus. I had to make these displays eye-catching before the crop tonight.

I stood back and frowned. Too many shabby chic styled layouts were hung side by side. I took one from the display board near the door and moved it down to the fourth wooden panel. The layout, a mixture of pinks, greens, and brown pattern paper in a flower motif, looked perfect hanging next to an entry using a linear style with black and white and a subtle placement of teal blue as an accent color. The entries complemented each other and brought out the others composition.

The scrapbooker of the linear layout had enlarged the photo to an 8x10 and placed it on the left of the 12x12 sheet of white cardstock. The black cardstock was used as a mat around three sides of the photograph. In the picture, Sierra and I stood in different corners of the booth helping potential customers. I stood near the man examining the layout with the fish wire.

This was right before the announcement of the murder. I leaned forward and studied the photo, hoping something in the captured image pointed to Marilyn's innocence. Wait. Was that Hank in the background? In civilian clothing? I thought he was working security at the event. That was why Sierra brought the boys.

"I can hang a few," Linda said, bumping into me.

I leaned forward and nearly toppled into the display boards. I placed a hand over my thumping heart and willed it to slow down. I handed her a layout. "Sure. I'm trying to balance the designs, make sure any aren't overlooked because they blend into one another."

"That's why you're studying them so hard." Linda smiled and found a lovely spot for the cream and pastel lime layout.

"I just like seeing what was happening that day. See who was around. Maybe ask them if they have a layout they'd like to enter." I took another from the pile and turned it toward Linda. "Aren't the pages fantastic? It'll be hard to pick a winner."

"Details in the photographs are what will be the deciding factor for me." Linda pinned up another layout, making sure the pin went through the page protector and not the actual page.

Grandma Hope's concerns flashed through my mind. Maybe if I showed I was interested in making friends, she wouldn't be so concerned about forcing some on me. "Linda, would you like to join me for lunch?"

Linda gaped at me.

Sierra who was manning the register also looked at me with shock. Now I felt like a heel. In the three months Linda worked with us, none of us had offered a hand of friendship.

"Sure," Linda stammered. "When did you want to go?"

"I think we can have this last batch of entries on the display in about fifteen minutes." I smiled at her.

Linda looked over at Sierra.

"That works for me," Sierra said, grinning. "Hank plans on taking me out for a late lunch. He got the job!"

Maybe I could ask Hank a couple of quick questions about him doing security at the Art Benefit Show. Like what happened to items left behind. Linda left her layout in my and Sierra's possession, so it was only right to inquire about it.

"That's great!"

Linda and I finished in ten minutes and headed over to Home Brewed.

"Changing the crop class into a singles mixer was a fantastic idea," Linda said, opening the door.

I shrugged off the praise. "It wasn't actually my idea, just going with the flow."

"It sure grabbed the town's interest." Linda sighed. "One day I might attend one. It gets lonely at times, but I'm not ready. My son thinks I should start going out more."

Besides scrapbooking, Linda and I also had people dictating our social life in common. "Everyone is different. Some people prefer staying home. Some people need a longer time with their memories before getting into a relationship after they lost someone."

"Did you lose someone, Faith?" Linda rummaged around in her bag. "Besides your parents?"

I ignored the question. "The special looks really good today. The mozzarella, tomato and fresh basil sandwich on sourdough bread is calling my name. What about you?"

"That does sound good."

We reached the front of the line and ordered. Linda refused my offer to pay. Dianne quickly prepared our lunch and handed it to us without a long wait.

We picked a table in the back and sat down, staring at each other for a while. The only sound was Linda opening up a bag of chips.

I decided to be the brave one and open up the dialogue, since this was my idea. "Wow. I can't believe how many entries we've received."

Linda nodded.

"It's going to be fun to see who wins since none of us know who actually made the entries."

"If it's not Darlene, I don't know if I want to be at work when the announcement is made."

"Maybe we can have Ted stop by that day, since the man has handcuffs."

"He'll already be at Scrap This. He seems to like the store...or someone in it."

Not a topic I wanted discussed. "Are you enjoying working at the store?"

She quickly drew back and tears flooded her eyes. "This is the 'I'm sorry but we have to let you go' lunch isn't it?"

I guess we hadn't done a good job of keeping our financial situation a secret. Or employees caught on that if customers didn't walk into the store and buy, it equaled no income. I shook my head and held up my hands. "No. I just wanted to know if you liked working with us."

"I like it." She started eating her sandwich.

That response pretty much shut that topic. Scrapbooking. Art. We had that in common. "At the Art Benefit Show, did you see anything interesting?"

Her eyes widened, then quickly narrowed, looking like an owl who got hold of some caffeine. She patted her chest a few times, then coughed. "Sorry. Something got stuck."

I pushed a glass of water closer to her. "I didn't get a chance to look at any of the displays. Did you see any designers or art techniques we might be able to incorporate into scrapbooking?"

Linda shifted uncomfortably. "The truth is, I'm not really an art person, so I didn't pay attention. I only took up scrapbooking because of the job."

"Your layout of your husband and son is really nice," I said.

"You have my layout. Why haven't you given it back?" She clenched her right hand around the fork. If she wanted to stab me with it, she had the right grip.

I casually eased back. "I saw it the day of the show. Sierra asked me if I could fix it. I haven't seen it since. But I promise to look. I'm hoping it got placed in one of the product boxes. You really have a lot of talent. Have you thought about making a memorial album? There's a company that's running a contest with a large cash prize."

"I'd rather not." Red splotches decorated her cheeks. "I didn't mind having it up at the store's booth, but I don't want strangers seeing it. It's too personal."

"I know it's hard to share private moments. Sometimes scrapbooking can help a person work through their pain." I felt like such a hypocrite as I spoke. I just wanted Linda having some confidence in herself. This was the first time I seen some life in her.

"And sometimes people want their choices respected." Linda grabbed her plate and plastic fork and headed to the trashcan.

Ouch.

TWENTY-THREE

Linda and I returned from lunch in record time and Sierra had the good sense not to ask any questions. The three of us worked in silence preparing for the crop. Fifteen minutes later, the door opened. The sound of children—boys—drowned out the jingle of the bell.

"Mom!" Three similar voices cried out in glee.

Sierra crossed her arms and gave her husband a stern look.

Hank smiled sheepishly. "School had a half day, sweetheart."

The boys gagged at the term of endearment and pressed their bodies into the front of the counter.

Ten years and three children later, Sierra and Hank still got starry-eyed around each other. Their boys complained about them being all huggy, even around other people. I thought it was sweet, but the boys thought it only one step from the worst act ever committed: parents kissing.

I saw two pair of eyes and just the top of Howard's head. He needed to grow a few inches before he could spy.

"School-wide or selective?" I asked Hank.

He grinned. "Hello to you, Faith. How's the private eye biz?"

I shot him my best evil look. It didn't faze him. Must come from having children. "Very funny."

"From what I hear, it isn't very safe," Hank said.

"But she knows how to shoot." Harold looked at me with obvious admiration.

Hank nodded. I didn't want to know why, or where, that turned into a topic of conversation at the Brodart family dinner. Hank sent me a beseeching look and pointed at the boys. He needed a babysitter.

I waved my hands in protest. "Out of the question. I'm working."

"They'll behave. It'll only be for an hour. Come on, Faith. How much trouble can they get into in an hour?" Hank asked.

Twenty different scenarios popped into my head of what they could do with paper, stickers, adhesive, and metal items. Not to mention the cutting tools. The last time I babysat, within ten minutes they flooded their kitchen, set off the fire alarm and kidnapped Mrs. Evans' poodle.

"The boys promise to be good. They won't touch anything without your permission." Hank nudged his oldest, Harold.

Harold still looked at me with awe-filled eyes. "Miss Faith, we'll do everything you say."

Henry nodded solemnly, puppy dog eyes fixed on me. He tilted his head and sighed. "We'll do anything you ask."

Howard's hair flopped up and down as he nodded. "Anything."

Hank grinned at me. "See, what did I tell you?"

I looked over at Sierra who watched her crew with morbid fascination. She knew they were up to something.

"Hank, this is not a good idea," I said.

"I concur." Sierra crossed her arms.

"Boys, do you want to disappoint Miss Faith?" Hank asked.

"Never!" All three responded.

The who-me shock in their voices filled me with dread. Definitely up to something. The Hooligans were never this calm and agreeable, unless they already had mischief plotted.

Linda walked to the front, a bright smile spreading across her face. "I can handle the register. There aren't too many customers right now, so I don't think the children will disturb anyone."

Payback time.

"See, Faith, it'll be okay." Hank got down on one knee and clasped his hands together. "Please, one hour is all I ask."

"Hank, I think Faith is right. It isn't a good idea to leave the boys here." Sierra eyed her children suspiciously even though they stood at attention in front of the counter.

"They'll behave. I promise. We promise." Hank's pleading gaze on his wife switched to smoldering. Sierra blushed.

The boys bobbed their heads in solemn nods. All three pairs of eyes filled with wonder locked onto mine.

I crossed my arms and narrowed my gaze. "No touching anything unless I say it's okay."

The Hooligans nodded.

"No running, jumping, or screaming."

"We'll just look at the pictures on the board," Harold said. "Just like this." He placed his hands behind his back and flattened them in an I've-been-arrested fashion.

I shooed Sierra and Hank. "All right. One hour."

Then Hank owed me. I had a couple of small questions needing answers.

"Thanks." Hank grabbed his wife's hand and took off out the door, tugging her behind him. The man was probably afraid I'd change my mind.

I looked at the boys who remained rooted to a spot on the carpet in front of the counter. "You can look at the layouts on the board, but don't touch any of them."

They crossed their hearts and then carefully walked over to the boards, their hands behind their backs.

I stood beside Howard, determined to discover their plan. He smiled shyly at me and averted his gaze. Howard always talked. Matter-of-fact, it was the main reason he got in trouble at school. Whenever I phoned Sierra, it took fifteen minutes to get Howard to stop chatting about his day so I could hear about his mother's.

A comment Harold made popped back into my head. "Harold, who told you I know how to shoot?"

"Dad did. He told us you were in the Army."

Henry nodded. "We watched some movies that showed what people in the Army do."

Wonderful. Hank figured the best way to get his boys to behave was letting them think I could destroy them. "I learned how, but I never shot anything. Except for a target."

"People in the military can also blow up bridges," Henry said.

Harold showed me two thumbs-up. "Patton was cool."

At least the movies they watched weren't the popular gore fests. And they boys were behaving. For now. I shuddered, envisioning the day the Hooligans decided re-enacting the *Bridge on the River Kwai* was an awesome summer project.

Howard leaned forward, his nose almost touching one of the layouts.

I rested my hand on his shoulder. "What are you looking for?"

"I want to find Mom. I heard Dad tell Buddy she looked hot that day."

"Really?" Henry's eyes widened. "Man, I wonder if steam is coming from her ears."

"Maybe lasers from her eyeballs." Harold quickly walked to the other side. "I'll look over here. You guys look over there."

I suppressed my smile as I left the boys looking for a picture of their mom turning into a fireball. With the mad shopping rush earlier, some of the sticker sheets were left unrolled and a few puddled on the ground. I rolled them up.

"Miss Faith?"

I smiled at Henry. "Do you need something?"

"We were wondering if you had a magnifying glass. Some of the people in the pictures are so small we can't tell if it's mom. There's one lady with white on top of her head. I say steam. Harold says it's old lady hair."

"I'll go in the office and get it, but you stay here."

"Okay. Do you want me to fix the stickers for you?"

He looked so earnest, I racked my mind for a task he could complete without damaging anything. Someone had opened a package of paperclips and flowers, probably figured no reason to buy the whole package when they wanted only a couple, and dumped the remainder on the floor.

"Henry, can you get a basket and pick up all the paperclips and flowers from the ground for me?"

"Okay."

As I walked away, I heard Henry happily muttering that now I'd like him best. It took me a few minutes to find the magnifying glass. I handed it to Henry.

After saying thanks, he thrust the basket at me and scampered toward his brothers. How disappointed Henry will be when he finds out that it was a white-haired woman and not his mom with steam coming out of her head.

I spent the next thirty minutes putting pattern paper back into the correct slot and listening out for the Hooligans.

"That is too Dad," Harold said.

"No, it's not," Howard said.

"Don't yell, Miss Faith is going to get mad," Henry whined.

The three voices lowered to a loud whisper.

"Is too."

"Is not."

"We promised."

"Shouldn't you go see what that's about?" Linda asked.

Yes, I should.

I stood behind the boys, towering over the trio. Some of the few people I could achieve that effect with. "Okay, guys, what's going on?"

Harold pointed at a photograph on one of the layouts. "Is that Dad? Howard says no, but I bet it is."

"Dad is never mad," Howard said.

I held out my hand. "Let me look with the magnifier."

Harold passed it to me and I placed the glass almost on top of the photo. If I didn't know any better, I'd say that was Hank, not in a security uniform, arguing with someone near the hallway leading to the vending machines. Near where Michael Kane's body was found.

"I can't tell. Let's see if we can find your mom. Maybe she's turning into a fireball like a superhero."

Harold's eyes lit up.

"You don't think Mr. Kane will be in any of them?" Howard's

voice trembled and he squished himself against my leg.

I ruffled his hair. "No. Mr. Kane wasn't in this area when he was...hurt."

"Okay." Howard sounded convinced but remained glued to my side.

The bell jangled.

Hank raised his arms in triumphant. "We're back."

The boys rushed over to him. "We were good. Really good."

Henry beamed at his dad. "I helped clean up."

"What?" Hank lifted up his middle child.

"Stuff people took out of the little plastic boxes. Not us." Henry smiled at me. "Isn't that right, Miss Faith?"

"Best behavior I've ever seen them display," I said. "Mind if I talk to you, Hank?"

Sierra glared at the boys. "What did they do that you don't want me knowing about?"

"Just wanted to get the names of the movies the boys were talking about."

Hank grimaced and flushed red. "Yeah, that. Sure, I can explain. Plus, I'd like to thank her for helping out."

"Hank?" Sierra planted her hands on her hips.

"I promise it won't be the way I'll thank you for all your support this last year." Hank winked at her then followed me.

Sierra blushed crimson red.

I tugged open the maroon curtains and Hank slipped through the opening.

"I shouldn't use your military experience as a threat against the boys."

I waved that way. "It worked. I'm just curious why you weren't wearing a uniform at the art show? Were you undercover security?"

Hank took a step toward me. "Just knock it off, Faith."

The menacing, quiet tone startled me. I inched back. "I was just wondering. The boys thought they saw you in one of the pictures."

"No. I wasn't in uniform. As if that is any of your business. And stop bringing up the car to Sierra. She's thinking something's going on."

But something was going on if Hank wanted that kept a secret. "I didn't know it was a private matter between us."

"I had an errand to run I didn't want Sierra to know about," Hank said. He clenched and unclenched his hands, drawing in deep breaths.

"If it was a surprise for her, you could've said so."

"Since when do you have to know everything?"

"Sierra always shares what the boys do. It's what friends do."

"But you don't need to be sharing what I do." Hank pointed a finger in my direction then poked himself in the chest. "And we're not friends."

I stepped forward and jabbed a finger at him. "Remember that next time you want a babysitter or to borrow my car for whatever clandestine—"

Hank pressed a hand against my shoulder and pressed me away from him. "Shut up or—"

A gasp filled the small space.

Linda held the curtains open, only her head peeked through the opening. "Sierra took the boys outside. They were getting a little rambunctious. I need Faith. A woman's on the phone asking what brands of albums we have. I don't know them all."

Never once did she take her gaze off of me.

"Hank!" Sierra's voice rang out.

"Thanks for the help." Hank opened the curtains and bowed. He snagged Sierra around the waist and gave his wife a very thorough goodbye kiss. The boys made retching sounds as Hank led them away.

Linda placed an arm around me and scooted me off into a private corner of the storage room. "Are you okay? Do you want to call someone?"

I shook my head. "I'm fine. Forget about what you thought you saw."

"I know what I saw. That man shouldn't get away with that."

Fire lit Linda's blue eyes.

"It was nothing."

"It was something." Anger gripped Linda's features. "Don't you ever let some man push you around."

I smiled at Linda. "I appreciate you sticking up for me and the advice. But don't worry. I won't let some man bully me."

"If you say so. But if he comes in here again, there might be another pair of scissors missing."

TWENTY-FOUR

To our utter delight, and probably that of our banker, a horde of women rushed through the door to attend the first official Scrap This singles mixer. It looked as if our best event was one we hadn't even thought of planning.

Linda offered to stay, but she looked worn out. She had spent the rest of the afternoon readying for a battle with Hank. Twice I stopped her from sharing our secret with Sierra, so I encouraged Linda to leave at her normal time. The truth was I wanted to approach Sierra alone. She'd take it better from me, and without an audience. I'd rather not bring it up, but I wanted to make sure my friend was safe.

Linda waved and weaved her body through the croppers to outside.

"Bye," I called out.

"This is quite a turn out," Cheryl said.

"I'll go see if we have any snacks left." Sierra headed for the break room to rustle up food for the croppers.

Hope headed for the door. "I'll go get goodies from Dianne. It'll be a great way for her to advertise. Plus, she'd love for her daughter to attend."

I didn't know how happy Clarissa would be getting that call from her mother. At thirty-two, Clarissa made it clear to everyone—besides my grandmother and her mother—she planned on remaining single.

Cheryl gave out the tip sheets on basic techniques and recommended supplies for starting their first album. The women took hold of the sheets and glanced around the room. I could see the question pounding in their heads and hearts: Where were the men?

I hurried to the break room. Sierra was opening and closing cabinets, a frowned slashed across her face. "Nothing," she muttered.

"Hope went to get some goodies from Dianne."

"Great. Because we're kind of low on food." Sierra knelt down and opened up the bottom cabinet. "We do have two bags of miniature chocolate bars and a bag of pretzels."

"That'll work for now." I took the bags Sierra held over her head.

"Even better, we have three two liters of diet soda and one of regular. Plus, a case of bottled water." Sierra lifted up the large box and placed it on the counter. "I'll put some in the refrigerator. If we don't have any cups, maybe Dianne will give us a stack."

"I'm sure she would." My heart fluttered. How did you ask a friend a question about their husband's temper?

Sierra's eyes narrowed and then she moaned. "What are you up to now?"

"Nothing."

Sierra rolled her eyes. "You're still investigating Marilyn's case. And now you want to drag me into it."

"This isn't about Marilyn." I let out a deep breath, hoping my fear went out of me along with the air. "Is everything okay between you and Hank? He seemed a little...angry."

Sierra crossed her arms. "This is about the car thing. I told Hank to let it go. It was his fault and not yours. So what did he say?"

"He wasn't too happy that I was making a deal about it. If I'd known there was a surprise involved, I wouldn't have said anything."

A softness entered into her eyes. "A surprise. I wished he would've told you that instead of some silly story."

"Yeah, that would've been better."

"He said you were so wrapped up about playing detective, he was afraid you'd make something out of it."

He should be afraid since he was lying about more than car troubles. "I just wanted to make sure you were okay."

Sierra's eyes widened. "Hank wouldn't hurt me, if that's what you're thinking."

I kept quiet.

Sierra rubbed my arm. "Listen, honey, men get angry, even yell, that doesn't mean they hit their wives. It doesn't always work that way."

My face scrunched up. "What?"

Sierra leaned against the counter. "Marilyn and I talk about you."

I crossed my arms. "Gee, thanks."

"You never talk about your time in Germany. Friends you made. Any fun stories about your job."

"There weren't any. It was boring."

"I highly doubt living in Germany and working in JAG was so boring nothing stuck in your mind." Sierra held up her hand and stopped my next pronouncement. "It's your decision what you want to talk about. It just makes us wonder what happened, and with your concern about Hank and how involved you are in Marilyn's case, I'm thinking a man did you wrong. Badly."

I cradled two of the bottles of soda in my arms. "I'll take half and you can take the other half."

"I got it. Subject off-limits." Sierra followed me back into the store.

The front door flung open, the bell jostling a merry tune, as Gussie toddled into the store, her left leg in a walking cast. Wayne and Wyatt followed behind their mother, both of them with their arms outstretched, acting as a catcher in case she tipped backwards or tumbled forwards.

Four women eyed the men with interest. Six other women craned their necks, probably waiting for Steve and Ted to come through the door.

Gussie must have noticed the marriage-eyes because a grin splashed across her face. She took one of the sheets from Cheryl and lowered herself into a chair. "I'd like to get two of everything on these lists for my boys." Gussie fanned herself with the paper. "Where's that niece of mine?"

Cheryl snatched up a basket and headed down the aisle, a bounce in her step.

"Bobbie-Annie will be here soon," I said. Or at least I hoped. But with Gussie present, her boys would be on their best behavior. I remembered once in the fourth grade, Gussie marched into class and plopped herself on the floor right next to Wyatt's desk. I'd never seen him so well-behaved.

Sierra seated each of the women in the crop area and they chose a piece of cardstock for their background. "It's time to get started."

Wyatt and Wayne shuffled over to an unoccupied table. Two young women scrambled to their feet and planted themselves into the chairs beside the unattached men. Wyatt and Wayne exchanged petrified looks, but kept quiet. Gussie grinned, her gaze roamed to the wedding albums.

The bell jingled and a blast of cool air filled into the room. I could almost hear the eyelashes fluttering. Either Steve or Ted just walked in. I turned, smiling. The expression vanished when I saw Steve and Ted standing there, neither of them happy. Bobbi-Annie trailed in behind them. She avoided looking at me and made her way to a vacant seat far from her cousins.

"There's a space here, Detective," a perky redhead chirped. She patted the chair beside her.

"I came tonight for inspiration, not to crop. Sorry. Creative block today." Roget tapped his forehead and walked over to the display boards and looked at the layouts. The women oohed and aahed in sympathy.

"Are you cropping tonight or gathering inspiration?" I smiled and waited for Steve's response. And waited. The sustained smile strained my cheek muscles. I shifted my weight from foot-to-foot and hoped he answered soon. The class watched us with keen interest.

"I need some help choosing my..." He snapped his fingers.

"Embellishments," I said.

"Exactly." He stepped aside and I led the way.

I headed for the back of the store and stood in front of the stickers, waiting for Steve's explanation. We stood side by side with our backs facing the students. Steve crossed his arms and stared straight ahead. To make this shopping excursion halfway believable, we needed props. I grabbed a package of beach stickers and handed it over.

"Hank said you accused him of killing Michael." Steve tapped the strip across his palm.

I was now thinking it, but didn't accuse him. "I just wanted to know why he borrowed my car when his wasn't broke, like he said. And why he wasn't in a security uniform the day of the Art Benefit Show. Those are questions, not accusations. Someone should get the man a dictionary."

Steve turned his head slightly, one eyebrow raised.

"Not that this is any of your business."

"I'm a prosecutor for this town, so murders, and who's accused of them, are my business." Steve flicked the edge of a packet of gel stickers. "Others in the police department, and at the courthouse, are wondering why it's a scrapbook store employee's business."

I drew in a breath. Okay, this wasn't the type of gossip I wanted to be a part of. Well, actually no type of gossip really, but I'd rather have people wondering if I was hooking up with Steve or Ted.

"Hank has been hurt by rumors in the past. That's why he's had such a hard time finding and keeping work. He doesn't need you starting anymore."

"You think I've been spreading rumors about Hank? Got him fired?"

Steve believed Hank already. He wasn't even letting me explain. I thought I could depend on him. Steve said I could depend on him. He lied. I trusted him. Never again.

Memories and emotions from the past attacked. Fear. Humiliation. Handcuffs cutting into my flesh. Adam entering a plea agreement. He'd give them information about a murdered German citizen if they forgave him for selling goods on the black market. He led me to the slaughter to save his own skin. If it wasn't for that one person, that one MP, I'd be in prison instead of Adam for the murder he committed. I panicked. I pushed past Steve and fled down the hall. My breaths came in painful spurts. I needed to get outside. I barreled into the storage room. The curtains tangled around my body. I flailed my arms, fighting the entrapment of the fabric, but my frantic movements made it worse.

"Let me help you." Steve placed his hands on my shoulder. I swatted the curtains along with Steve.

"Don't touch me." Tears flooded my eyes and the darkness became blurry.

"I'm trying to help," Steve said, frustration growing in his voice. "Settle down before half the people in the store come over here."

I stopped struggling. "Don't boss me."

"How about you let me handle this, Davis," Ted said.

Just what I wanted, another witness to my humiliation. The tears pooling in my eyes rolled down my cheeks.

"I'll take care of this, Roget."

"Is that so? Cause I could've sworn I heard the lady say leave her alone."

I remained quiet, tears dripping down my chin. If I said one word, the men would know I was crying. Crunching up some of the fabric, I brought it to my face and dried the tears from my cheeks, the velvet soft and comforting.

"Steve," Cheryl called out. "Can you grab the box of scissors from the stock room?"

"Sure." Steve's body brushed mine as he maneuvered around me.

"You get into quite the predicaments don't you, Faith?" Ted unwrapped me from the red drapes.

I blinked from the intrusive light.

Ted took a light, but firm, hold of my elbow. "Let's go outside for a minute. Come on."

The cold air struck my body and the sharp twang in the air zapped the heaviness in my limbs and my head. Why did Ted think I wanted his help as opposed to Steve's? Matter-of-fact, Ted started this whole mess. I glared at him. I bounced from foot to foot, keeping my ire under control.

He grinned. "Now that's the feisty woman I know."

"Why did you come to the store?" I crossed my arms and schooled my features to portray an I-don't-care attitude. "You said you weren't cropping tonight."

He ran his fingers through his hair. "I wanted to check on you. I kind of lit into you and it wasn't fair of me."

"Gee, why the sudden change of heart?"

Ted looked down at the ground.

"You told your brother and he laid into you."

"He said I'd never find a woman if I kept being police detective all the time." Ted looked up and grinned. "I did tell him I was taking up a hobby."

"Annoying me," I said.

"Possibly."

"Find a different one."

"I hope to." Ted's voice lowered. He cleared his throat and tapped the handcuffs attached to his belt. "Do I need to use these on Davis?"

I gaped at him. "For what?"

The humor left Ted's face. He brushed his fingertips across my cheek. "Whatever he did that scared you so much. I saw you running and he was chasing after you."

"Nothing."

"It didn't look like nothing. You want me to have a talk with him?"

"He didn't hurt me. Not like you think."

Ted frowned, his fingers tightening around the cuffs.

"Memories. Something he said brought back things I don't

want to remember." I rubbed my hands up and down my arms. "Do I really need to explain all of this to you? Steve hurt my feelings. That's not an arrestable offense."

"Maybe if you didn't keep it all to yourself, they'd go away. Or at least not feel like you're being tormented if they sneak up on you."

My brain hurt. I rubbed my temples and leaned against the door. I didn't want anyone's advice about how I handled my past. It was mine to deal with, not anyone else's and I'd been doing fine. If it wasn't for Michael's murder, I'd still be doing fine.

"I'm going home." I tugged the door handle of my car. Locked. I shoved my hands into my jean pockets. The keys were in my purse. In the store.

"Do you want to talk about it?" Ted stood behind me and draped a jacket around me.

"I left my keys in the store."

"I figured that out." He kneaded my shoulders. "Steve doesn't know about Adam."

The mention of my once-upon-a-husband locked the breath into my throat. The cold intensified around me and I sat on the car hood to keep from falling over.

"Damn, what did that man do to you?" Ted caressed my cheeks then captured my hands in his, rubbing them back and forth. "You're so cold."

"I didn't want anyone to find out about him. Ever."

Ted buttoned his jacket around me. "Faith, when you started interfering—poking—helping with the Kane case, I had to check you out. Especially when I discovered you kept quiet about your time out of Eden."

I wiggled my arms into the jacket sleeves, the fabric puddled around my hands. "I figured that might happen."

"But you took the risk."

"I couldn't let Marilyn go to jail for a crime she didn't commit. I know what that feels like. Even one day is too long." I shuddered.

Ted sat on the hood and wrapped an arm around me. "Want to

tell me what happened? The details I dug up were pretty slim."

"Here's the short story. I loved him. I thought he loved me, but all he wanted was an Eve defense."

"An Eve defense?"

"You know, the woman made me do it. When he got caught selling military goods on the black market, he tried getting out of it by pinning a murder on me. That's when I realized he never loved me. He needed a fall guy. Fall girl. He was a respected captain. I was just some enlisted girl from a Podunk town in West Virginia. And it would've worked except one military police, a Specialist, actually listened to me."

"Good man."

"Woman," I said. "But it didn't matter. People still treated me like a criminal. A traitor. People believed the worst about me because they thought they knew him better."

"That's why you keep barreling into this case. One person believed in you."

"Believed me and saved me. I want to do that for Marilyn."

"What if you're wrong, Faith? What then?"

I didn't know the answer. I didn't want to know. "Now I'm hurting people." I laughed, a bitter sound. "I guess I'm like all those other people. All that matters is my truth."

"You're not like them. You're trying to find the truth so Marilyn isn't spending her life in jail if she is innocent. That isn't heartless." Ted smiled at me. "Annoying, but not heartless."

"Doesn't make me feel any better."

"And that is the biggest difference between you and Adam. You feel pain over your actions because others were hurt."

I remained still. I wanted Ted's words to soothe me.

"Why didn't you tell your grandmothers what happened?" Ted asked.

"Embarrassment. Shame. Tired of being judged for a lapse of judgment. What he did followed me to my next duty station. Some people couldn't trust me because they believed I had to have helped him. And others couldn't trust a soldier who so easily fell for a con.

My grandmothers gave up their lives to raise me after my parents died."

"From what I've gathered you are your grandmothers' life. The only reason I wouldn't say anything to them is because they'd go after that guy."

A smile fluttered on my lips.

"Taking on Cheryl seems like quite a task, but I have a feeling Hope is the one to really fear. It's always the quiet, polite ones that will do a person in quick and swift." He stood and held out his hands to me. "How about we go in there and get some contesting, cropping, whatever you call it, done?"

I took his offered help, sliding off the hood. I kept my hand in his as we headed for the door. "I think I should give you a warning."

He paused and looked at me, mischief twinkling in his eyes. "Now what are you up to?"

"Me? Nothing." I batted my eyelashes at him. "But those women in there came to find themselves a man."

"It's only one night of pasting pictures to a page. How bad can it be?"

I raised my eyebrows and grinned.

He reeled me into his arms, his gaze lingering on my mouth. "Can't I just tell them that I already have my eye on a woman?"

"No." I pulled away from him. "They'll demand a refund. You are one of the bachelors they came to see."

"Wonderful." He growled and then a broad grin filled his face. "On the bright side, Davis must be ready to scream uncle."

I shook my head. "My grandmothers are protecting him. They've already staked a claim on him."

"Isn't he kind of young for both of them?"

I rolled my eyes and dragged Ted into the store.

TWENTY-FIVE

Friday morning, I pulled into the back lot of Scrap This, feeling better about the fact Ted wasn't planning to arrest me even though he knew about Adam. The secret no longer haunted me. It was nice knowing there was someone I could be open with. Not that it made me want to announce my annulled marriage and almost court-martial to the world, my grandmothers, or Steve.

Enough of the past. Today was all about the present. This afternoon the customers would vote on the layouts, and tomorrow morning, we'd announce the winners. I'd better hurry inside before Darlene beat the door down.

Plus, between the contest and the new singles mixer crop, our bank account was filling up like the fire hall on designer purse bingo day. Lots to be excited about. I waved at my grandmothers who had parked beside me, then unlocked the door. Hallelujah, it opened on the first try.

I rushed over and whipped back the curtain. I screamed and dropped my purse. The contents scattered onto the floor.

"Faith!" My grandmothers' cries carried from the parking lot.

Shredded layouts littered the linoleum, the once full boards now bare. Anger coursed through my veins. I wanted to hit something. Someone. Why would someone break into our store and destroy the precious work of our customers? I stepped farther into the room and examined the other damage.

"The police are on their way!" Cheryl shouted. "Faith, where are you!"

"They're destroyed." I knelt beside the ripped paper and photographs.

"What is— Cheryl gasped.

"Oh my goodness." Hope gripped my shoulder.

In the crop area, near the large trimmer, more destroyed layouts were strewn over the floor. Brads, shredded ribbon, and chipboard pieces mingled among the torn cardstock and pattern paper. Glossy pieces of photographs peeked out from the carnage.

Stunned, I turned around in a circle and examined the rest of the store. Nothing else was touched. Every item for purchase was in the proper place and neatly arranged.

"I'm calling Sierra," Cheryl headed to the phone. "She closed up last night."

"Grandma, I unlocked the back door." Though it had been rather easy this morning. Maybe the lock hadn't engaged all the way. I reached for the knob on the front door. "I'll check this door."

"Don't touch it," Hope said. "The police might be able to get fingerprints from it."

Sirens filled the air, and barely two minutes later, Jasper and Ted entered into the store.

"Gee, Faith, who'd you go and make mad?" Jasper asked, a humorous lilt to his voice.

I buried my head in my hands.

"Be quiet, Jasper," Roget said. "Did you see any sign of a break-in, Faith?"

"No." I mumbled into my hands.

"Did anyone touch anything?" Roget asked, rubbing my back lightly.

I raised my head and looked at him. "I almost did."

He offered a small smile. "Almost isn't the same. You have an idea who could've done this?"

"No." I moaned and rubbed my temples. "How are we going to explain this to our customers? We can't have the contest without layouts. "

"Why don't you sit while we look around?" Ted tried leading me behind the counter.

I shoved away from him. "I'm not a damsel in need of protection."

"All of them were destroyed?" Jasper asked.

"I have one. It's in my purse." I pointed to where it laid by the back door.

Hope and Cheryl followed Jasper around as he looked for evidence.

"That's one big purse." Ted walked over and picked up the page protector. Another layout slid out. "Actually you have two in here. Why are they in your purse?"

Two? Was the other one Linda's layout? I wanted to get a look at it before I mentioned it. No sense getting her hopes up. I explained Darlene's concern and request.

"And you agreed to do that for her?"

"It was a simple thing to make her happy."

"How important was winning this contest to her?" Ted handed me the layouts and snapped open his leather-encased notebook.

I shook my head and waved my free hand in a cutting motion. "Darlene wouldn't do this. She couldn't get into the store and leave undetected."

"This contest sure did irritate someone," Ted said. "I witnessed how upset she was about it, especially about people cheating."

"I know. But I just can't see her doing this. She wants to win fair and square, not by default."

"I'll stop by the Bennett's house and see what their grandchildren were up to last night." Ted held up his hand to block my argument. "They probably didn't do it, but considering what happened with the window, I need to check on it."

"People are going to wonder why the city homicide detective is investigating vandalism."

Ted shrugged as he stood. "I reckon they will. Some guesses will be more entertaining than others. I'll stop back later."

Customers and spectators lined the sidewalk trying to figure out why the police were at Scrap This. Again. I leaned against the locked front door. Cheryl took Hope home. Her pale complexion worried us. This latest stress of the destroyed contest—or rather our customers' reaction to it—wore her out.

Sierra and Linda were on their way, but until they arrived, the contest participants, sales, and clean up rested on me. Sighing, I unlocked the door and the people poured in. Darlene walked inside and her gaze fixed on the display area.

"Where are the layouts? I thought the customers were going to judge them this morning?"

Other women murmured their agreement and confusion.

"They were damaged," I said, motioning to the mess on the floor.

Questions erupted from around the room.

"All of them?"

"Damaged?"

"How?"

"Why?"

My head pounded. I rubbed my throbbing temples and felt someone step beside me. I glanced and saw Darlene.

She raised her hands into the air and clapped. "Let's give Faith a chance to explain."

"Someone broke-in, destroyed the layouts. All of them," I said.

Hands fluttered toward mouths as the group sounded a collective gasp.

"The police are investigating," I assured them. "If you hear anything, please tell Detective Roget or Officer Jasper."

Darlene rolled up the sleeves of her silk blouse. "Tell me what you need me to do."

Another woman lifted her purse into the air. "Just going to run this to my car, then I'll help, too."

The anger and tantrums I expected didn't come, instead offers of help and total understanding from the women. I knew how much effort and love scrapbookers put into their layouts, and now those creative works were destroyed.

The phone rang. I snagged the receiver from its base. "Scrap This."

"Hi, honey, it's Grandma," Cheryl said. "Is everything okay at the store?"

"It's actually really good. The contestants have been very understanding."

"We have good people in Eden."

We did indeed. "How's Hope?"

"She'll be fine."

"You both keep saying that, but she hasn't felt well all week."

"Hope is a natural worrier and the accounting has stressed her beyond her limit. After today, I'm handling the finances. She's much better at the promotion stuff."

After assuring Cheryl that I was truly fine, and that no, I didn't need Steve's help, I hung up. A little less worried, but still sad.

My attention kept slipping from managing the store and volunteers to wondering who could've destroyed the layouts. If it wasn't about winning the contest, then what was it about? The only thing that made sense was the Art Benefit Show. All the pictures on the layout centered on that day. The day Michael Kane was murdered.

Had someone accidentally captured something that maybe gave away the killer?

Like something to disprove someone's alibi? The only person with a solid alibi was Annette Holland. And Hank freaked when I mentioned him being in a picture. He had access to the Scrap This keys. Could he have done this?

There was one person who could find out. I prayed Sierra would forgive me.

"Detective Roget."

"Have time for lunch?"

"Who's this?" His voice was suspicious.

Gee, he really did have a thing for me. I hunched over the receiver, whispering into the phone, "Faith."

"For you, yes."

"How about I pick you up in front of the station and we eat at the park?" I asked.

"That'll work. I'll be out front in an hour. And try to stay out of trouble until then."

Now what did I do?

I ordered two turkey sandwiches with all the trimmings, minus the mayo, two bags of chips, two large coffees and a large piece of chocolate cake to go. I hoped Ted would share the dessert. I left Home Brewed and walked around the back of the building so Linda and Sierra didn't spot me through the display windows.

I got into my car, eased from the employee parking spaces, and headed for the police station. When I reached the station, I slowed down and craned my neck, trying to spot him. I really didn't want to go inside and find him. The door of a cruiser opened and Ted stepped out. I stopped.

He opened the passenger door, carrying a white sack, and settled into the seat. "Let me guess, you want to make a citizen's arrest."

I ignored the sarcasm and held out the brown sack with Home Brewed splashed across it. "I brought lunch."

"So did I. Annabelle brought chicken and waffles."

The smell filled the car. My mouth watered. "Let's go with yours."

"We'll go with yours. I'm saving this for dinner."

"What if I don't want to share?"

Ted buckled up. "No problem. You eat your lunch and I'll eat mine. Whether for lunch or dinner, I'll still get chicken and waffles."

"Tease."

"I try."

I jerked the wheel and got the car back on the road.

"Someone needs a safety course in driving." Ted reached for the radio.

"Someone needs to stop distracting the driver." I swatted his hand.

"I'm a distraction. Not sure if I should be flattered or not."

"Not. Definitely not."

"So what kind of sandwich? Or is that a distracting question?"

"It might be if I decided to shove you out."

"That would fall under assaulting a police officer." Ted held on tight to the chicken and waffles.

"Might be worth the consequence."

"Come on, Faith, we both know you're not that type of girl."

I flashed him a wicked grin. "You have no idea what type of girl I am."

"I'd be willing to find out." His tone grew huskier and darker.

Why had the tempo of my pulse increased? I did not like Ted. He was aggravating.

I found a space near the park and pulled into it. "Stop messing with me or you can eat lunch by yourself."

Ted held up his hands in surrender. "Fine. I'll even share the chicken and waffles."

I grabbed the coffee and shut the door, following a few paces behind him. He kept glancing over his shoulder at me, the expression on his face unreadable. My nerves bounced. Was I walking into a trap? Enough with the paranoia, I scolded myself. If someone planned to do me in, they wouldn't do it in the middle of the day in plain view of the courthouse.

Ted sat at the first bench and I dropped down beside him. Behind us, I heard children laughing and arguing while women gossiped, the topics ranging from the new pastor and his fashionable wife to Michael Kane's murder.

"We could go somewhere else," Ted said, casting a sympathetic gaze at me.

I shrugged and wriggled a little further away from him, the woodsy scent of his aftershave created a roller coaster effect in my stomach. Dizziness washed over me, I really should've eaten something. I took a sip of coffee and it landed in my empty stomach like a rock.

Ted handed over a piece of chicken. "You feeling okay?"

I nibbled at the chicken. "I'm great. Just got busy and skipped a meal here and there."

Anger seeped into his gaze. "How hard did Hank shove you?"

The chicken slipped into my lap and I stared at him.

Ted settled back against the bench. "Linda told me. I interviewed all the employees this morning. She said Hank cornered you in the backroom. He shoved you. What the hell was that about?"

This was the second time I heard Ted curse. Both times when he thought someone physically harmed me. I gave him the brief version.

"I'll have a talk with him. You should have told me." Ted bit into a chicken leg.

"I was planning on telling you during lunch."

Ted chewed and eyed me, doubt on his face.

"I was going to tell you about Hank getting upset, the layout I saw him in, and that he had access to the key, but not the other thing."

"It's not another thing, Faith, it's a threatening action. Just because it's not a punch, doesn't mean you accept it."

"I didn't."

"Good."

We ate in silence for a few minutes.

"You're not going to tell my grandmothers or Steve, are you?"

"No," Ted said. "I don't want another murder in this town. I don't think we have enough room for the three of them in the jail."

"Bobbi-Annie would let them out."

"The chief would let them out. He has a soft spot for Hope."

That was new. Chief Moore's wife died three years ago from cancer. He was a kind and fair man, two years older than Hope. I should send him an invitation to the next crop mixer.

"What are you plotting now?"

"A date for my grandmother."

Ted smiled. "Give it a few more months and there'll be no reason for plotting. The chief is a take charge kind of guy."

"What kind of guy are you?" I couldn't help asking.

"Patient."

* * *

I returned to the store with Ted's comment floating in my mind. What had he meant by that, or did I really want to know. I went with not. There were some items better left in the realm of the unknown.

"You okay?" Sierra asked.

"Peachy as can be." I picked up a few remnants of a layout and tossed them into the trash.

"The customers were asking about the contest."

"Customers or Darlene?" I knew the woman's compassion couldn't last too long.

"Darlene and others. They spent a lot of time and money on their layouts." A grimace twisted Sierra's mouth.

I joined Sierra behind the counter. "What?"

"I hate to say this."

Groaning, I leaned over and placed my forehead on the cool surface. "Just say it." How could the day possibly get worse?

"Darlene is convinced this vandalism was an inside job."

I had my answer, the day could get worse. I thought like Darlene.

"She thinks we didn't want to award the die cut machine so—"

"We destroyed the layouts ourselves. Because everyone knows that would help our business."

Sierra rested a hand on my shoulder. "No one is going to believe her."

I stared at her.

"Okay. Not for very long. By Monday, this conspiracy theory of hers will bring us sympathetic shoppers and nothing more."

"I hope you're right."

"Of course I'm right. Right now people are in shock and want to be a part of something scandalous."

Only those never involved in a real "scandal" wanted one popping up in their life. "And that will change by Monday."

"Absolutely." Sierra grinned. "They'd all have sitting in a pew on Sunday."

"Or they're going to announce it during prayer request time, then everyone will join in."

Sierra lightly swatted my arm. "Stop being pessimistic. Have some hope, faith and patience."

I narrow-eyed her. "Really? You're going to go there?"

Sierra pressed back a smile and nodded. "You aren't a caver-under. I know that."

"A what?"

"That's what Harold calls a person who quits because something looks hard. Don't give up, Faith. We'll get through this."

I just hoped it was all in one piece.

TWENTY-SIX

Sierra's words had helped and for the first time this week I slept soundly. The weekend was off to a good start, even though I did have to field calls about refunds. The conspiracy river was flowing fast and wide, but at least the newspaper ignored Darlene. Not that she hadn't tried, but even Karen England had standards.

I was feeling stronger until Hank stormed into Scrap This.

Sierra blanched and ran toward her husband. "Is it the boys? Did something happen? What did they do?"

"They're less trouble than your so-called 'friend.'" Hank glared at me and tried stepping around Sierra.

She slipped back in front of her husband. "What are you talking about?"

"She's worried about Marilyn, and what being labeled a murderer will do to her and her family, but not about you." Hank clenched and unclenched his fists. "Great friend she is. The only reason Faith agreed to watch our boys was to see if she could find herself another suspect since blaming Annette didn't work out for her."

"What are you talking about?" Sierra looked at me, confusion tugging down her brows and mouth.

"Why don't you tell her, Faith? Or do you only stab people from the back?"

Apparently Ted talked with Hank. "I'm not the one who's been hiding something. It's not my fault you got called out on it."

Sierra pivoted and faced her husband. "What is going on?"

"Ask Faith."

Sierra pointed at her husband. "I want you to tell me."

Hank took in a deep breath. The anger evaporated and he looked at his wife with hurt and sadness in his eyes. "I asked Faith the other day if she'd quit talking about me borrowing her car. I didn't want you to know I was going out that night. So I lied and told Faith the boys tampered with ours and needed hers."

Sierra bit her lip. "Why would you lie about that?"

"Because I didn't want you to know I was signing up for the cage match they're having at the high school tonight."

"What?" Sierra and I both said.

"I should be the one supporting my family, not my wife." Hank looked at the ground. "If I win, I'll make five hundred dollars for one night's work."

Sierra's hand fluttered to her mouth. "That's not work. That's dangerous."

"What choice do I have? No one would hire me," Hank said. "It might be easier now that Michael isn't around."

"Michael got you fired?" I asked.

Hank's eyes turned cold when he looked at me. "Yeah. Want to run off and tell that to the Detective? Michael enjoyed sharing our exploits as kids. Except he'd leave out the kids and him part from it. I showed up the morning of the art show, but the security team leader told me they didn't need me anymore. Heard about my 'brushes with the law.'"

I shifted my weight from foot to foot. I didn't know he had brushes with the law. Hank must have guessed what I was thinking because he rattled off the details.

"There was hiding our third grade teacher's purse. Of course, I only buried it under the beanbag chairs, but Michael told it as if I stole it and only returned it when the authorities were called. Then there was the stolen county vehicle. Michael's dad was on the school board and put a huge magnetic sign on the driver's side door. Michael and I borrowed the car one day and his mom reported it stolen."

I remembered that car. It was a big joke among the students at the high school. We always wondered if Michael's dad had a badge and a uniform to go along with it. Michael had always been a good storyteller, weaving tales that had everyone rolling with laughter, especially the ones about his and Hank's recreational activities.

"Faith thought since I didn't tell her the real reasons I borrowed her car, and since the boys saw someone who looked like me in a photo, that I'm the murderer."

"You told the police that Hank killed Michael?" Sierra gaped at me.

"I didn't say that! I just told them about the inconsistencies in what Hank said—" I started explaining.

"Don't forget you said I had access to the store key and a motive for destroying all the layouts," Hank finished.

Sierra tossed her hair over her shoulder, anger smoldering in her eyes. "Is this your new way to get Marilyn off the hook, pointing the finger at Hank?"

"I'm not pointing the finger at anyone. I told Detective Roget the truth, just like I did with Marilyn. You told me I did what I had to do and shouldn't feel guilty about it. Now it changes because it's Hank coming under suspicion?"

"It changes because you're using bits and pieces of information, not the whole story, to find someone else to blame. If Hank being in a photograph, having access to the store key, lying about why he needed a car, getting fired from a job, all adds up to his guilt, then why doesn't the evidence found by the police add up to hers?"

That was a good question. And I didn't have an answer.

I tried sleeping, but the distant and near past collided in my head. Pictures of the day Michael died, the crop where Marilyn whacked away at her husband's image, Adam's court-martial, my near court-martial, the betrayal on Sierra's face, the fact I did to Hank what others had done to me. I assumed his guilt on random details that pointed to what I wanted to believe rather than the truth.

Pushing myself up on my elbow, I looked at the clock on my

bedside table. Midnight. For two hours, I re-lived my life and my mistakes and each time arrived at one conclusion: if there was a way to miss the obvious, I managed it. Tossing off the covers, I stood and pattered barefoot down the stairs. The only way I would clear my head was shake off the unhappiness swirling around me.

I needed to scrapbook.

Working on layouts reminded me of the pleasant times of my life. I saw the love of my grandmothers in the photos. Some people scrapped the good and bad times in their lives, but I was strictly a "happy" scrapper. The photos of shameful and painful times were kept locked in the closet. I relived them enough in my mind, I didn't need them documented in an album. But for the happy moments, I needed a physical reminder to prove they occurred more often in my life.

I made a quick stop in the kitchen. Opening up the refrigerator, I peered inside and found fruits, vegetables and a chunk of cheese. I shut the door and searched the cabinets and found a half-empty bag of chocolate chips, noodles, soup and crackers. Cheese and crackers would have to do, plus a handful of chocolate chips. I tossed the rich morsels into my mouth as I prepared a healthier late night snack.

Carrying my plate of cubed Monterey Jack cheese and butter crackers, I walked over to the craft table. I juggled the items while I cleared off a spot in the corner. I never finished cleaning, so I'd simply have to create amidst the chaos. Appropriate considering the state of my life.

Nope. Only pleasant and happy thoughts allowed.

The easiest way for me to reach a peaceful state of mind was focusing on the business side of my life rather than the personal. We took photos at every single Scrap This event and I planned on creating pages for advertising use. Photos of Roget and Steve working on layouts would've been great.

Humming a made up tune, I gathered up photos and white textured cardstock. The photos would pop off the page rather than using the color of the cardstock to grab a person's attention. I placed the choices onto the table and sorted through the pictures. After choosing three from our last customer crop, I put them on the cardstock and arranged, then rearranged, them. Once I settled on the placement, I reached for the adhesive.

None. I searched through the supplies on the table, but came up empty. When was the last time I used the dispenser?

I closed my eyes. My cropping tote appeared in my mind. I took scrapping necessities to the Art Benefit Show in case any layouts needed fixing. The packed bag still sat by the front door where I placed it on Saturday.

My stomach rumbled and I snagged a cheese and cracker sandwich as I headed toward the front door. My purse was on top of it. Linda's layout. I could fix hers and have at least one co-worker happy with me. I carefully carried it to my work table.

A jagged hole marred the pattern paper and the tip of the photograph near her husband's head. I cringed. Poor Linda. I studied the layout, turning the page in different directions as I contemplated the best way to repair the rip while maintaining the integrity and style of Linda's page.

The easiest solution was placing a fabric flower over the hole, but the embellishment didn't complement the photo of her husband and son. Linda's handsome son grinned out, his arm draped around his dad's shoulder. The older man had his head turned toward his son, a look of pride and affection glowing on his face.

I examined the products in my craft space. A piece of ribbon or fabric twisted and stapled to form a remembrance ribbon would give the layout a feeling of reverence. I ran my fingers across the glass jars on the shelf. The soft pastel colors spoke of femininity.

Until tonight, I had no need for masculine colors when I cropped at home. The photographs I did have from my time in the Army were kept in a box in my closet, under an old blanket. I didn't destroy them because totally obliterating my past left me nervous, almost as if I would repeat my doom by not having a reminder of it.

I reached for a jar containing a light beige ribbon with a white strip stitched down the middle and placed it on top of the layout.

The light brown clashed with the tone of the page. I rummaged in the jar and none of the other choices fit. The colors and shades gave the layout a cheery, almost comical tone. I'd hold off on adding the embellishment until tomorrow when I had the store's stock to choose from. This wasn't a case of just repairing a display project, but mending a work of the heart for a grieving widow. Picking up the protected layout, I studied it for any more damage. A brad crinkled up the beginning of the journaling box, smashing a few words of the text.

With care, I slipped the page from the protector and laid it on the table. Using my nail, I smoothed out the corner of the four-inch text box. The paper twisted and I sucked in a breath. Please don't let me have caused more damage. Another slip of cardstock peeked out from underneath. The brad had been used for a hidden journaling panel.

Should I check the hidden box? It wasn't fair to invade her privacy, even with good intentions. As I moved the top layer back into place, newsprint slid into my view. It was an article, probably her husband's obituary. The nice thing to do was make sure the document was intact. If needed, I could go down to the newspaper and get a replacement copy.

The article was attached to black cardstock by a piece of white ribbon tied at the top of the mat. Another journaling box peeked out from underneath. Gently, I lifted the obituary.

My stomach plummeted and I felt light-headed.

"Widow's claim denied." On the left hand side of the newspaper article was a small picture of Michael Kane walking down the courthouse steps.

"There might be another pair of scissors missing." Linda's comment from the other day entered my mind. Detective Roget hadn't publically spoken about the scissors. How did Linda know there was a pair missing?

Don't start conjuring up another suspect. Get facts, not guesses.

I went upstairs and searched online for more information

about the accident that claimed Jim Anderson's life. A logging truck had overturned on a winding road one foggy evening and the trees rolled off the truck. One of the logs crashed into Jim's car and crushed him. I shuddered.

According to some accounts of the accident, the truck driver had fallen asleep. The driver denied the accusation, claiming Jim Anderson's small compact car collided into his rig. That didn't add up to me. How could a small car cause so much damage to a large rig that it jackknifed? Did the driver notice Jim Anderson's car at the last minute and swerve, causing the load to tip and break the chains holding the logs in place?

Jim had been given a ticket early that night for driving ten miles over the speed limit during poor weather conditions, and it factored into the jurors' verdict, giving them reasonable doubt. It was possible Jim Anderson didn't heed the warning and continued driving at an unsafe speed, thereby contributing to the accident—and his own death.

Poor Linda. How awful to sit in the courtroom and hear your beloved spouse blamed for his own death. I wished I could read the court transcript. What questions did Michael Kane ask the driver of the logging truck? Did Michael's defense help the driver get off scot-free and leave Linda Anderson destitute?

Linda had come in one day begging for a job. She mentioned her husband died and left inadequate insurance. She had no job skills since she'd been a stay-at-home mother, then a stay-at-home wife, for the last twenty-five years. My grandmothers took pity on her and offered her a job on the spot even though our finances were probably as dire as Linda's. My grandmothers' compassion outweighed any business concerns.

What would I do with this information? Linda had a good—or a potentially good—reason for wanting Michael dead. I leaned back in the chair and stared at the screen. But just because she had a good reason didn't mean she had the opportunity, means, and temperament to do it.

I've cried wolf so many times, nobody would believe me even if

I had a written confession and a YouTube link of the murder.

I scrubbed at my eyes as weariness settled into my bones and my soul. I hated when people had blamed me for a crime based on no real evidence, and I'd been doing it to others to help Marilyn. Hadn't Linda been through enough? Did I really want to walk up to her tomorrow and ask for her alibi? I could do it with a little more finesse.

Or could I? Wasn't that my biggest problem right now with Ted? Every time I tried to help Marilyn, I made matters worse. I wasn't a subtle sleuth. I could do the smart thing, hand over all the information to the police. But what information did I really have? Michael Kane was a defense attorney for the truck company whose driver drove the semi that killed Jim Anderson. Was it fair to drag Linda into this mess just because I believed Marilyn innocent? It was one thing to take a good hard look at Annette Holland, but quite another to go after a widow because of one coincidence.

A quick check of our inventory would clear it right up without creating more unnecessary drama. Our town had enough of the necessary kind right now.

I kept hearing Annette say Michael told her he was afraid of "her." What if he hadn't meant afraid of his wife, but the woman he ensured lost a wrongful death settlement? Another issue I needed to clear up before I brought my new theory to Ted.

The insurance company was victorious. Jim Anderson slandered. Linda heart-broken and destitute.

Where was Linda when Michael was stabbed? If anyone had a solid motive to kill the man, it was Linda.

TWENTY-SEVEN

My plan for doing more Monday morning quarterbacking of Detective Roget's decision to arrest Marilyn was in jeopardy. And the day had just started. I needed a "plan B" and I had spent all of Sunday coming up with a "plan A." A simple yet brilliant plan thwarted by Grandma Hope.

Yesterday, I had pretended to be sick and skipped church. Having a run-in with Sierra and Hank was inevitable and I'd rather have it happen at the store than in the sanctuary. Not everyone needed to know about my meddling. Mrs. Newsome had gotten a new smartphone and would have any "discussion" up on her blog before the pastor got the words of the first hymn on the overhead.

Apparently, my moaning and whimpering were worthy of an Oscar as Hope had marched into my bedroom this morning to take me to the doctor. I had two choices: admit I lied yesterday, or be taken to the doctor like a child. I saw the doctor. Even scarier than tracking down a murderer was admitting to my grandmothers I lied about church.

When I finally arrived at work, a stack of layouts were on the counter and Hank was repairing the display boards. I smiled and waved but he—and Sierra—ignored me. This was going to be a long day. I slipped my purse under the counter.

Linda gave me a friendly smile and patted my arm. "It'll work out."

If she knew what I found out, she might not be so happy about it working out. "Thanks for coming in and helping. I was running way behind today."

"It's nice to be able to return the favor."

I fingered the layouts. "The croppers redid their layouts?"

"After church, Linda and I helped your grandmothers' come up with a plan. We extended the contest three days and decided the contestants could use photos from the show or any other one that illustrated how art is important in their life," Sierra piped up from the display racks.

"Thanks for letting me know."

"You would've already known if you hadn't ditched your responsibility to them because you were too interested in hanging out with the detective."

"I wasn't—"

Sierra gave me the I'm-done-with-you hand.

"Ignore her," Linda whispered. "She'll see the truth soon enough."

Or I would if Linda went home. "I appreciate all your hard work and filling in for me. Since I'm here, you can take off if you'd like." Please, please, please.

Linda pouted slightly. "If you don't need me, I'll go. But I don't mind working today, even if you can't pay me. It's better than my quiet house."

"No. That's not it. We're doing fine." I grinned. "I just wanted you to go about your day if you had any plans. Lunch out. Gardening. Reading a great book. Whatever."

"I'll just put the layouts up on the board," Linda said.

Sierra shot a questioning look over at me.

This time I ignored her. I needed Linda out of the store so she didn't see me check the inventory and put two and two together. Of course, that would only matter if she was the murderer.

While Linda put the layouts up, I scanned the inventory sheet Jasper left and jotted down the number of scissors the police took. Now to figure out a way to compare it to our current inventory. If a pair of scissors was missing, then I needed to figure out if Linda helped the scissors find their way into Michael's chest.

"Going down a checklist?" Sierra asked as she walked toward the back of the store. "Who you accusing next?"

"I'm sorry I hurt your feelings. I only answered what the detective asked."

"I'd be careful if I were you, Linda," Sierra sang. "Faith is being awfully friendly lately. Might be a motive there besides friendship."

Linda paled.

"That's not fair, Sierra." Though actually spot on.

Sierra rolled her eyes and continued reorganizing the supplies. "Whatever, Faith."

My friend's words and attitude bruised my spirit. I needed to talk to someone who'd give me the benefit of the doubt, even when it appeared I didn't deserve it. My grandmothers would, but I didn't want them knowing what I involved myself in this time.

Grabbing the strap of my purse, I yanked it out. Papers slid out along with my purse. Sierra could clean up the mess. I headed for the front door. A nice brisk stroll would cool me off.

"Where are you going?" Sierra asked.

"Out. You and Linda have everything under control."

"Say hi to Detective Roget for me."

I slammed the door and marched across the parking lot. Let Sierra think what she wanted. Though I wished she kept it to herself. My low-key look into Linda's possible involvement blew up before I even started.

In fifteen minutes, I made it to the courthouse and tugged open the door.

"Morning, Faith." Mrs. Dawn Altwright, my former Bible school teacher, said. "Haven't seen you here. Anything I can help with?"

"Just wanted to visit Steve." I held in a groan. The man was working. What if he had a client in his office or was in court? "Do you know if he's available?"

She winked at me and pointed the way. "For you, darling, I'm sure he is."

I walked down the hallway and stopped in front of the door with the name Steve Davis on it. Taking a deep breath, I pushed open the door and hoped I wasn't making another mistake in my quest for justice.

I stepped inside and froze. I had never been in Steve's office before. Unlike his immaculate house, which looked like he didn't really live there, his office was a poster child for chaos. Papers and folders took up every available space. In the corner was a table holding a microwave and a box of clean plasticware.

What would my grandmothers say upon learning Steve wasn't perfect?

"Give me an hour and I can get the info for you." Steve signed off from his telephone call. "This is a shock."

No kidding.

"Something amusing about my office?" Steve plucked a small stack of folders from a chair. "In case you'd like to sit. Don't want you thinking I'm bossing you around."

Okay, I had been a little rough on Steve lately, but it was important I establish some boundaries as my grandmothers ramped up their match-matching duties.

Photographs sat on the window sill behind him. There was one of Steve as a young child on the beach with his parents. Another showed an adult Steve with his dad at a golf course, and the one next to it was taken at last year's Christmas tree lighting. I was in between Hope and Cheryl. Hope had her arm linked through Steve's and her head leaned toward him.

The bookshelf held a paddle ball set, a handheld video game, and stacks of law books. In the corner behind his desk were a pillow and a blanket.

He caught my wandering eye. "I need an unwinding method during the day."

"Do you live here?" I sat on the soft cushioned chair.

"Sometimes it's necessary. There's a couch in the lounge."

Steve walked around from behind the desk and sat on the edge. Closer to me.

The scent of his cologne revved up my pulse. There was just something about the man that made me think wicked thoughts. Maybe it was because he was off-limits. Or perhaps the combination of conservative mixed with biker was irresistible. "If you're ever stuck here, you can give me a call and I'll bring you some dinner."

"I'll do that."

We stared at each for a while. The room felt hotter than it had a moment ago. One of us needed to get to the conversation and it had to be me since I was the one with the topic.

"I wanted to talk to you about something." I licked my lips as my mouth had somehow grown dry.

Steven nodded, never taking his eyes off me.

I squirmed.

"Please don't let this be about the Kane case."

I felt a little bad. Steve might have held some hopes I was popping in because I missed him. He had stopped coming by my house unannounced. "I found out something that might be the proof of Marilyn's innocence."

"Stop right there." Steve held up his hands in a don't-come-any-further gesture. "I don't want to hear anymore and I don't want to know anymore."

"I need your help," I pleaded, barely refraining from pouting.

"No."

No? I didn't expect that from Steve. "Why not?"

"It doesn't look good for a prosecutor to take on a side job of private investigating. And I refuse to help you mess up your life."

I sprung from the chair. "Mess up my life by finding the truth?"

Steve slowly stood. "Mess up your life by being so stubborn you hurt other people. That's not you, Faith."

"I'm helping, not hurting."

"Sierra?"

My shoulders slumped forward. One person.

"Yourself." Steve tipped my chin up with his finger. "I won't take part in that."

I jerked back a step and my knees hit the back of the chair. I flopped into the chair and pushed myself right back up. "I'm not."

At least I didn't think so. I didn't want anyone controlling or managing my life for me. I'd make my own decisions, good and bad. I needed support, not advice. Well-meaning or not.

"I won't be used." Steve walked around the desk and stood behind his office chair, the desk a barrier between us.

"I'm not..." The remainder of the sentence stuck in my throat. The intensity in Steve's fathomless brown eyes rendered me silent.

He leaned forward, never breaking eye contact. "Your grandmothers raved about you and I was intrigued. When I saw you the first time, I knew I wanted to get to know you better. But you were reserved, leery of me and everyone else, except for Cheryl and Hope. I didn't know why, but I knew you needed space. I respected that. "

"I appreciated that."

For the first few months, he treaded carefully around me, and my grandmothers. It was hard as my grandmothers had depended on him for so long and he was a part of their life. I liked having a hot guy around. He was wonderful to look at and having my grandmothers' focus on him gave me the breathing room I needed.

He offered friendship. I accepted it. Even added in some harmless flirting. It was nice knowing a handsome man found me attractive. Steve was safe. He never crossed the line I drew, which was both disappointing and a huge relief.

"I apologize for overstepping your boundaries," Steve said. "I never intended for my concern to come across as controlling. Your grandmothers wanted you safe. I wanted you safe, and like most males, figured if physical harm came from your investigating, I could handle that better than you."

"I know you meant well." I twisted my fingers in the hem of my shirt. Steve and I never had a conversation like this. We hinted around about our feelings and joked with each other. I wasn't sure how I felt about laying it all out like this. Or at least Steve doing it. My contribution so far was clichéd one-liners.

"I want you to need me, Faith, because you need *me*. I want you to want me, Faith, because you want *me*."

"I don't think you understand me," I croaked out. "I want you in my life. Need you."

With each word I said, Steve walked closer. "I don't think you understand me."

Steve wrapped an arm around my back and pulled me closer. His mouth settled over mine. Shocked, I remained still except for my trembling knees, threatening not to hold up my weight. Not a real problem as one of Steve's arms tightened around me while the other hand trailed up my back and cupped the back of my head.

My hands inched their way from his chest, to his shoulders, then clasped around his neck, increasing the pressure of his mouth on mine. Reality was so much better than fantasy. Steve's lips left mine and disappointment swelled in me. The feeling left when his fingers tangled into my hair and he dropped a feather-light kiss onto my cheek.

"Steve..." I breathed his name.

He cradled my head to his chest. "When you come to the place where you're ready to trust again, Faith, let me know."

I nodded and moved back a few inches.

"I'll tell Cheryl and Hope that I'll come to your aid, as they put it, if you request it." A flash of humor broke into the seriousness of his expression. "You know where I work and where I live. Knock. Yell. Send your cat over to caterwaul at my window. Whenever you're ready, I intend to be there. But I can't promise I'll wait forever."

TWENTY-EIGHT

On shaky legs, I walked back to Scrap This. Was Steve stepping out of my life unless I specifically asked for his attention? That's not what I wanted. I liked him stopping by on occasion. I liked knowing I brightened his day. It was nice being wanted by somebody, even if I had no intention of the friendship progressing into a relationship.

But was that fair to Steve?

I tugged the door open and stepped inside. I saw Sierra and three shoppers, but no Linda. "Did Linda go home?"

Sierra finished ringing up a customer. "Yes. That's what you told her to do."

"Thanks. I'll be back in the office. I need to check on inventory."

"Just make your private phone calls out here." Sierra walked from behind the counter. "I'll go clean up the break room before I head home. It got messy last night since we were short staffed. Linda will be back for the afternoon shift. Poor lady is probably just sitting around the corner waiting to return. Happy prying."

I ignored Sierra and pulled up the store's inventory on the front computer. We usually didn't check from the main computer, didn't want any confusion if one document was updated and another wasn't, but Sierra wasn't cooperating. My heart plummeted. One pair of scissors was missing.

The phone rang. It stopped just as I reached for it. Sierra picked up in the break room. Maybe there was a small chance she'd forgive me soon. Then I'd start the process all over with Linda. If I was wrong. If I was right...

How would I approach Linda this afternoon? Hopefully with

more finesse than I handled the situation with my other "suspects."

By late afternoon, I started worrying about Linda. She was usually ten to twenty minutes late, but not two hours. Had Sierra's hint that Linda was next on my suspect list make her skip town? Or knowing the real truth was coming out, she went—I shuddered and stopped my mind from completing the thought. Maybe I should call the police station and have someone check up on her.

I picked up the phone and called Sierra at home. "Did Linda call and say she couldn't work this afternoon?"

"Yes. And I don't blame her for not coming back," Sierra's tense voice attacked me through the phone line. "She's not as stupid as she looks. She figured you out."

"I'm not this evil person you've made me out to be."

"Come on, you've been hiding her layout from her. What kind of person does that?"

"What?" I had put her layout in my purse. Was that what slipped out? There went half my evidence.

The boys were screaming in the background and Sierra sighed. "There is a battle being re-enacted in the bathroom, something about sinking a ship. I need to stop it before my house floods."

Before I said goodbye, Sierra hung up the phone.

Perfect. I'd lost a friend and my evidence. I didn't know how to repair the friendship, but maybe there was another person who might have some evidence for me. Annette. I needed to hurry because her office closed at six.

"Allan, Taylor and Gilder," a bored voice answered.

"I'd like to speak to Miss Holland, please."

The voice tightened. "This is her."

"Annette, this is Faith Hunter."

"I don't want to talk to you."

"I'm sorry," I blurted out. "I hurt you. I know you loved Michael."

"I still do," she whispered. "Even though he's gone, I can't just stop loving him."

My heart commiserated with her. "I hate to bring you any

more pain, as you're still grieving."

The line was silent for a full thirty seconds. "Thank you," Annette said, tears evident in her voice.

"For what?" I asked, surprised at the trace of gratitude in her voice.

"For knowing Michael's death hurts me." She sniffed. "What would you like to ask?"

"If this isn't a good time..." I trailed off, now feeling bad for bringing up this painful topic while she was at work.

"What do you need?"

"Did Michael say he was scared of Marilyn? Did he name her specifically?"

"No."

"Could it have been someone else?"

"I guess." She hesitated. "But I don't know any other woman who was mad at him. Besides his wife. And her mother. And, well, actually his mother."

Interesting to know, but I doubted either of the mothers killed him. "You said a woman came up to you at the show, said something happened to Michael."

"Yes."

"Can you describe her?"

"Late fifties, gray hair, average height, a little overweight."

It sounded like Linda. "Can I bring a picture by and show you? Tomorrow morning. It would be a huge help."

"Actually, I'd rather you not stop by here. My boss isn't happy with the firm getting this type of exposure."

"Would you mind stopping by the store then?"

She paused so long I thought she might have hung up. "Fine. But I can't be there until seven-thirty."

"Thank you, Annette. This means a lot. I'll see you at seven-thirty tonight."

She mumbled a goodbye and hung up.

Steve didn't want to know about the case anymore. Detective Roget didn't either. Someone needed this information so Marilyn could go home to her family.

Bob Roget! Okay, the PI said he wouldn't take the case, but I'm sure he could give me advice on handing off the information.

There was more than one woman in her fifties with gray hair in Eden. But how many would know Annette was Michael's girlfriend? Who was I kidding? Any of them who lived in Eden, worked in Eden, or listened while they spent even five minutes in Eden.

I quickly called Bob, but it went straight to voicemail. Did I want to leave a message? While I contemplated my decision, Bob's strong, friendly voice gave me an emergency contact number. Before I dialed, I looked up the number, making sure Bob's emergency number wasn't the non-emergency number for the Morgantown police department. Clear.

I punched in the number.

"Bob Roget."

"Hi Bob, this is Faith. We met the other day."

"Yes, how could I forget my younger brother's nemesis."

"I'm not actually his nemesis."

"Annoyance. Pain in the tush."

"I'll go along with that."

A deep rumble echoed across the connection. "What can I do for you, Faith?"

"I'm calling for some professional advice."

"While I enjoy needling my brother now and then, this might be taking it too far."

"Please. I don't have anyone else to bounce my ideas off of. Everyone has already said no."

"I hate saying no to a beautiful damsel, but I'm not sure this is a good idea. My brother is the detective on this case."

"Ted firmly believes I'm the annoying lady crying wolf and that I might be using this to show my interest in him."

"Really?" Bob sounded interested in my plight now.

"Steve believes I'm being stubborn—"

"Whoever Steve is, he has a point."

"A prosecutor in Eden, another reason he turned me down.

And I can't ask my grandmothers' for help—"

"Okay, enough. I certainly don't want sweet, older women be-coming involved in a murder. My mother would kill me. She raised a gentleman."

I should have a talk with her about Ted.

"Give me the details," Bob said.

After taking in a deep breath, and uttering a prayer of thanks, I launched into my newest theory. I heard a tapping over the phone. Was Bob sending out Morse code over the wires or pounding out an email for Ted to arrest me?

"You at home right now?" Bob asked.

"No. I have to close the store first." And wait for Annette.

"Why don't you see if one of the other employees can come in? Keep you company as I sort this out."

Now Bob sounded worried. "My grandmothers had today off and I don't want to call them. I'll be done in about an hour. And Sierra is—"

The backdoor rattled.

Very forgiving. "Looks like Sierra decided to come in since Linda never showed."

"Good. I'll give you a call back. I want to check on some of this information."

"Thanks." I disconnected the call.

I rang out the register and started work on reconciling the re-ceipts. "I'm doing the receipts, Sierra. Can you return the merchan-dise to its proper place? I appreciate you—"

The curtain jerked opened. "I'm not Sierra."

TWENTY-NINE

Linda stalked toward me, her right hand behind her back, lips pressed together and brows drawn low over her eyes.

I forced out a friendly, non-suspicious smile. "Hey! I'm glad to see you. You did a great job hanging up the layouts."

Linda whipped her hand from behind her back. She pointed a pistol at me. "Put your hands on the counter."

I gaped at her.

"Don't act surprised." She tightened her finger on the trigger. "Hands on the counter. Now."

I complied. I had finally figured out the culprit, but felt no satisfaction in being right.

"It's good no one remembered Marilyn's key." Linda shook the gun at me. "Her mother had no problem giving it to me. It was nice someone trusted me. You never did."

"That wasn't a lack of trust, Linda. It was a lack of cash. We couldn't afford to get another key made." I inched my hand toward my cell phone.

"Hands on the counter and keep them still." She stomped a few steps closer.

I pressed my hands back onto the countertop. Linda destroyed all the layouts. She must have been afraid one of the photos from the art show would prove she killed Michael. The Hooligans searching for their mom must have scared Linda. Made her realize there could be proof of her whereabouts, or lack thereof.

"Come out from behind there." She waggled the gun at me. "And keep your hands up."

I raised my hands and walked around the counter. "Why did

you kill Michael?"

"Don't play dumb, Faith. You know exactly why. Does it really matter anyway?"

She had a point. Dead was dead. And murdering someone for any reason, unless it was self-defense, meant prison. Of course, killing two people upped the number of years on a person's prison term.

I tried talking sense into her. "We can't let Marilyn go to prison for something she didn't do. Think of her children."

"You should have stayed out of this."

"And I would have, but you blamed Marilyn." Not to mention the small guilt of ratting out a friend.

"I didn't!" Tears plopped from Linda's chin to the floor. "I sent Annette Holland over to Michael. I figured the police would blame her, find her next to him. What kind of man flaunts his girlfriend to his wife?"

I remained silent.

"I knew what kind of man. The kind of man who said lies about my husband. Lies that stole my son from me. He moved away because he couldn't handle the gossip about his father's death."

I started to feel bad for her, actually wanted to hug her, but kept my hands on the countertop.

She raised the gun and aimed at my head. "Why did you steal my layout?"

I noticed Linda knew as much about guns as she did scrapbooking techniques. Not much. The safety was on. "I'm sorry Michael hurt you and said those horrible things about your husband. He was wrong."

"I can't go to jail." She sobbed. "Just give me the layout Darlene made. That's all I want."

She thought I still had one piece of evidence proving her guilt. "I don't have it. The police do."

"You're lying."

"So are you."

She gaped at me and her hand shook.

"How stupid do you think I am? Now that I know you killed Michael, you won't let me walk out of here." I knew she couldn't shoot me, but she could still attack me. I needed something to defend myself with.

And thanks to Ted, we didn't have any dangerous scissors on the shelves.

The back door rattled. Linda pivoted toward the storage area.

Shrieking, I charged Linda. The two opposing noises, people ramming through the back door and my banshee scream, confused her. She fumbled with the gun, fingers twisting and turning as she tried pulling the trigger. She pressed the trigger back. Nothing.

Confused, she stared at the gun. I grabbed her around the waist with one arm and reached for the gun with my other hand. Wrapping my left leg around her right leg, I tugged with more strength than I knew I had. We both fell to the ground. My elbow smacked the floor and pain shot up my arm, but I held on so tight it was like we were duct taped together.

Linda struggled under me, wailing, screaming, desperate to keep the gun in her possession.

I ducked as she swung the gun at my head. I pinned Linda with my forearm and yanked the pistol from her hand.

Breathing heavily, I tossed it to the side.

"Police! No one move!" Ted, Jasper and Steve filled the room.

I kept Linda flattened on the floor. "Didn't anyone ever tell you not to play with guns? You're lucky you didn't kill yourself."

"Faith, are you okay?" Steve dragged me off of Linda. Ted yanked her to her knees, then cuffed her. I pushed strands of hair out of my face and dusted off my pants.

"She couldn't have hurt me. The safety was on." I stood. "She killed Michael."

"We know." Steve and Ted exchanged a look.

"Isn't that great?" I jammed my hands on my waist. "You both knew and neglected to tell me my employee was a murderer."

Ted rolled his eyes. "Look how well that worked with Marilyn."

Jasper led the wailing Linda out the back door.

"I'll be right back," Roget said, following Jasper and the criminal mastermind.

The adrenaline in my body evaporated. Lightness filled my head and I swayed.

"Want help?" Steve wrapped an arm around me, drawing me close.

"I need to sit."

Steve lowered us to the cool tile floor, now wrapping both arms around me.

For a moment, I allowed myself the luxury of basking in the safety and snuggled into his embrace. My eyes drifted closed and I wished I could stay there. Steve smoothed a hand down my hair then rested his cheek on top of my head.

"I should've listened to you. Thank God Roget's brother did." He whispered into my hair. "She could've..." He cleared his throat.

I forced my lids opened and looked at Steve. The feelings he had for me were clear in his eyes. I took in a deep breath. "You can't like me like that."

A small smile flashed on Steve's face then faded. "And why not?"

"Because it would hurt you if you did."

He trailed a finger down my cheek. "It hurts me when I pretend I don't."

It was time. See if he stayed or went. "I was almost a convicted felon."

"Then maybe I should look into working for a defense firm. I'll change careers. I can be a carpenter. A private eye." A light sparked in his eyes and he placed a quick kiss on my lips. "Don't worry, Roget wouldn't have arrested you. I think he finds your interference a little amusing."

I didn't elaborate, allowing Steve to think I meant Ted. Now wasn't the time for confessions. Besides, I'd rather let things continue as they were: friendship with a soul-shaking kiss every now and then.

I pushed out of his embrace. "Don't do that."

"What?" He pulled back and traced a finger around my mouth.

"That. And get into the detective business. Trust me, it's a lousy job."

"Remember that the next time you think about getting involved in a case." Steve stood and helped me up.

"I seriously doubt there will be a next time. How did you and Ted figure out it was Linda?"

"I wanted to help out by making a layout for your contest. I went through my pictures from the show and noticed some near the scene of the crime. I took the memory card to Roget and he enlarged the area."

"And he saw Linda."

"Yep. Then Bob called and we came straight here." Steve nodded toward the front window. "There's also the fact Annette Holland saw it all through the window."

Annette's nose was pressed against the glass. She waved to me and held out her cell phone.

Bright and early the next morning, Marilyn raced into Scrap This. "Thank you!" She wrapped her arms around me and squeezed.

I hugged back, then gently pried her grip from around my neck. "You're welcome."

No sooner had I escaped her clasp, Sierra pushed past me and hugged Marilyn.

"I'm so glad you're back. Let me tell you what's been going on here." Sierra draped an arm around Marilyn and bumped me out of the way with her hip.

So that was how it was going to be. Well, Marilyn was grateful for my sleuthing, so she'd give me the opportunity to tell her the real story.

Darlene maneuvered around us and hung up the new entries that trickled in. Being down two employees, and short on cash, convinced my grandmothers and me to accept Darlene's offer of free help.

Over her head, my eyes caught the sight of a handsome assistant prosecuting attorney. Steve wore faded jeans and a dark blue t-shirt, a hint of tattoo showed where his t-shirt bunched up from holding a motorcycle helmet under his arm. On a work day. Steve was revealing another side of him. Maybe there was more "bad boy biker" to him than I knew.

My heart twittered and then spun out of control when I spotted Ted standing in the corner. He stared at me, an unreadable expression on his face.

Hank and the Hooligans had arrived with a balloon bouquet and a cake. "Heard there was a need for a party. Welcome back, Marilyn."

"I knew I could count on you," Sierra rushed over to her husband and linked arms with him. The happily married couple shot a glare at me, then focused on Marilyn, all smiles and laughter.

"Good job, Miss Private Eye." Steve placed one around my shoulders and the other around my waist and reeled me into his arms. He frowned when I remained rigid.

"I didn't do such a good job." I nodded toward the newcomers.

"Sierra will come around. Give her time." Steve tipped my chin up, his gaze devouring my lips.

"My grandmothers are watching," I whispered.

Laughter rumbled from him. "I don't think they'll mind." Seriousness deepened the chocolate brown of Steve's eyes. "Do you?"

Ted saluted me and walked out the door. My emotions felt like a roller coaster. Up and down, fast then slow, high in the air with anticipation and then plummeting to the ground in dread.

Steve cupped my face in his hands and lowered his mouth to mine.

Behind us, two little boys made retching sounds while a third burst into tears.

"But I cleaned up all the mess," Henry wailed. "I thought Miss Faith liked me best."

Reader's Discussion Guide

1. Faith finds herself guilted into helping a friend. Have you ever been in a similar situation and how did you react?

2. Do you think Faith's decision to keep her past hidden stops her from moving past it? Do you think she is being unfair to her friends and family by not allowing them the opportunity to help her through it? How do you think her keeping her past from her grandmothers will affect their relationship?

3. Faith risks the skeletons coming out of her closet to help a friend. Do you find Faith's willingness to risk her reputation for a friend as a strength or weakness in this situation?

4. This story offers a glimpse into the competitive side of the hobby. Did this view surprise you or not?

5. After Scrap This is vandalized, a reporter writes an inaccurate description of a class and it works in the scrapbook store's benefit. Have you ever had an error work out in your favor?

6. Do you think Faith's drive to right the wrongs done to her hampers her ability to solve the case? Because she makes impetuous decisions? Or do you think her experience helps her to keep strong when others doubt her?

7. Detective Ted Roget's feelings toward Faith change as the case progresses. Does his growing attraction affect how he pursues the case? Do you think his attraction factored into his decision of revealing to Faith what he learned about her?

8. During the course of the investigation, Faith discovers information that places a friend's husband on her suspect list. Do you think Faith handled this twist well? Do you think her friend's reaction was fair?

9. Steve finally voices his feelings to Faith rather than just showing them through his actions. Why did his words have a bigger impact on Faith than his actions? How does the declaration now change their 'safe' relationship?

10. Part of Faith's job is coming up with classes for the scrapbooking store. Have you ever taken a scrapbook class, or any class, to learn a new hobby or skill?

11. When she's feeling overwhelmed, Faith finds scrapbooking lessens her stress. What activities do you find as a pick me up? Do you enjoy them as often as you should?

12. Faith had previously closed herself off to relationships, now she's willing to reconsider that stance. Who do you think is the better fit for Faith: Steve or Ted, and why?

CHRISTINA FREEBURN

Christina Freeburn wrote her first book in the ninth grade, mostly during algebra class (which she doesn't recommend). She served in the JAG Corps of the US Army and also worked as a paralegal, librarian, and secretary. She lives in West Virginia with her husband, children, a dog, and a rarely seen cat except by those who are afraid or allergic to felines. When not writing or reading, she can be found in her scrapbook area among layouts, paper, bling and stuffed Disney characters. Her novel, *Cropped to Death*, brings together her love of mysteries, scrapbooking, and West Virginia.

Henery Press Mystery Books

And finally, before you go...
Here are a few other mysteries
you might enjoy:

LOWCOUNTRY BOIL

Susan M. Boyer

A Liz Talbot Mystery (#1)

Private Investigator Liz Talbot is a modern Southern belle: she blesses hearts and takes names. She carries her Sig 9 in her Kate Spade handbag, and her golden retriever, Rhett, rides shotgun in her hybrid Escape. When her grandmother is murdered, Liz hightails it back to her South Carolina island home to find the killer.

She's fit to be tied when her police-chief brother shuts her out of the investigation, so she opens her own. Then her long-dead best friend pops in and things really get complicated. When more folks start turning up dead in this small seaside town, Liz must use more than just her wits and charm to keep her family safe, chase down clues from the hereafter, and catch a psychopath before he catches her.

Available at booksellers nationwide and online

Visit www.henerypress.com for details

DOUBLE WHAMMY

Gretchen Archer

A Davis Way Crime Caper (#1)

Davis Way thinks she's hit the jackpot when she lands a job as the fifth wheel on an elite security team at the fabulous Bellissimo Resort and Casino in Biloxi, Mississippi. But once there, she runs straight into her ex-ex husband, a rigged slot machine, her evil twin, and a trail of dead bodies. Davis learns the truth and it does not set her free—in fact, it lands her in the pokey.

Buried under a mistaken identity, unable to seek help from her family, her hot streak runs cold until her landlord Bradley Cole steps in. Make that her landlord, lawyer, and love interest. With his help, Davis must win this high stakes game before her luck runs out.

Available at booksellers nationwide and online

Visit www.henerypress.com for details

BOARD STIFF

Kendel Lynn

An Elliott Lisbon Mystery (#1)

As director of the Ballantyne Foundation on Sea Pine Island, SC, Elliott Lisbon scratches her detective itch by performing discreet inquiries for Foundation donors. Usually nothing more serious than retrieving a pilfered Pomeranian. Until Jane Hatting, Ballantyne board chair, is accused of murder. The Ballantyne's reputation tanks, Jane's headed to a jail cell, and Elliott's sexy ex is the new lieutenant in town.

Armed with moxie and her Mini Coop, Elliott uncovers a trail of blackmail schemes, gambling debts, illicit affairs, and investment scams. But the deeper she digs to clear Jane's name, the guiltier Jane looks. The closer she gets to the truth, the more treacherous her investigation becomes. With victims piling up faster than shells at a clambake, Elliott realizes she's next on the killer's list.

Available at booksellers nationwide and online

Visit www.henerypress.com for details

DINERS, DIVES & DEAD ENDS

Terri L. Austin

A Rose Strickland Mystery (#1)

As a struggling waitress and part-time college student, Rose Strickland's life is stalled in the slow lane. But when her close friend, Axton, disappears, Rose suddenly finds herself serving up more than hot coffee and flapjacks. Now she's hashing it out with sexy bad guys and scrambling to find clues in a race to save Axton before his time runs out.

With her anime-loving bestie, her septuagenarian boss, and a pair of IT wise men along for the ride, Rose discovers political corruption, illegal gambling, and shady corporations. She's gone from zero to sixty and quickly learns when you're speeding down the fast lane, it's easy to crash and burn.

Available at booksellers nationwide and online

Visit www.henerypress.com for details

ARTIFACT

Gigi Pandian

A Jaya Jones Treasure Hunt Mystery (#1)

Historian Jaya Jones discovers the secrets of a lost Indian treasure may be hidden in a Scottish legend from the days of the British Raj. But she's not the only one on the trail...

From San Francisco to London to the Highlands of Scotland, Jaya must evade a shadowy stalker as she follows hints from the hastily scrawled note of her dead lover to a remote archaeological dig. Helping her decipher the cryptic clues are her magician best friend, a devastatingly handsome art historian with something to hide, and a charming archaeologist running for his life.

Available at booksellers nationwide and online

Visit www.henerypress.com for details

THE AMBITIOUS CARD
John Gaspard

An Eli Marks Mystery (#1)

The life of a magician isn't all kiddie shows and card tricks. Sometimes it's murder. Especially when magician Eli Marks very publicly debunks a famed psychic, and said psychic ends up dead. The evidence, including a bloody King of Diamonds playing card (one from Eli's own Ambitious Card routine), directs the police right to Eli.

As more psychics are slain, and more King cards rise to the top, Eli can't escape suspicion. Things get really complicated when romance blooms with a beautiful psychic, and Eli discovers she's the next target for murder, and he's scheduled to die with her. Now Eli must use every trick he knows to keep them both alive and reveal the true killer.

Available at booksellers nationwide and online

Visit www.henerypress.com for details

PORTRAIT OF A DEAD GUY

Larissa Reinhart

A Cherry Tucker Mystery (#1)

In Halo, Georgia, folks know Cherry Tucker as big in mouth, small in stature, and able to sketch a portrait faster than buck-shot rips from a ten gauge -- but commissions are scarce. So when the well-heeled Branson family wants to memorialize their murdered son in a coffin portrait, Cherry scrambles to win their patronage from her small town rival.

As the clock ticks toward the deadline, Cherry faces more trouble than just a controversial subject. Between ex-boyfriends, her flaky family, an illegal gambling ring, and outwitting a killer on a spree, Cherry finds herself painted into a corner she'll be lucky to survive.

Available at booksellers nationwide and online

Visit www.henerypress.com for details

FRONT PAGE FATALITY

LynDee Walker

A Headlines in High Heels Mystery (#1)

Crime reporter Nichelle Clarke's days can flip from macabre to comical with a beep of her police scanner. Then an ordinary accident story turns extraordinary when evidence goes missing, a prosecutor vanishes, and a sexy Mafia boss shows up with the headline tip of a lifetime.

As Nichelle gets closer to the truth, her story gets more dangerous. Armed with a notebook, a hunch, and her favorite stilettos, Nichelle races to splash these shady dealings across the front page before this deadline becomes her last.

Available at booksellers nationwide and online

Visit www.henerypress.com for details

PILLOW STALK

Diane Vallere

A Mad for Mod Mystery (#1)

Interior Decorator Madison Night has modeled her life after Doris Day's character in *Pillow Talk*, but when a killer targets women dressed like the bubbly actress, Madison's signature sixties style places her in the middle of a homicide investigation.

The local detective connects the new crimes to a twenty-year old cold case, and Madison's long-trusted contractor emerges as the leading suspect. As the body count piles up like a stack of plush pillows, Madison uncovers a Soviet spy, a campaign to destroy all Doris Day movies, and six minutes of film that will change her life forever.

Available March 2014

Visit www.henerypress.com for details